"MAYBE I SHOULD COME OVER AND GIVE HIM A LESSON."

The corners of Tyler's mouth lifted. "I think that's a very good idea. I can't think of a better way to start a morning than greeting the day with a beautiful woman and some good coffee."

His stare was so intense upon her that she felt her cheeks heat. She couldn't exactly say thank you since he hadn't said she was that beautiful woman he'd been referring to, but the implication had been there. Judging by the look in his eyes as they focused solely on her, his meaning was clear.

"Then I'll see what I can do . . . about Rohn's coffee, that is. It's the least I can do to pay you back for your work on the fence." Desperate to get out from under his gaze, she threw out that response and then turned toward the counter to add sugar to her own mug.

"I'll look forward to it." There was amusement in Tyler's voice as it came from much closer to her than she expected.

He leaned past her to set the container of half-and-half on the counter next to her. The move put him close enough that the combined scents of manly deodorant and good clean sweat hit her. That, along with the warmth radiating off his body as he brushed against her before moving back, had her hyperaware of Tyler. He was a man and she was a woman. Her body knew it and didn't care he was younger and she was a fool to even think of him that way.

MIDNIGHT
Ride

CAT
JOHNSON

ZEBRA BOOKS
KENSINGTON PUBLISHING CORP.
http://www.kensingtonbooks.com

ZEBRA BOOKS are published by

Kensington Publishing Corp.
119 West 40th Street
New York, NY 10018

All Kensington titles, imprints, and distributed lines are available at special quantity discounts for bulk purchases for sales promotion, premiums, fund-raising, educational, or institutional use.

Special book excerpts or customized printings can also be created to fit specific needs. For details, write or phone the office of the Kensington Sales Manager: Attn. Sales Department. Kensington Publishing Corp., 119 West 40th Street, New York, NY 10018. Phone: 1-800-221-2647.

Zebra and the Z logo Reg. U.S. Pat. & TM Off.

First Printing: May 2015
ISBN-13: 978-1-4201-3621-0
ISBN-10: 1-4201-3621-6

First Electronic Edition: May 2015
eISBN-13: 978-1-4201-3622-7
eISBN-10: 1-4201-3622-4

10 9 8 7 6 5 4 3 2 1

Printed in the United States of America

ACKNOWLEDGMENTS

John Dollar, the inspiration for my tattooed Oklahoma bad boy, Tyler.

The Alaskan cowboys, Rohn and Colton, for the use of their names.

The bloggers and reviewers who support me— Slick, Kelly, Dawn, Terri, Kathy, Kim, Tanya, Brenda, Anna, Laura, and Moddiker, just to mention a few of the many.

Eliza Gayle, my sounding board and fellow strategist in navigating the many twists and turns of this crazy publishing world. Together, we chased our dream, and made it all the way to the top of the *New York Times* bestseller list.

The Joseph's Fine Foods crew in Drumright, Oklahoma, who I finally got to meet in person.

My fellow authors, always there with a kind word, a hearty congratulation, a kick in the butt for motivation, and a strong shoulder to lean on.

The men who are my consultants and inspiration, whether they wear combat or cowboy boots.

My cowboy-loving Tweethearts around the world— you know who you are. Some I've met, and some I haven't, but I feel as if I know you all.

Chance Butterfield, the Canadian steer wrestler who took time to answer my question on Twitter.

The Book Obsessed Chicks who have so generously welcomed me into their hearts and homes. You know how much I love you!

Finally, my readers, old and new, near and far. Too many to mention by name, but all important. Some make me handmade gifts. Others send cards. Some, I'm amazed and humbled to say, have tattoos of my tagline. More than all that, every one shows me they care and encourages me to go on when it would be too easy to quit. For that I will be forever grateful.

Chapter One

There was something about a really good, down-home barbecue joint that made Tyler Jenkins happy, deep down all the way through his stomach and to his very soul.

Of course, to meet his very high culinary standards, it couldn't be one of those bullshit places that pretended to be real. It had to be authentic, or why bother? If all the restaurant did was slap some sauce on a piece of meat and call it barbecue, he might as well go to a fast food chain.

To be worth his time and money, there had to be smoke, and lots of it. He wanted to smell it in the air as they slow-cooked the meat out back. He wanted to taste it the moment the food hit his tongue.

Like most things worth doing, getting that kind of result took time. Hours. All day, in fact. Only the best places devoted that kind of time and effort. Where he sat now was one of those places.

It looked like nothing from the road. A run-down shack with an old RV parked next to it. A couple of wooden picnic tables inside and a couple more out front by the parking lot, each with a roll of paper towels set out on top for customers to wipe their hands and mouths.

That was the extent of it, except for the most important part—the smoker. The big steel barrel pumped a mouthwatering cloud of meat-laden smoke into the air.

Yes, sir, there was everything right with this place. Incredibly good food that was fast and cheap—everything Tyler looked for.

As he sat with the sun beating down on his shoulders and the wide brim of his cowboy hat shading his eyes, he was in heaven. He shoved another piece of marbled brisket between his lips, and a burst of flavor filled his mouth. He couldn't help the sound of appreciation that rumbled from deep within him.

It might very well be hereditary in the Jenkins men—this appreciation for fine barbecue. Tyler's older brother Tucker had his own favorite place in Drumright. Tuck would travel quite a distance if he had to, and drive hours to get his favorite smoked meat. It must be in their genes, right along with the other Jenkins traits—dark hair, blue eyes, an appreciation for the gentler sex, a love of all things rodeo, and, of course, the ability to sniff out good food.

Closing his eyes to better enjoy every subtle nuance, he absorbed how the smoky taste stuck around for a while. He could feel it settling in on the back of his throat for a nice long stay, even after he'd swallowed the beef.

Another sound of pure appreciation grumbled from within him. Two things made Tyler purr like a house cat from total contented satisfaction, but only one of them was something he could do out in public. "Mmm, mmm. This right here is good enough to make you want to smack your own ass."

With a forkful of jalapeño macaroni and cheese poised in midair, Tyler's boss let out a laugh. "You ain't kidding. How'd you find this place to begin with? There isn't even a sign out front."

Tyler laughed at the older man. "Rohn, please. There are two things I can always find—women and food. I've been working for you at the ranch for long enough, you should know that by now."

The truth was, the scent of smoked meat and the telltale trail from the smoker rising into the air like a beacon had first led him here.

The building was partially hidden from the road by a hardware store in front of it. The OPEN banner blowing in the breeze from a pole stuck in the dirt along the road hadn't told Tyler what the hidden establishment sold, but the scent in the air sure had. He could sniff out good barbecue a mile away. He was certainly glad he'd swung the truck onto the dirt of the parking lot that day.

His dining companion dipped his head. "You're right, Ty. My apologies. You are the master when it comes to all pleasures of the flesh."

"Thank you." Tyler accepted the compliment from the older man with a tip of his hat.

"How old are you again?" Rohn asked between mouthfuls.

"Twenty-four. Turning twenty-five shortly." Single, young, healthy, and living the dream. Tyler couldn't ask for anything more. Well, maybe another order of cornbread.

"Twenty-four." Rohn shook his head. "Damn. At that age I was already married to Lila and working my ass off to pay the note on the ranch." The man got the same faraway look in his eyes Tyler had seen there whenever he talked about his late wife.

Rohn had lost her to cancer a few years ago, but it was clear he still missed her badly. It had to be lonely living on the ranch with nobody for company except the guys he hired to help him out with the stock during the day.

Tyler couldn't bring Rohn's wife back, but he could do something about his boss being alone and cooped up in that house every night. "So, Colton and I are fixin' to go out. Why don't you come with us?"

Rohn's hair and his closely cropped beard had already begun to show strands of steely gray, but it suited him. The man probably hadn't turned fifty yet. He kept himself in good shape, physically. There were a lot of women who'd find him plenty attractive, but he sure as hell wouldn't find them while hunkered down in his living room.

"Me? Go out with you two tonight? What the hell would I do out with you and Colton?" Rohn's brows rose beneath his cowboy hat.

"I don't know. There's plenty to do at the bar." Tyler shrugged. "You could knock back a few cold ones. Shoot some pool."

"Look like a fool hanging around with you two young bucks and sniffing around women young enough I could be their father?" Rohn laughed while shaking his head.

"Aw, come on. That's not how it would be at all."

"No?"

"No. I've seen some old—er men and women at the places where we go out." Tyler had had to scramble to cover that he'd almost called his boss *old*. He hid his cringe and tried for some damage control. "Hell, it's never too late. I know a guy who's forty. Logan Hunt. He grew up next door to my parents' house and is real good friends with my brother. Anyway, he just got married for the first time in August and now he and his wife have a baby."

If his longtime friend Logan could meet a woman, get married, and have a kid at forty, Rohn should at least be able to go out and have a little fun.

Rohn swung his head from side to side and let out a snort of a laugh. "Yeah. Thanks for the words of encouragement, but no. You two have fun. Just don't come in to work dragging your ass tomorrow morning. We got a shitload of work to get done."

"Yes, sir." He stabbed his fork into another piece of meat. The marbled brisket would serve well to coat his stomach in preparation for the beer he'd be consuming later. He was intent on his barbecue until Rohn let out a sigh that had Tyler glancing up. "What's wrong?"

"Having young guys like you and Colton and Justin at the ranch . . . it's starting to make me feel old."

"You're only as old as you feel, and that's exactly the reason you should come out with us tonight." With his brisket still poised on his fork, Tyler made sure he emphasized the point before he finally shoved the meat into his mouth. It was a sentiment he truly believed.

"Maybe next time." The tone of the older man's answer said pretty much the opposite of his words.

It wasn't in Tyler to give up easily, but there wasn't much he could do if his boss was dead set against coming. He swallowed and nodded. "A'ight. We'll be at the Two-Step, if you change your mind."

"The Two-Step? Jesus." Rohn laughed. "Is that place still standing?"

It was a valid question. The local hangout had been around forever. It had definitely seen better days, but Tyler loved every rickety old board of it. The whole run-down, hometown atmosphere.

Tyler grinned. "It is, but the floor is so crooked that the last time I was there I had to shove some shims under one end of the pool table just to keep the balls on the felt long enough for a game."

That had been a good night. He'd walked out with a wad of cash from winning at pool and with a girl on his arm to warm his truck seat for an hour or so.

Life got hectic sometimes, and it had been too long since he'd visited the Two-Step. He was glad Colton had suggested going tonight.

"I used to go there when I was your age. That floor always did lean a bit toward the back bar. I can tell you, I would use that fact to my advantage when I was shooting pool against any out-of-towners who didn't know about it." A twinkle lit Rohn's eyes and Tyler saw hope. He might be able to get him to come out after all.

"They've got a two-for-one beer special tonight."

He dangled that carrot as inspiration to sway Rohn's decision.

The Two-Step had dollar drinks for ladies, too, which was the main reason he and Colton were going. Tyler didn't think the possibility of many— not to mention very drunk—women being at the bar would encourage Rohn to join them, so he kept that tidbit to himself. Plenty of time to ease the man back into the world of dating, but first they had to get him out of his house. Baby steps.

Rohn screwed up his mouth beneath his mustache. "Nah. You guys go and have a good time."

"Oh, we will. Don't you worry about that." He'd work some more on Rohn and his love life later on. As for tonight, Tyler was going to have a whole lot of fun, hopefully while surrounded by a whole lot of women.

A man was only young once. He was going to take full advantage of this time in his life, because when he settled down, it would be for keeps. When he asked for a woman's hand, he intended it to be for a lifetime. That, however, hadn't happened yet, and it probably wasn't going to for a long while, even if all the single people around him seemed to be pairing off.

It seemed most folks he knew were dropping like flies after being bitten by the love bug. His brother Tuck had gotten married again, just when they all thought he never would after the disastrous end to his first marriage. He seemed happy enough.

Hell, even his little sister Tara was settled down

and seriously dating Tuck's buddy Jace. That was all fine and good for them, but not for Tyler . . . yet.

He didn't discount the fact that it could happen at any time. He just hadn't found the person he wanted to spend more than a few weeks with, never mind a lifetime. He certainly didn't plan on finding the future Mrs. Jenkins at the Two-Step's ladies' night.

Nope. Tonight's goal was to consume a good amount of hops and barley, and sow some wild oats. That way, when he finally did meet the right girl and the time came for him to retire his single status, he'd be good and ready to do so. He'd settle down and turn in his player card after he'd lived a full life of fun, but not one minute before.

As for the here and now, Tyler was good and ready to devour some more of his tasty barbecue. He and his boss had to finish eating before they headed back to the ranch, where they'd left Colton to handle the last of the afternoon chores.

The lumber that Rohn and Tyler had picked up while in town was in the back of the truck. They'd all unload that, and once they'd dumped the wood behind the shed they'd be fixing tomorrow, Tyler's workday would be done. He'd shower and then he and Colton would be off for fun and good times at the Two-Step.

All the best stuff in life was right there within his grasp. Life was good and he was going to live it to the fullest. With that thought, Tyler tucked into the remainder of his brisket.

He let the flavors take him away to his happy place—the place where his belly was full and there were cold beer and hot girls in his near future.

Chapter Two

The ringing of Janie's house phone on the kitchen counter was a welcome interruption. Cooking dinner for one person had to be the most depressing task on earth. Especially after having cooked for her husband and their crew for over a decade. She put down the spoon she'd been stirring the chili with and reached for the receiver in the charger.

She didn't recognize the number, but it was a local area code, so she hit the button to answer. "Hello?"

"Mrs. Smithwick?"

"Yes." She didn't recognize the voice any more than she did the number, but the man on the phone seemed to know her.

"Hey, there. It's Colton Travers. I'm a hired hand over at Rohn Lerner's place next door."

"Oh, hi." Having the ranch hand's name didn't help Janie much since she didn't know any Colton Travers, but at least her neighbor's name was familiar, even if Colton's was not.

"I just wanted you to know that a tree limb took down part of the fence in your south field. Must've happened during that wind we had the other night. I was out riding our line and I noticed it. I took a chance and looked up your number in the phone book in Rohn's office and sure enough, you were listed in there, so I called. I figured you'd want to know."

And there it was—more bad news she didn't need. It wasn't enough that prices were so low it had hardly made it worth selling the stock, or that just the deductibles on her husband's medical bills were so high she was still trying to pay them off nearly a year after he'd died. Nope. Now Mother Nature was dumping tree limbs on the fence in the only field where she had stock left.

She couldn't help the sigh that escaped her. "Did any of my animals get out?"

"No, ma'am. The tree branch is working pretty good to block the opening for right now, but I wouldn't count on that lasting forever. You know how cattle can be."

She supposed she should thank God for small favors that none of her cows had figured out they could walk over the limb while the barbed wire was down.

"All right. Thanks for letting me know. I'll take care of it."

Of course, to take care of it she'd have to figure out how, when, and with what help. She'd also have to sideline dinner for the moment and drive out to see how bad the damage was. Then she could determine what she needed to buy for the repairs and if this was something she'd be able to do herself or if she'd have to find a guy to hire and pay with money she really didn't have to spare.

"No problem at all. Have a good day, ma'am."

Not likely. "Thanks. You, too."

The polite and oh-so-young-sounding Colton hung up before she could talk to him about possibly fixing the fence in exchange for some of the chili on the stove. Sad but true, that was about all she had to spare to pay a hired hand right now.

Alone, widowed, and in debt up to her eyeballs on a ranch she couldn't maintain but couldn't bear to think about selling, all at thirty-six years of age.

Janie had to wonder how her life had turned out like this. She wasn't living in the untamed Old West, when men died too soon and young widows were commonplace. This was modern times, and only a couple of hours' drive from Oklahoma City, for God's sake. Yet here she was, worlds away from where she thought she'd be back when she'd been a young starry-eyed bride marrying the older man who'd swept her off her feet. Long before Tom's diagnosis with pancreatic cancer had changed both their lives.

Blowing out a loud breath filled with frustration, Janie flipped off the burner. She grabbed the truck keys from the counter and shoved them in her pocket before bending to retrieve her paddock boots. Sitting to pull them on over her socks, she felt the bone-deep exhaustion that had hung over her for months. Like a black cloud in the sky darkening everything beneath it.

It was really no surprise she was tired. Just keeping

up with the ranch and teaching riding lessons kept her busy from sunup until sundown, and worrying kept her up all night. Sleep would be good, but she wasn't the type to use the crutch of sleeping pills. After Tom's death, yes, she'd given in for nearly a week, drugging herself into oblivion where reality didn't creep in until consciousness returned eight hours later. Pills weren't a long-term solution. She needed to move on, and foolish as it might be, she wanted to do it on her own without any medications, not even the over-the-counter stuff.

As she rallied the last bit of strength in her, she braced one palm on the kitchen table and hoisted her weary body from the chair. She had to wonder how much longer she could keep this up before something broke—either her mind or her body. She guessed that as long as she was still managing to put one foot in front of the other, that was a worry for another day.

Out in the truck, she pulled herself into the driver's seat and shoved the key into the ignition. The lights on the dashboard told her that the gas tank was nearing empty. Fuel would cost her another fifty bucks, and at current prices, that wouldn't even fill up the tank. She wasn't to the point of starving or losing the ranch that had been her grandfather's before she'd taken it over, but that didn't mean she liked spending money she really couldn't spare on fuel that cost far too much nowadays, in her opinion.

Janie was getting accustomed to the constant sensation of unease that worrying caused inside her. It was a familiar presence that hovered in the background and shadowed every waking and sleeping moment. Used to the tightness in her chest and the turmoil in her stomach, she pushed herself past it and into motion.

On autopilot, she fired up the truck's diesel engine and threw the transmission into gear. The drive to the field where Rohn's hand had said the fence was down was a short one. Once there, it didn't take her long to spot what he'd seen. She saw the fallen tree limb lying across a broken section of fence, just as he'd described.

The few head of cattle she'd kept when she'd sold the rest lifted their heads at the sound of the truck approaching. At least they were still contained. As long as they had grass to eat in the pasture, and the pond to drink from, they likely wouldn't go looking to escape, but the fence had to be fixed nonetheless. The sooner the better.

It looked like one upright had snapped and the barbed wire was down. She'd have to buy a new fence post, but that was the least of it. Getting the old one out of the ground and sinking the new one would be a lot of work. Not to mention securing the wire to complete the repair.

This was the kind of thing Tom and their ranch hands would have taken care of. Now the job fell to her. Even without the much larger herd they used to maintain, owning a large tract of property and keeping even a few animals meant a lot of work.

The modern woman inside her liked to think she could deal with things as well as any man, but when it came to handling eight-foot-long locust fence posts by herself, she had to face the fact that this time, that might not be the case.

One thing at a time. She'd run out and buy the post tonight before the lumberyard closed and she'd worry about the rest tomorrow. Maybe, if she found she couldn't handle the repair on her own, she could hire one of the kids from the lumberyard on the cheap. Or beg a favor from Rohn and get one of his hands to help her. She hated playing the widow card—taking advantage of the sympathies of friends and neighbors by asking for help—but desperate times called for desperate measures. Hard to admit, yes, but the woefully sad situation in her bank account was just that since Tom's death—desperate.

After one more appraisal of the situation, Janie felt confident enough to leave the herd in the field. The repair could wait until morning. The few head of cattle she'd kept when she'd sold the rest of the herd were happily munching on the summer grass, huddled well away from the breach in the fence that was being blocked by the tree limb.

Drawing in a bracing breath, she climbed back into the truck. Next stop, town, to get fuel and a fence post. Then straight home and possibly directly to her empty, lonely bed. That would be after she put the chili away for tomorrow. What with the interruption, she didn't really have an appetite for it any longer.

Chapter Three

They were barely inside the door of the Two-Step when Colton nudged Tyler with his elbow. "I get the blonde."

Tyler's brows drew low. "Why do you always want the blondes?"

Colton shrugged. "I don't know. I like 'em. I guess I have a type."

"Fine. You get the blonde." Tyler rolled his eyes. A *type.* What bullshit. Tyler's type was any pretty young thing with the potential to make his evening more fun.

There had to be a dozen women in the bar, all enjoying, in volume, the ladies' night dollar drinks. There were all colors, shapes, and sizes. Far too many for Tyler to even have gotten a good look at in the short time since he'd walked in.

The evening was still young. There was no need to make a choice as quickly as Colton had. Tyler wasn't even sure which blonde it was that Colton had his eye on since he'd spotted at least three, but it didn't matter. There were more than enough to choose from. If his friend really wanted to limit himself to this one girl—whoever she was—Tyler wasn't about to argue. That still left all the brunettes and the redheads for him.

"Come on. Let's go get a beer." Apparently satisfied that his claim had been staked, Colton led the way to the far end of the bar.

When they arrived, there was indeed a blonde. She was leaning up against the wooden rail, posed for maximum impact and displaying a good amount of skin. More importantly, and what caught Tyler's attention, was the fact she also had a friend—a dark-haired friend who was fair game for him to pursue.

The girls turned at their approach.

"Ladies." Tyler tipped his hat at them. The brunette followed the move with her eyes and smiled.

Colton moved around to the other side, closer to the one he'd called dibs on, and leaned in to signal the bartender. "We'll have two drafts, and two more of whatever they're drinking."

"Sex on the Beach." With a fingertip, the blonde slid her nearly empty glass across the surface of the bar top. "Thanks."

"Two more Sex on the Beach it is." Colton nodded with a smile, looking as amused at the name of the drink as Tyler.

He met Colton's gaze and grinned. This night was getting better with every moment.

"I got first round." Tyler tossed cash on the bar and then turned to the brunette. "So tell me, what exactly is in that drink?"

"I don't know, but it sure tastes good."

Maybe it didn't matter what the ingredients were.

He liked it already just judging by the name. He extended his hand to her. "I'm Tyler."

"I'm Libby." Her fingers felt cool against his from the ice-filled glass she'd been holding. He shook her hand, lingering for a bit longer than necessary before he released his grip.

"Well, Libby, I sure hope to get a taste of this Sex on the Beach of yours sometime." He'd fully intended the suggestion behind his words.

"Here. You can have a sip now." She pushed her half-empty glass closer to him, but he shook his head.

"Nuh-uh. There are far nicer ways for me to take a taste than out of that there plastic straw." His focus moved from the drink in question to her plump, pink lips.

By the time he dragged his gaze back up to her eyes, she was smiling at him. "All right."

She fisted the front of his shirt and pulled him closer before she crashed her mouth into his.

Oh, yeah. Coming to the Two-Step had been a good decision. He'd achieved lip-to-lip contact in less than five minutes. That had to be some sort of record, even for him.

Libby thrust her tongue between his lips and he tasted the remains of the sweet drink inside the heat of her mouth. She stayed right there, French-kissing him like a woman on a mission.

Never one to deny a lady what she wanted, Tyler reciprocated wholeheartedly. He rested his hands on her hips, slid his thigh between her legs, and leaned back against the bar, settling in for a nice long make-out session.

This was going to be a very good night, and all for the bargain price of a dollar a drink. That would no doubt be the least expensive sex on the beach or sex anywhere that he'd ever gotten.

Tyler was aware of the bartender planting the two beers and two drinks on the bar, and of him taking the cash and delivering change. All of that action seemed far off in the corner of his consciousness as he enjoyed some attention from the lovely Libby. He didn't know how Colton was faring with his blonde, and he really couldn't rally the concern to care all that much.

Libby pulled away from his mouth and raised her gaze to his. "How about we take this outside?"

"Sounds good to me." He grabbed his beer and downed a few gulps. He had a feeling he'd be working up a thirst shortly. As he set the glass bottle down, Tyler shot Colton a look. "I'll be back in a bit."

His friend raised a brow, but dipped his head in a nod. "A'ight."

Right about now Colton was probably second-guessing his spur-of-the-moment decision to go for the blonde. In this situation, it sure looked as if brunettes had more fun.

Tyler looped his arm around the girl's shoulders and led her out the back door. For one, it was closer to where they stood than the front door. More important, it conveniently led directly to the parking lot. They'd arrived at sunset, so it was beginning to get dark out. There weren't as many lights out back as there were in the front of the building. That would provide them with some privacy. Not to mention they'd left Colton's truck parked in the back lot and the doors were unlocked. He and Libby could crawl in there for some added privacy for their fun.

The quiet of outside replaced the noise of the bar as the heavy door slammed shut behind them.

"So, you wanna—" Tyler didn't get to finish asking if she wanted to get comfortable in the truck. He couldn't as she slammed him up against the wall of the building.

With her hands on his belt buckle and her mouth covering his, the time for talking was apparently over. He guessed doing whatever it was they were going to do right there against the building was fine with her since it seemed she was driving this bus, not him. He was simply along for the ride.

She broke away for a moment and Tyler used it as an opportunity to breathe and get a few words in. "You're sure . . . enthusiastic tonight."

"I'm mad."

Libby concentrated on his buckle as she struggled to open it. It gave him a second more to ask, "Who are you mad at?"

"My fiancé."

"Fiancé? Whoa, wait a minute." He would have taken a step back from her if he weren't already pressed against the wall. He made do with grabbing her hands to stop her from stripping him further.

Having already conquered his buckle and the top button of his jeans, she was in the process of lowering his zipper. He held her still to stop her progress before she got her hands inside his underwear.

Ironic, that. Usually Tyler was all for a girl getting into his pants, and vice versa, but not when there was a fiancé in the picture.

"Why are you so mad at him?" He figured it had to be pretty bad to get her angry enough to be doing what she was with him, a total stranger.

A frown creased the brow above her eyes. "He was staring at some girl's tits. I saw him doing it. Right there inside the front door, plain as day."

He started to suspect that the drink he'd seen her with wasn't her first one of the evening. Her speech was a little slurred, her eyes a bit unfocused. Her reasoning was definitely off, too. Even if her guy had been eyeballing a girl, that was nowhere near equal to what Libby was trying to do now with him.

"Maybe you were mistaken. Did you ask him about it?" Tyler tried to talk some sense into the girl, even though odds were she was past hearing him.

"I can't. I'm not allowed to talk to him when he's working. He's too busy." She wrinkled her nose and did an unflattering imitation of a man's voice, clearly showing her displeasure. "But you can bet I will later, as soon as the other bouncer gets here and he can take a break. Until then, I figure I'm free to do whatever I want, and I intend to."

She stepped closer and pressed her pelvis against his as tidbits of what she'd said began to penetrate Tyler's brain. Like puzzle pieces, they started to fit together, and the resulting image was not a pretty one. While she moved both of their hands down the front of his jeans to connect with the tip of his burgeoning length, he managed to picture the bruiser who'd been manning the front door of the bar and checking IDs as they'd walked in.

"Wait. Libby, hold up. Are you saying he works here? Jesus, please tell me he's not the guy out front tonight." He could only pray he'd misinterpreted her drunken babbling.

The back door flew open, smashing against the wall and bouncing back to where it was intercepted by the beefy forearm belonging to one hell of a big—not to mention angry-looking—guy.

Tyler didn't have to wait around for Libby's answer. One look at the murderous expression on the man in the doorway and he figured he had all the information he needed. He wasn't about to risk bodily injury by sticking around any longer.

There were times when a man should stay and fight, and there were times when it was wiser to cut and run. It was clear to Tyler that this was the latter.

Shoving the woman he'd been kissing just moments before out of the way, he clamped his hat lower on his head and took off at a sprint as her bruiser of a fiancé followed him.

Cowboy boots weren't meant for running, but Tyler managed it. He sure had incentive. Avoiding being pummeled into the ground by a jealous fiancé served as fine inspiration. He knew the truck was unlocked, but he didn't have the keys to start the engine. Colton had those with him inside the bar. Tyler wasn't about to lock himself inside a truck when he couldn't flee, not with an angry lunatic hot on his tail, so he kept running.

The terrain worked in his favor, as did the darkness while Tyler crashed into the woods off the side of the parking lot. Branches whacked into him as he dodged between them. He twisted an ankle when one foot landed on a rock, but he kept going, limping in a half run. A pine bough caught him across the face, blinding him as he squeezed the injured eye tight and the tears began to flow. Still, he forged ahead. His life depended on it.

Chapter Four

The woods broke into a clearing and Tyler realized he was behind the lumberyard right off the main road in town. He slowed to a fast walk when he hit the concrete and glanced around him.

He needed to get somewhere safe and tend to his eye, which hurt like hell and was still tearing up. And he needed to zip his jeans and refasten the belt buckle the girl had undone, all while she'd kept to herself that one important detail—that the fiancé she was mad at was working the door of the bar. That would have been good information for Tyler to have. He also needed to make sure his cell phone hadn't fallen out of the back pocket of his jeans so he could call Colton to come and rescue him. But before any of that, he had to make sure the man in hot pursuit hadn't followed him this far.

A crash in the woods behind him, followed by a loud cuss, told him the lunatic hadn't given up yet. Damn, but this guy was persistent.

Tyler took off running again, though at this point it was more of a fast hobble. He had to hide.

A pickup truck parked in the lot in front of him provided his only hope. He should just take the truck and drive away. It wouldn't be stealing. He'd only be borrowing it. He could bring it back as soon as life and limb were no longer in jeopardy, but he didn't know if the owner had left the keys inside and he couldn't waste precious seconds checking.

Maybe it was dark enough that if he lay flat and still in the back, he might not be seen. But if the guy looked closely and saw him hiding, he'd be a sitting duck.

It was a chance he was going to have to take.

Running out of time, he sprinted to the back of the truck, planted both hands on the tailgate, and vaulted into the bed. When he landed inside, he knew his luck was holding. There was a big green tarp in the bottom of the truck bed. He flipped it over himself and held his breath, trying to move as little as possible to not rustle the thick plastic covering him.

While he waited to be discovered, or not, he figured praying couldn't hurt. Silently, he vowed that if he got out of this night unscathed, he'd never make out with a stranger in a bar again.

As his heart pounded, he heard heavy footsteps in the lot and then a few more loud cusses and what sounded like a bear—or a really big man—crashing back through the trees.

Long minutes ticked by in silence, and the crazed fiancé didn't come back to whip the tarp off him and beat him to a pulp. Against all odds, he might just be safe. Out of the woods, literally.

In light of that, Tyler decided to add a small

amendment to the deal he'd made with God. It would probably be all right to hook up with girls he met in a bar. However, he would be sure to ask them if they had a boyfriend or any kind of significant other *before* he kissed them and let them unbuckle his pants.

Satisfied that was a promise he could live with, and hopeful that the guy had given up the chase, he was about to take a peek to see if the coast really was clear when he heard footsteps heading toward the truck.

It sounded like two people walking. They hadn't come from the direction of the woods, but rather from the building. He was most likely safe from being maimed by his pursuer, but he definitely was not in any position to be socializing with anyone. His jeans still hung wide open, his eye remained squeezed shut, and he was hiding under a tarp in a stranger's truck.

It wasn't as if he could pop up and say *hey*, but he also couldn't stay hidden. If the owner of the truck drove away, who knew where he could end up?

Tyler was weighing his limited options when he heard a female voice say, "Hang on. Let me move this and then you can slide it right inside."

He lay helpless as she whipped the tarp to the side and exposed him to the beam of the parking lot light. At the sight of him, she screamed and jumped back.

Truth be told, he nearly screamed, too. He scrambled to sit up before he realized he might not want to be sitting up. He still wasn't convinced the scorned fiancé had really gone.

"Hey, Tyler." There was amusement in the male voice that came from his left.

Still partially blinded, Tyler turned his head to the side to see a guy he'd gone to high school with standing next to the truck and grinning as he balanced a fence post on his shoulder.

Hell of a time for a high school reunion. Not having much choice, Tyler tipped his head in greeting. "Hey, Jed."

"You know him?" the woman asked.

"I do." Jed grinned wider. "Don't worry. He might not look it right now, but he's harmless."

She let out a breath and held her hand to her chest. A fall of dark hair brushed her shoulders as her gaze swung from Jed to Tyler. "You scared the hell out of me. What are you doing under there?"

"Um, it's a long story." Sitting up, Tyler glanced at the woods and decided to take his chances with the crazed bouncer rather than look like more of a fool by continuing to lie in this woman's truck bed. He pulled himself all the way upright and went to work fastening the open fly of his jeans.

"Oh, don't worry, Ty. We have the time to hear your explanation, no matter how long it is. I'm sure it will be worth it." Jed grinned.

Jed hadn't missed the fact Tyler's pants were hanging wide enough to expose his underwear. Neither had the woman. Tyler saw her bite her lip to control a smile as she averted her eyes. Didn't it figure? A beautiful woman who drove the crew cab, dual rear wheel pickup truck he'd always wanted to own, and he looked like a complete ass in front of her.

He cursed his belt as buckling it with his shaky hands confounded him. Finally, Tyler got his clothes put back together. Jumping down from the truck, he felt a twinge in the ankle he'd twisted, but it held his weight. No broken bones, and his eye had finally stopped tearing, so he figured he was good to go.

He turned toward Jed and reached for the fence post. "Let me help you with that."

Jed took a step back. "Oh, no. You don't get out of telling us what's going on that easily."

Tyler shook his head. "Ain't nothing to tell. Just a simple misunderstanding is all." Grabbing the post off Jed's shoulder, he guided it into the back of the pickup and angled it so it wouldn't stick out more than a couple of inches past the tailgate. "There. It's in there pretty good. You won't need a warning flag on the end of it."

Glancing over, he saw both of them watching him and felt the need to keep talking. He turned to the woman. "Where are you going with that? Do you need some help unloading it when you get there?"

Jed laughed. "You need a ride home, don't you?"

"No." Technically, Tyler wasn't lying. "My truck's not at home. It's at the Double L. And I can call Colton for a ride, if I need one."

Of course, his friend would only be able to come get him *if* the bruiser hadn't gone back to the bar and taken his anger out on Colton because he couldn't find Tyler.

"You talking about Rohn Lerner's ranch?" the woman asked.

"Yup." Tyler nodded. "I work there. Do you know

him?" Sometimes this town was too damn small for his liking.

"Yeah, I do." She tipped her head toward the truck. "Hop in. I can drive you back there."

"You sure? You don't have to if it's out of the way. I can—"

"Get in. It's fine. It's on my way home." She dismissed Tyler's concern and turned to Jed. "Thanks for carrying that for me."

"No problem, ma'am." Donning another smart-ass grin, Jed turned to Tyler. "I'll see you around."

"Yup." Tyler hoped it wouldn't be for a long while. He kept that to himself and reached for the passenger door handle.

The woman climbed into the driver's seat and he realized he didn't even know her name. "I'm Tyler Jenkins, by the way."

"Janie." She glanced at him as she turned the key in the ignition.

Tyler appreciated the rumble of the powerful engine vibrating through him as she threw the truck into gear. He pushed his lust for the truck aside and concentrated on doing some more damage control. "I do apologize again for the whole truck thing."

She laughed as she pulled out of the parking lot and onto the main road. "Don't worry about it. This is the most excitement I've had in a long time, even if I did come in at the tail end of your mysterious adventure."

"I swear, I'm not usually getting into trouble—"

"Aren't you?" She raised a brow as her gaze cut sideways. "I somehow have difficulty believing that. I think your friend back at the store might, too."

His cheeks heated at being caught in the lie. Tyler let his chin drop before forcing himself to look at her. "You're right. I guess . . . sometimes . . . I can get myself into situations that maybe I shouldn't."

Her smile reached all the way to her eyes before she focused back on turning off the main drag and onto the side road that would take them to the ranch. "You do have a way with words. I bet that talented tongue of yours gets you out of many of those situations."

His mind went to bad places at her mention of his tongue and its talents. Visions of what he'd like to do with it—and her—flashed through his brain. He glanced at her left hand where it gripped the steering wheel and saw the glint of a gold band. It was a damn shame that she wore a wedding ring, because he wouldn't mind getting to know her better.

Disappointed, he dragged his attention back to the road. "That's the turn. Coming up on the right side up there. Rohn's place is the next driveway after this one."

A smile bowed her lips. "I know. That's my drive we just passed. We're neighbors."

Tyler frowned as the pieces fell into place. "You're Tom Smithwick's widow?"

"I guess I am." She let out a short, breathy laugh. "Widow. I think that's the first time I've heard someone call me that."

His eyes opened wide as he realized how badly he'd screwed up. Her husband hadn't been gone for that long. The grief was probably still fresh and there he was bringing up her loss. "I'm so sorry. I didn't mean anything by it."

"No, it's okay. Really. I mean, I'm sure they're all saying it when I'm not within earshot. I just never heard anyone say it. Besides, it's perfectly true. That's exactly what I am. It's just strange hearing it, you know? It's even stranger saying the words." She drew in a breath. "I'm a widow. At thirty-six years old."

He scrambled to make up for putting his foot in his mouth. "You don't look thirty-six."

She didn't look at all like what he'd always imagined a widow would, either. Tyler hadn't been working for Rohn for very long when her husband had died. In that time, he had only met Tom Smithwick a few times, and he'd never met his wife. He'd pictured her being older. Less vibrant. Definitely less hot, and not nearly so curvy. . . .

"Thanks." She treated him to a small, sad smile as she pulled up to where his truck was parked in Rohn's drive.

Not ready to say good-bye and let her leave quite yet, he hooked a thumb behind him. "So, what are you going to do with that fence post in the back?"

"A tree limb took down part of my fence and broke the upright. I'm going to see if I can replace it tomorrow."

"Alone?" He figured she'd have to dig the broken post out to sink the new one.

"Yeah. I let our crew go after Tom died and I sold the bulk of the stock, so I don't have any hired hands right now."

"Do you need some help?" Digging postholes was no job for a woman, in his opinion.

She shook her head. "No, really. You don't have to—"

"I know I don't have to. I want to." He shrugged. "Besides, it's the least I can do to pay you back."

"Pay me back for what? The ride? I told you, I was driving by here anyway."

"The ride." He laughed. "And the spot to hide out in the back when I needed it most."

She smiled. "You still haven't told me why you needed to hide."

The last thing on earth Tyler wanted was for this woman to know the embarrassing truth about what had happened tonight. It looked bad enough already, he was sure. "How about this . . . I don't tell you and I help you fix that fence instead?"

One brow cocked up before she nodded. "All right. Curious as I am, I could use the help, so I'll take that deal."

She extended her hand. He pressed his palm to hers and shook. "Good. I'll come over first thing in the morning."

As he felt the firm grip of Janie's hand, so tiny compared to his larger one, Tyler had to think he'd made a pretty damn good deal for himself. Not only did he get to save face, he also got to see her again tomorrow.

"Sounds good. I'll be home. And thank you for the help." A smile tipped up the corners of her mouth.

He couldn't stop his gaze from dropping to the Cupid's bow of her lips. "You're welcome."

The pleasure would be all his.

After getting out and calling a final good-bye, Tyler watched her back up. She spun the truck around, heading out the driveway and toward her own place, conveniently located right next door. He'd definitely be paying her a visit tomorrow morning.

When the glow of the taillights had disappeared, he strode to his truck while fishing out his cell phone. Inside the cab, by the glow of the dome light, he typed a message to Colton, telling his friend he was going home and wouldn't be back to the bar tonight. Before sending the text, Tyler added one final sentence.

You might want to leave. I pissed off the bouncer.

Satisfied he'd issued a proper warning, he hit SEND and tossed the phone into the console. Time to head home. He had a fence to fix bright and early in the morning.

Chapter Five

The sun had already risen over the horizon and lit the sky with a blaze of color when Tyler saw Colton's truck turn from the side road into Rohn's drive.

Standing near the shed, Tyler knew the moment Colton spotted him across the yard. He'd slammed the driver's side door so hard the sound traveled across the acres and had the bulls grazing in the pasture lifting their heads.

Gaze down and his step determined, Colton strode forward. His intent to confront Tyler was clear in the cadence of his quick stride. When he got to where Tyler stood waiting for the explosion, Colton pinned him with a glare.

"So let me get this straight . . . I miss my chance at getting any action with the blonde because two minutes into the night you pissed off the bouncer by sucking face with his fiancée. Does that about cover it?"

"Yup. Sounds about right to me." Tyler nodded

and escaped from his friend's icy stare by turning toward the tool shed.

Of course, a good portion of the blame belonged to Libby, who'd neglected to tell Tyler what the real situation was, but it was no use nitpicking details when Colton was in this kind of mood.

It was way too early in the morning to argue, and technically, what Colton had said was true. It was partially Tyler's fault that last night hadn't worked out as planned for either of them, but he'd learned an important lesson from the mad dash through the woods to save his life. From now on he'd ask questions first and kiss the girls later.

"Where are you going?" Colton's question came from behind Tyler as he walked.

"To get the tools I'll need to fix a fence."

"Why?"

"So I can fix the fence." Tyler answered Colton's nosy question with a purposely vague smartass response.

"What fence needs fixing?" Colton followed Tyler all the way to the door of the tool shed.

He should have gotten to Rohn's earlier that morning. That way he could have been in and out with what he needed and over at Janie's before Colton and his dozen questions had arrived.

There'd be no possibility of getting away from Colton or the inquisition now, so Tyler figured he might as well take advantage of the situation and lighten his own burden. "Part of the fence over at the Smithwick place is broke and I'm gonna replace it. I'm glad you're here early so you can help."

Colton let out a sigh, as if sinking one fence post

was a huge weight added to his workload. "A'ight. I'll come with you. Rohn won't mind we're taking the time to help her, I reckon. She is a neighbor and all. Besides, I feel sorry for the old lady having to tend to the place alone since her husband died."

Old lady?

"Do you know her?" Tyler asked, even though it was obvious Colton had never met Janie Smithwick. If he had, he sure as hell wouldn't have called her old.

"Nah. I knew Tom, but I never met his wife. Talked to her on the phone yesterday, though. I called to let her know about the fence before her stock got out. I guess you must have seen the tree limb down in her south pasture, too."

"Uh, yeah. That's right. I did. Right there in the south pasture, like you said." Tyler saw no need to bring up the sore subject of last night's bar debacle by revealing how he really knew about the fence. How Janie had told him about it after she and her conveniently parked truck had saved him from a certain beating in the lumberyard lot.

"What tools are you planning to take over?"

"Shovel. Posthole digger. Sledgehammer." Tyler talked as he reached into the shed and started grabbing what they'd need. "Better grab a pair of leather gloves from your truck, too. We'll be working with barbed wire."

"A'ight. You know, she's gonna need a new upright. The old one looked like it was snapped right in half when I saw it."

"Yeah, she knows. She already bought one." Tyler realized his error when he saw Colton's frown.

"How do you know that?"

The jig was up. He let out a breath and braced himself for the confession. "I helped her put the fence post into her truck at the lumberyard last night before she drove me back here."

"I was wondering how the hell you got home." Realization dawned visibly on Colton's face. His eyes opened wide. "You walked from the Two-Step all the way to the lumberyard in town? That's far."

Distance hadn't been the issue. Fear of death had been.

"More like ran, actually. It's not that far when you cut through the woods . . . and a man intent on snapping your neck is chasing you."

Colton burst into a bout of laughter that had him doubling over and trying to catch his breath. When he finally controlled himself enough to talk, he wiped his eyes and said, "Holy shit. No wonder you didn't come back to the bar to meet me."

Tyler raised a brow. "Would you have if you were me?"

"Nope. But then again, I wouldn't have had my tongue down some girl's throat I'd known for all of thirty seconds."

"You're just jealous."

"Yup. That's right, bro. I'm jealous. You caught me. I wish I could have run for my life all the way to town, too. Because, you know, that sounds like such a blast. Way better than having a cold one and enjoying the company of some ladies." Colton glanced sideways at Tyler as they walked toward the truck with the tools. His brow drew low. "Hey, is that why you're fixing her fence and I'm stuck helping you? Because you owe her for driving you back from town last night?"

"No. We're fixing her fence because it's a nice thing to do for a woman who's recently widowed and needs some help." And because he wanted an excuse to see Janie again, but he sure as hell wasn't telling Colton that. "Come on. Toss that stuff in my truck and let's go. I told her I'd be over first thing."

He intended to keep that promise. It was the neighborly thing to do, and she was the most enticing neighbor he'd seen in a long time.

Chapter Six

The sunlight sneaking through the blinds of the bedroom window pulled Janie out of that gray zone between being asleep and being awake. A state she was used to being in since Tom's death, caused by worry keeping her mind working even when her body was exhausted.

Hell, she hadn't really slept since his diagnosis, so she should be accustomed to being tired.

That made it easier for her to drag herself upright and plant her feet on the floor. She needed to get up, get dressed, and get moving. It was very possible she'd have a visitor this morning. She shook her head and smiled just remembering Tyler hiding in the bed of her truck. Breathless with his jeans undone and the color in his cheeks so high, she'd noticed his blush even beneath the parking lot lights.

That cowboy was trouble with a capital *T*. She could see that right off. In another lifetime, one where she was ten years younger, he'd be tempting in spite of the trouble that surely came with him.

She should have heard the story rather than

agreeing to his helping with the fence instead.
There was no guarantee he'd show to help her even
after shaking on the deal, and that story of his was
bound to be interesting. She'd be lying if she didn't
admit to being more than a little bit curious about
what had happened leading up to their strange
meeting in the parking lot.

Odds were it had to do with a woman. When a
man that good-looking and wild got into trouble,
the cause was usually a female. Tyler certainly was
both, handsome and wild, and the last thing she
needed to be doing was thinking about him.

She shouldn't think about how the cowboy hat
pulled low over his sky blue eyes only made his
jawline look more chiseled. Or how his well-defined
muscles had flexed beneath his T-shirt as he'd
hoisted the fence post effortlessly into the back of
the truck. And she really, really shouldn't be remembering his hand sliding down his flat, hard
stomach as he tucked that shirt into his open jeans.

Damn. He was making her think things she
hadn't thought about in a very long time, and that
had to stop. She'd never been a wild woman herself.
She'd gotten married young to an older man. Things
had been good with Tom, but the sex had never
been romance novel–worthy.

Sex hadn't even been a thought in her head all
through the rapid decline in Tom's health. She certainly hadn't thought about it since his death. She
was too stressed over simply surviving. Maintaining
the property and paying the bills occupied every
ounce of her resolve.

It seemed odd that one brief meeting with Tyler

had her craving the wild sex she'd never known and had never thought she'd been missing out on. Fantasizing about a man, especially one so much younger than herself, was about as foreign a concept to Janie as being a widow at thirty-six and trying to hold on to the ranch alone.

Stranger things had happened in her life lately than having inappropriate thoughts about a hot, young cowboy. Given that, she'd just chalk this up to stress. She decided not to worry about it, though it might be best if he did renege on their deal and failed to show up to help with the fence. She didn't need the image of him sweaty and breathless from work adding more fodder for her libido's already overactive imaginings.

Her crazy thoughts were most likely caused by sleep deprivation. It was time to get her head on straight and get moving for the day. The best way she knew of to do that was to get her butt in motion and make some coffee.

Simple enough, but even that was not without its challenges. Walking into the kitchen every morning and finding it empty had been the hardest change to get used to since Tom had died.

He'd routinely been up before her. She'd married a man much like her grandfather. A farmer, born and bred. Tom had always been outside working with the hired hands, checking on the stock at sunrise. By the time she woke and had dressed, washed, and gotten ready for the day, which still was only about an hour past dawn, he and the guys would be on the way back to the kitchen in search of coffee.

Considering how much she dreaded facing that empty kitchen each morning, it shouldn't be a surprise to her she'd gotten into the habit of lazing around in bed. She glanced at the clock on the nightstand and saw how late it was already.

With no hands to cook for and not much in the way of stock on the property, there wasn't usually motivation to get up extra early. Today, however, she did have incentive. Tyler could be arriving any moment. It would be rude to keep him waiting when he'd come to help her with the fence.

Even though it was spring and the days could get hot, it felt cool this morning. Janie threw on a long-sleeved T-shirt, jeans, and boots, and then headed for the bathroom to finish getting ready.

With the toothbrush in her mouth, she evaluated her reflection in the mirror and tried to see herself as a stranger—as Tyler—might. Her brown hair desperately needed a trim. It was much too long, past her shoulders. The last thing she'd thought about in close to a year was going to the salon.

Her lack of sleep showed in the rings beneath her eyes—the green eyes with flecks of gold that Tom had always said first made him take notice of her all those years ago. She'd never believed him that it had been her eyes that attracted him.

Back then, when she'd been barely twenty and he'd been just over thirty, she'd had a pretty great body, if she did say so herself. Barrel racing and tending to the horses on her granddaddy's ranch had kept her in good shape. She'd been tan and toned, with sunny golden highlights in her hair and color in her cheeks.

Tom had taken one look at her at the stock sale she'd been attending in Texas and swore he'd fallen in love that day. It had taken Janie a little bit longer than a day, but a few years later, after she'd graduated from Oklahoma State and was working full-time with her grandfather, Tom had asked her to marry him. She'd said yes. How could she not love a man who'd been willing to sell his own place and move to help her and her aging grandfather on his spread?

What a difference the years made. No more sun for her. Nowadays she put on sunscreen and wore a hat, and tried not to look too closely at the changes in her figure. And as far as family . . . one by one she'd lost the most important people in her life. Her mother gone. Her father moved away across the country. Her grandfather, gone. Tom, gone. And here Janie still was, holding down the farm, alone.

She rinsed her mouth and stared some more at her reflection. Widowed or not, she was only thirty-six. So why did she feel more like fifty? Thank God she didn't look as old as she felt. At least she didn't think so. Not yet. Hopefully, she'd keep it that way.

With a sigh, she washed and dried her face and slathered on some moisturizer—the kind with built-in sunscreen. Just because she was a widow, that didn't mean she didn't care about getting wrinkles from sun damage.

Janie considered putting on makeup, but the urge only lasted a few seconds before she rolled her eyes at herself for even having the notion. If Tyler showed up at all, it wouldn't be for a social call.

She wasn't entertaining company today. She was having a ranch hand over to give her some help. However she looked would just have to be good enough.

Honestly, how ridiculous could she be? She was heading outside to fix a fence. That she was even worrying about her appearance at all was crazy.

Flipping off the bathroom light made it impossible for her to criticize her reflection any longer and put an end to her internal debate. She thrust all thoughts of makeup out of her head and turned toward the kitchen, where the coffeepot awaited her arrival. She needed to be quick about it, too. It was later in the morning than she'd planned.

Facing the counter, she poured whole beans into the grinder and hit the button that started the machine whirring as it pulverized the coffee with a noise loud enough to wake the dead.

Though if that were true, Tom would be walking through the door about now. He loved his morning coffee more than anything else. Possibly even more than he'd loved her. It was one reason why even though they'd made do with the stove that had been here since her grandfather's day, they had a top-of-the-line grinder and coffeemaker.

The day she'd purchased the machine, she'd had to have the instruction booklet out just to figure out how to brew the first pot. The memory made her smile even as she felt the kitchen's emptiness more keenly than usual.

The grinding finally complete, she grabbed the carafe and filled it with water from the sink. This morning, just in case Tyler did show up, she didn't set the machine to brew the minimum number of cups for just herself. She made a full pot. It wouldn't go to waste since she could always microwave it later and drink it herself if he didn't show.

A punch of the BREW button and she was done with her part in the task. Nothing left for her to do but wait and maybe think about food. As unhealthy as all the experts said it was, she'd gotten into the habit of not eating until lunchtime since Tom's death. It just didn't seem worth making breakfast for only one person. Of course, today she had someone to cook for. Tyler might be hungry after she and he finished working on the fence. . . .

Janie stopped herself from opening the refrigerator door and taking out a pound of bacon. She was thinking way too much about this wild cowboy she'd known for all of twelve hours. The truth was he might not show at all.

With a huff of annoyance at herself and her obvious innate need to tend to a man—any man, apparently—she turned to get a mug out of the cabinet next to the sink.

A dark shape, its bulk blocking the window of the back door, caught her eye. Startled, she jumped, but managed to hold in the scream that threatened to sneak out past the hand she'd pressed to her mouth.

Logic replaced fright soon enough and she recognized the cowboy hat and the cowboy beneath it. Living alone had made her jumpy. She wasn't used to company. She moved toward the door and swung it wide.

"I'm so sorry I scared you again. I seem to keep

doing that. I didn't mean to." He bowed his head in a move that would have looked contrite on anyone else. On Tyler, with a cocky smile lighting his face, it only made him look amused.

"It's okay. I was expecting you. I just got startled, is all." Janie figured it was simply a symptom of living alone after having people around the place for so many years.

"This here's Colton." Tyler stepped to the side and hooked a thumb in the direction of the blond cowboy behind him. Not only had Tyler arrived as promised, but he wasn't alone. Good thing she had made that extra coffee.

"Howdy, ma'am." The man introduced as Colton tipped his hat to her in greeting. "We spoke on the phone yesterday."

"Yes, we did." She had to wonder when ranch hands in Oklahoma had gotten so young and so handsome.

They certainly hadn't seemed so when she'd had a crew working here. Then again, her husband had done all the hiring. Tom had always chosen older, plainer, married men to work for them. It seemed Rohn leaned toward hiring a crew way younger than she was used to having around her own place.

Janie realized she was being rude, leaving them standing in the doorway, and took a step back. "Come on in, both of you. And thank you for calling and letting me know about the fence. I appreciate it."

"Not a problem." Colton dipped his head. "I didn't think it would be good to chance having your cows break out and somehow get in with our bulls."

She laughed. "I don't know about that. Considering

the bulls on your property, I might have me some prize-winning bucking stock in a few years if that were to happen."

"If you're thinking about breeding your heifers, I could talk to Rohn for you—"

"No. That's okay." Janie interrupted Tyler's offer. "I know full well that Rohn's bulls are potential champion buckers. My stock consists of a few heifers and some cows I was too sentimental to sell with the rest of the stock last year. It would be silly to even think about breeding them with your bulls."

Tyler shrugged. "Well, if you change your mind, just let me know."

"I will. And thank you." A beep from the counter behind Janie signaled the pot was done brewing. The fence would wait long enough for them to drink the coffee while it was fresh and hot. "Coffee's ready. Can I pour you two a cup before we head outside?"

"Yes, ma'am. That would be great." Colton nodded. "Black, lots of sugar if you've got it."

"Yeah, I've got it." She smiled as she poured. That was how her husband used to take his. She handed Colton the mug. "Sugar is in that big canister right there on the counter. Spoons are in the drawer just below."

She'd long ago given up on trying to keep one of those cute little sugar bowls full with Tom and the other guys dipping into it all day. Even though it had been nearly a year since she'd been drinking her coffee alone in the morning—and she only took one teaspoon of sugar in hers—she'd never put the oversized sugar container away. It was too familiar, too much a part of the kitchen, so it remained where it had always been.

Tyler took the mug Janie handed him. "I take cream and sugar in mine . . . if you've got any. I'm afraid I'm not as hard-core as Colton here."

Always the charmer, he treated her to the same self-deprecating smile she'd seen the night before during their odd encounter. Janie smiled.

"Don't worry, so do I. There's a quart of half-and-half in the fridge. Top shelf." Coffee without cream and sugar was torture, as far as she was concerned. It didn't matter how good the beans were or how fancy the machine brewing them.

"Thank you, much. I'll grab it for us both, then." He nodded, sending the cowboy hat into a dip as he turned to open the refrigerator. Tyler turned back to her with the container in hand. "Then when we've all had our coffee, you can come outside and see if Colton and I did a good enough job on the fence for you."

Janie drew her brows low. "You fixed it already?"

"Yes, ma'am." Colton leaned back against the counter with his mug in his hand.

"I was going to help—"

Tyler's burst of air cut her short. "No gentleman worth anything is gonna let a lady help him do something like dig out a fence post. We handled it just fine on our own."

"Yup," Colton agreed. "Wasn't a problem at all."

Their kindness threatened to bring tears to Janie's eyes. "I don't know how to thank you."

"This here fine coffee is thanks enough." Tyler

smiled. "Don't tell Rohn I said so, but he makes the worst coffee I've ever tasted."

Colton let out a laugh. "Ain't that the truth. Tastes like he scooped it out of a tire rut after a rainstorm."

Janie couldn't control her smile. "Maybe I should come over and give him a lesson."

The corners of Tyler's mouth lifted. "I think that's a very good idea. I can't think of a better way to start a morning than greeting the day with a beautiful woman and some good coffee."

His stare was so intense upon her that she felt her cheeks heat. She couldn't exactly say thank you since he hadn't said she was that beautiful woman he'd been referring to, but the implication had been there. Judging by the look in his eyes as they focused solely on her, his meaning was clear.

"Then I'll see what I can do . . . about Rohn's coffee, that is. It's the least I can do to pay you back for your work on the fence." Desperate to get out from under his gaze, she threw out that response and then turned toward the counter to add sugar to her own mug.

"I'll look forward to it." There was amusement in Tyler's voice as it came from much closer to her than she expected.

He leaned past her to set the container of half-and-half on the counter next to her. The move put him close enough that the combined scents of manly deodorant and good clean sweat hit her. That, along with the warmth radiating off his body as he brushed against her before moving back, had her hyperaware of Tyler. He was a man and she was a woman. Her body knew it and didn't care he was younger and she was a fool to even think of him that way.

Janie took her time adding cream to her mug. When she finally had no more excuse to hide in the corner, she turned. She was in time to see Colton shoot an amused look at his friend before his mug covered the smirk on his lips.

Tyler was a flirt. Colton knew it. Jed from the lumberyard had known it. Deep down, Janie realized it, too, which made it even more ridiculous that she was letting him get to her. He was a young, cocky ranch hand enjoying life. Enjoying it a bit too much, as far as she could see.

She needed to get herself back on level ground. She was a mature woman who also happened to be the sole owner of a large tract of land, some damn good horses, and a few head of cattle. Things weren't ideal, but she was hanging on. Those accomplishments were nothing to sneeze at in this economy, especially after last year's drought, which had been bad enough to put some farms in dire straits.

Searching for a safe topic of discussion, she asked, "So how's Rohn doing? I don't get to see him much."

"He's real good," Tyler answered before taking a sip from his mug.

Colton frowned. "You think so? It seems to me he's lonely. When we're busy working he seems okay, but when things slow down at the end of the day, he looks kinda sad. I think he's still not over losing his wife."

Janie nodded. "That I can understand better than most."

"I guess you can." Colton's eyes settled on her. "I'd meant to say it before, ma'am. I'm real sorry about Mr. Smithwick's passing. I'd met him a few times. He was a good man."

"Thank you. He was." She'd reached the point where she could smile at the good memories and accept the kindness of those who'd known her husband without tearing up. Maybe things were improving after all.

"If you need any help, like with the fence, just give Rohn a call and Tyler and I will be right over. Our other hand, Justin, too. As soon as he's back to work."

"Thanks." When Janie glanced at Tyler, she noticed his odd expression as he watched the conversation between her and Colton, maybe because she hadn't included him in her gratitude. She could rectify that easily enough. "Thank you both. I appreciate the help more than I can say."

She directed that last to Tyler. For once, there was no amusement in his expression when he focused his piercing blue gaze on her. "It was my pleasure."

Uncomfortable beneath his scrutiny, she raised her mug. "I guess you'd better finish up so you two can go back to work before Rohn gets mad."

"He'll get over it." Tyler's gaze remained on her.

"Still, I didn't mean to steal his two best hands for the entire morning."

"No stealing involved. I came very willingly. Believe me."

Her cheeks heated at the implication in Tyler's

words. Watching her face, he smiled, a smile that reached all the way to his eyes.

Janie had a feeling she'd be seeing that smile and those eyes again real soon. Most likely the moment her head hit the pillow and she closed her weary lids, and she feared there wasn't a damn thing she could do about it.

Chapter Seven

Rohn's sigh was audible even from where he stood across the yard.

Obviously, the man thought his employees were pulling into the drive so late because they'd indulged in too much booze or womanizing last night. He was wrong. Yeah, a woman was involved, but not like he thought.

Tyler slammed the truck door and ambled toward his boss. Colton did the same on the passenger side. When they'd moved close enough, Rohn crossed his arms and shook his head. "Do you see how high that sun is in the sky?"

Looking up at the sun, Tyler said, "Yup."

"I fed the horses myself. With Justin hurt and home recuperating, there's too much work to do in a day even when you two manage to get here on time."

"There sure is a lot of work to do around here. You're right about that. I guess we'll have to work late tonight. Right, Colton?" Tyler glanced over at Colton, who only rolled his eyes at him.

"If you're not too hungover to work, that is." Rohn let out another huff of breath and looked agitated.

Since Tyler had gone to sleep early and sober last night, that comment was extra insulting. Sure, he was torturing his boss, purposely by not telling him where they'd really been and what they'd been doing, but that was what the man got for making assumptions.

"Rohn, we're late because we were over at the Smithwick place fixing a broken fence for Tom's widow." Colton, the Boy Scout, ended the game that Tyler had been enjoying so much. "I'm sorry. We should have asked you first."

The older man's eyes softened and he let out a breath. "Yeah, you should have told me first, but it's all right. I'm glad you went over. Janie could use the help." Rohn's gaze cut away from Colton, looking less charitable as it landed on Tyler. "And you . . . You let me stand here and lecture when all you had to do was tell me where you'd been in the first place."

Tyler folded his arms across his chest and leaned back against the fence. "Yup."

"You wanna tell me why?"

Tyler shrugged. "My granddaddy always said the best way to teach somebody something was to let them screw it up a few times so they could figure out their mistake on their own."

Rohn's brows rose high. "So you're teaching me a lesson?"

"Yup. Trying to, anyway."

"And that lesson would be what?" Judging by Rohn's tone, he was not happy with Tyler or his lesson.

"You should never assume, because when you do, you make an ass out of you and me." Tyler repeated the saying he'd heard since he was in middle school. Back when he had thought it was a big deal to say the word *ass*. The sentiment still held now he was an adult. And the saying worked well to further goad his boss.

"There's only one ass here," Colton mumbled under his breath. Tyler shot his traitorous friend a sideways look.

"God almighty, Tyler, if you weren't so damned good with the stock, I swear . . ." Rohn let out a breath and shook his head.

"Thanks, boss." Tyler grinned, knowing full well it wasn't meant to be a compliment, but choosing to take it as such.

"Hey, what are you saying? I'm good with the stock, too." Colton frowned.

"Yeah, Colton, you are, but you don't piss me off enough to want to fire you."

"Oh, okay." Colton visibly backed down. He probably figured he should quit while he was ahead.

"Um, are we done here?" Tyler glanced from Colton to Rohn. "Time's a wasting. It's already late and I really need to get to fixing that shed."

Rohn leveled his gaze on Tyler before he let out another sigh filled with frustration. "Yeah, we're done here."

"All right. Nice catching up with you." He pushed

himself off the fence and headed toward the shed. A few steps in, he glanced over his shoulder at Colton. "You coming or what?"

A frown creased Colton's brow. "Yeah, I'm coming."

"Well, come on, then." The last thing Tyler saw before he turned back around toward the shed was Rohn shaking his head.

Nothing more fun than being a pain in the ass. Teasing Rohn to frustration always had been fun. And Colton? Well, he deserved whatever Tyler dished out today. It had been Tyler's idea to help Janie, but meanwhile when they'd been in her kitchen, Colton was the one who was all, *We'll help you anytime, ma'am. Just call and I'll come running.*

The kiss-ass had better not have any ideas in his head about the lovely Widow Smithwick, because whatever Colton was thinking, Tyler had already thought it. That marked a prior claim in his mind.

He opened the door to the shed and waited for Colton to catch up to him so they could each take an end of the table saw and bring it outside. They'd need to cut the boards to length in order to make the repair to the back wall.

Opposite him, machine in hand, Colton hefted the weight up while he asked, "Are we going out tonight?"

"Nah. Don't think so." Tyler followed Colton out while holding the other end of the table saw.

"Why not? We don't have to go to the Two-Step."

"Set it down here." They'd reached a level spot in the yard, so Tyler tipped his head toward the ground and lowered his end. "And yeah, I think I shouldn't be going back to the Two-Step in the near future."

Colton grinned wide, still amused at Tyler's misfortune the previous night. "We can go to the Thirsty Squirrel instead."

"Nah. I'm not in the mood." What Tyler didn't tell Colton was why he didn't want to go out. "You should go, though. Hey, you could call Justin and see if he's up to it. He's probably going crazy cooped up in his house, not being able to work or ride."

"You're right. Maybe I will give him a call."

Tyler wasn't the kind to give up easily on anything, his interest in Janie included. He'd just have to figure out the smartest way to proceed. There was nothing like good hard physical labor to help a man think. He had a full day of work during which to come up with some plausible excuse to get him back over to her place. A plan he'd hopefully start implementing right after he finished working at Rohn's today.

Just the thought of seeing her again was enough to have him whistling while he worked.

Chapter Eight

Janie entered the cost of the fence post purchase into the ledger under *Expenses*. Her grandfather had taught her how to keep the records for the ranch. Thank God for that or she'd really be lost now that Tom was gone.

There was something else she'd recently purchased, but she'd be damned if she could remember what it was. Her grandfather would be sorely disappointed in her. His philosophy had been to never put off what you could do right away. He'd say she should have written down whatever it was immediately after she got home. She knew what she should do. It was actually remembering to do it that was the problem lately. To be fair, she did have a few—or a few hundred—things on her mind.

Pen poised in the air, Janie tried to remember the forgotten expense, but her thoughts turned toward that morning and Tyler and Colton's visit instead. She tried to wrestle her mind back to the task at hand and decided it was useless. She'd remember when she remembered or when she came across the receipt in the truck. If she didn't, then the records would just not be accurate to the penny this year. Worse things had happened.

Whatever she was forgetting couldn't be that big, or she'd remember it. With that in mind, she decided it was time to eat. Food might help her waning brainpower.

After the late start and the visit from the cowboys, the day had gotten away from her. It was now afternoon and the sun was riding low in the sky. It sent beams of light through the office window, making the particles of dust dancing in the air visible. There was nothing she could do about the dust. It was nearly impossible to keep a house on a ranch completely dust free. She'd long ago stopped trying.

With a sigh, Janie heaved her tired body out of the desk chair. It couldn't be normal to be thirty-six and feel this exhausted all the time. Of course, it probably wasn't normal to be this age and a widow, either.

She headed for the kitchen and the food in the fridge that would comprise her dinner for one. Most people would think it would be easier, not having to worry about cooking for anyone beside herself nowadays. It wasn't.

Feeling the loneliness full force, she took out one bowl and one spoon. It was easy enough to scoop a bit of the cold chili out of a plastic container and into the bowl. Three minutes or so in the microwave and her dinner preparations would be complete. No muss. No fuss. And only one dish to wash.

Yup. Living the easy life, she was.

Movement out in the drive caught Janie's attention

and interrupted her unhealthy wallowing. A closer look told her there was a truck pulling into the drive. It was the same truck that had been there that morning.

Her heartbeat kicked up a notch as the vehicle came to a stop not far from the house and the driver's door swung open. Her pulse quickened further when she realized only one cowboy occupied the cab, and by the look of him, it was Tyler. Here. Alone.

The urge to run to the bathroom to check how she looked after the long day told Janie she was thinking too much, not to mention the totally wrong things, about this man. She should be grateful he'd helped. She could be curious as to why he was back. But she really, really should not be waiting breathlessly for him by the back door.

His long legs and matching stride brought him to the door, where he stood in front of her before she was mentally ready to face him. Somehow she managed to remember to open the door.

"Hey." Tyler shot her what she was beginning to see was his trademark grin. The one that had over the years probably won him the hearts of countless females, both young and old, if the racing of her pulse from being on the receiving end of Tyler's smile was any indication.

"Hi." She had to wrestle to untie her tongue to return his greeting. She couldn't help but wonder what he was doing here, but she couldn't figure out a way to ask without being rude, so she went with the next best thing—polite small talk. "I didn't expect to see you back here today."

His grin spread wider. "Eh, you know. I couldn't stay away. You've won me over with your excellent coffee."

Tyler's smile was infectious, or maybe she just turned into a giddy schoolgirl around him, because she couldn't help smiling back. "I can make a pot, if you'd like."

"No need." He held up a hand to stop her as she turned toward the counter. "I really just came over to talk to you about your hayfields."

"My hayfields? Okay. Come on in."

"You need to harvest that hay."

"I know." Those fields were on the *To Do* list she'd come to hate. She let out a sigh. It felt as if the weight of the world rested on her shoulders. Or at least the weight of a field of alfalfa and another of grass, both of which needed cutting.

"Well, don't look so upset about it. It's a good thing. It'll make you some cash. I know Rohn ends up having to buy hay every winter when we run through what we cut. I'm sure he'd rather buy it from you than somebody else."

"We never sold it before." In past years, they'd used it to feed their own herd over the winter, but now that she'd sold off most of the stock, she wouldn't need it. "You really think it'll bring in good money?"

"Hell, yeah. You know, after the drought last year, there's a shortage of both grass and alfalfa hay inventory. Prices will be way up for good-quality hay."

"And is mine good quality?"

"Looks it to me. But I'd have your hired hand cut it

now, if I were you. While the buds are just blooming. That way you'll get a second cutting."

That made her laugh in spite of the truth. "I don't have a hired hand anymore. Last year, one of the guys who used to work for us before Tom died did it for me. But he hasn't worked here in almost a year now. I guess I could call him. I honestly was going to give it a try myself."

"Yourself." Tyler's lips formed a tight line. "You ever harvest hay before?"

"Um, personally? No, but I've watched."

A frown drew his dark brows low. It was a striking contrast, his dark hair and brows framing eyes as brilliant blue as a summer sky. "Are you here working this place alone? You've got no hired help at all?"

"Nope. Just me." It was probably stupid to admit that, but this man worked for the neighbor she'd known most of her life. Rohn and her grandfather had been friends even before she married and Tom took over running the ranch. She could trust Tyler with the truth, although he didn't look very happy with her answer.

"How are you managing it?" he asked, still frowning.

She shrugged. "Selling the bulk of the herd helped. So far, I've found I can handle most things myself."

He swung his head, as his lips remained pressed tight. "No. I don't want you trying to do it. I'll cut the hay for you."

It was a relief, knowing she wouldn't have to do it for the first time alone. And if Tyler was right and she could sell the crop, she'd have money to pay him for the work. "How much do you get paid?"

"Nothing."

"No, I can't let you work here for free." The microwave chose that moment to ding, signaling her dinner was ready. She was prepared to ignore it and the smell of spiced beef hanging in the air. Tyler was not.

He glanced at the counter. "It's suppertime and I'm interrupting you."

"It's okay. It's just leftover chili."

His smile returned. "I was wondering what smelled so good. You use chipotle?"

"Yeah. How did you know?"

He tapped his nose. "I have a nose made for sniffing out good food."

Tyler also had other body parts—lean, hard, muscled parts—that looked made for enjoyable activities besides eating. She yanked herself away from her shameless thoughts. For lack of anything else, she said, "Would you like some? There's plenty."

What the hell was she thinking, asking this hot young guy to dinner? The offer had been vague enough that maybe he'd just say yes to a plastic container to go.

"I'd love to stay and eat with you." His smile lit his face.

Or maybe not . . . "Okay. Great. I'll just grab another bowl and microwave some more."

"Sounds good. I got the spoon." He moved to the correct drawer and pulled out one of the big soupspoons to match the one she'd laid out on the table for herself.

This man not only remembered where the utensils were kept, but he was setting another place at her table without her asking him to. All after she'd only known him for one day.

He caught her watching him as he reached into the holder on the counter for a paper napkin. "Something the matter?"

His question knocked her out of her trance. She yanked open the fridge and took the container out for the second time that day. Talking while she worked seemed to make it easier. "Not really. I was just thinking that somebody raised you right."

Ugh. She sounded like some old granny talking about his manners. Tyler didn't seem to mind. He laughed and held up the spoon. "Or my mouth's just watering from the smell of that chili."

"Here. This one's hot." She took the piping bowl out of the microwave and set it on the table. "Sit and eat. I'll heat up more and join you in a minute."

Tyler eyed the steaming bowl on the table. "Ladies first. What kind of gentleman would I be if I started to eat before you?"

"No. Guests first. What kind of hostess would I be if I ate before you?"

"All right. You got me there." Conceding the point, he tipped his head. "Thank you much. I don't mind if I do."

He sat, his long legs and lean muscles filling the chair and the space beneath the table. She felt the strangeness of seeing a man at her table again after what felt like a long absence. He dug the spoon into the steaming bowl, and for the first time in a while, Janie felt a sense of accomplishment, pride in having cooked a good meal for someone to appreciate.

She turned her attention to her own meal. The microwave chugged away on the counter with her bowl of chili inside as she watched the seconds tick down. It seemed like as good an occupation as any. Far better than staring, or trying not to stare, at her guest as he ate.

"When's the last time that equipment of yours was tuned up?"

"I don't know. Tom handled all that. Probably last year—" Janie caught herself. Last year he'd been so sick, she couldn't be sure he'd remembered to tell the hands to service the machines. "Possibly the year before."

"Tractors, the mower, the baler—equipment like that needs to be checked regularly and maintained even when it's not being used in the off-season. I'll take care of it for you. I'm good with machines."

Good with machines. Probably good with his hands. . . . Janie imagined there wasn't a whole lot Tyler wasn't good at. But still, she couldn't let him do her any more favors. "I can't let you—"

He held his hand up to stop her protest. "Stop. I'm doing it."

"Then you have to let me pay you for your time."

"Nope. I won't hear another word about it. It's a little oil and some grease. Maybe I'll have to change the blades. That's all. Nothing to it."

She sighed. "I don't like that you won't let me give you anything."

"Well, I didn't say I wouldn't let you give me something." The tone of his voice was as suggestive as the look he shot her.

Janie opened her mouth but wasn't sure what to say.

"I might be convinced to let you cook me dinner again some night." Tyler saved her from the embarrassment she felt. He grinned and held up a spoon overflowing with chili. "This is really good."

"Thank you."

Her heart beat faster at the thought of cooking for him. Of Tyler being her dinner companion. The scene formed in her overactive imagination . . . the dining room table set with her good dishes and linens. The sunset visible through the lace curtains. Tyler, filling the dining room with his mere presence. Janie, unable to eat a bite of food as her stomach roiled with all the nerves she hadn't felt around a man since her first date with Tom all those many years ago.

How the hell much longer was this microwave going to take? She needed something to do with her hands and she needed to change the subject. As the timer ticked down to the final thirty seconds, she decided the chili had heated for long enough. She punched the door release with one finger and grabbed the bowl. Heated through or not, the food was done as far as she was concerned. Turning back to the table, she put the bowl down at her place and sat opposite him.

Feeling the need to make conversation, she said, "So, you have any plans for tonight? Any visits to the lumberyard?"

"Nope." He raised his eyes to hers but then glanced down to concentrate on his food.

He seemed embarrassed. Janie liked this side of him, though she liked the confident, flirty side of him, too.

"That's probably better, since I'm home. My truck won't be in the parking lot for you to hide in." She couldn't resist teasing him.

He rolled his eyes, but he was taking the teasing in stride, judging by the crooked smile that lifted one corner of his mouth. "I'm never going to live that down, am I?"

"Well, if you keep helping me out around here, I'll really owe you. I suppose I'll have to stop teasing about finding you under the tarp in the back of my truck." Out of deference to the fact that he was going to do her a huge favor by helping with the hay harvest, she left off the part about the compromising state she'd found him in, with his belt and jeans hanging wide open.

"If that's the case, then I'm starting work here tomorrow."

"Don't you have to work at Rohn's?"

"I do. Don't worry. I'm good at juggling multiple things."

She didn't doubt that. She'd bet multiple women were sometimes what he was juggling.

"Just please, don't get fired on my account." If

that were to happen, she couldn't afford to hire him on full-time to make up for the loss of the job.

He let out a laugh. "If I get fired, it'll be my own doing, not yours."

Somehow, she believed him.

"But don't worry," Tyler continued. "I'll tune up your equipment in my off hours."

Janie's mind went to a bad place at the thought of the many things in her life that had been neglected and could use a tune-up, and the thought had nothing to do with farm machinery. She yanked her mind out of the gutter. "Okay."

"I can take a look at it tonight and see what I'll need. That way I can pick up any lube or oil on my way home and get started bright and early in the morning." Unaware of the turbulence within her, Tyler chattered on.

Lube and oil. Her insides warmed, while Janie had to wonder when those perfectly innocent farm machinery terms had taken on such sexual connotations in her mind. Since a hot-as-hell cowboy had decided to take her on as a charity case, apparently.

"All right. Tell me what I owe you for all that stuff. I'll reimburse you for whatever you lay out."

He dismissed her with a flick of his wrist and Janie realized it was going to be a struggle to get him to take any payment from her, even for expenses he laid out on her behalf. There wasn't enough chili in the world to repay him for all the help he was promising.

Strangely, she believed he'd do it all, too. Unlike her first impression of him, when she'd doubted he'd show to help with the fence, he'd proven himself reliable. He'd gone above and beyond, handling the fence repair before she even woke up, and recruiting help to do it. And tonight, taking the initiative regarding her hay harvest. She wasn't exactly in a position to not accept his help.

"Thank you." The words didn't seem nearly enough to express her gratitude.

"Don't mention it." His gaze captured and held hers for a moment before he broke away and went back to poking his spoon into the ever-lowering level of chili in the bowl. She remembered she had yet to start on hers and took a bite herself.

"So, anyway, when the equipment is ready to go, I'll start harvesting."

"On top of your regular work at Rohn's."

He glanced at what Janie knew was a look of doubt on her face. "It's not a big deal. Really. We take a breakfast and a lunch break during the day. I'll just skip one or both. Work straight through, get done early, and head over here to work until dark. The sun sets later and later every night."

"You can't—"

"Sure I can. I'll get to Rohn's early and put in my day's worth of work over there. Then I can pop over here to your place in the afternoon. I like to wait until after the sun's dried the dew on the fields before mowing, anyway."

She let out a sigh. Who was she to argue? Tyler sure seemed capable enough and seemed like he knew exactly what he was doing. Better than she did, she supposed, even after having spent so much time here with her grandfather growing up.

"All right. It sounds like a good plan." As Janie spooned another mouthful between her lips, she formulated a plan of her own.

She'd have to run out and go food shopping tomorrow and figure out a schedule of meals to make for the week. If Tyler really was going to skip his meal breaks at Rohn's just to help her out, the least she could do was make sure there was a good meal ready and waiting in case he showed up hungry at her back door.

The worst part was, now that she'd anticipated his being around, she really liked the idea. Making plans about a wild cowboy based on not much knowledge and an association of only twenty-four hours was bound to end badly. Even given that, she couldn't hold down her mood as it lifted, simply from the thought of having his company.

She needed to get out more if the prospect of one visitor did this to her. But for the near future, she wouldn't worry about forcing herself out of the comfort of her home. Tyler would be coming to her, at least until the haying was complete.

God help her, just the thought of Tyler being around had her heart beating faster. She was surely doomed.

A glance at Tyler's bowl told Janie he was way ahead of her in the eating department. Then again, Tom and the hands always had wolfed down their food. She'd never known if it was because they had worked up such a big appetite during the day or if all men ate like that.

"I can heat up some more if you're still hungry."

"Nah. I'm good. Thanks." He leaned back from the table. "Gotta watch my girlish figure. Your chili's so good I'll eat until I bust if I don't stop now."

Wearing a grin, he ran a hand over his stomach. His abdomen was so flat, she doubted he had anything to worry about, but she accepted the compliment. "Thank you. I'm glad you like it."

"More than like it. If you keep feeding me like this, I'll be like a stray dog hanging around your back door day and night, waiting for table scraps."

Tyler sure had the charmer role down pat. Almost everything out of his mouth seemed to be a compliment—not that she was complaining. "Lucky for you, I'm a big softy. As a teenager, I never could resist a stray. Dogs. Cats. Once I adopted a baby raccoon."

"Raccoon?" He cringed. "I'm afraid I'd have to draw the line there."

She laughed. "Yeah. My grandfather wasn't too happy about it either. It was a good thing the animal moved on once it got a little older and could feed itself."

His bowl empty, Tyler braced his bulging forearms on the edge of the table and leaned forward a bit. "So, you've got family around here?"

"No." If she had, she wouldn't feel so alone. "My mom died of MS when I was in high school. Multiple sclerosis," she elaborated for him, just in case.

"I'm sorry to hear that."

"Thanks. Anyway, her illness was a strain on my dad. More than he could handle, I guess. He got married six months after Mom died. The woman had young kids from another marriage, so he moved away and made a new family with her." Janie tried to keep the bitterness from her voice. She wasn't sure if she had succeeded or not.

As an only child, the task of tending to her ailing mother had fallen to her. At fifteen years old, when other girls were hanging out with their friends, she'd gone directly home to take care of her mother. Right up until things had gotten so bad they'd had to get a nurse in. Meanwhile, judging by the speed with which her father remarried, she had no doubt he'd been seeing the woman before her mother died.

Tyler's eyes widened. "What about you?"

"I suppose I could have moved with him, if I'd wanted to. He wouldn't have abandoned me, but I moved in here with my grandfather instead."

"So this was your grandfather's place?"

"Yeah. My mother had grown up on this ranch. This is where I'd spent summers my whole life. It was better for everyone that I came here, believe me. Gramps was getting up in years, so it was good for him to have the company. And I'd always loved this place. There's history. He and my grandmother bought this ranch right after they got married. They built this house and added the outbuildings as they could afford them. There are good memories here." She realized she was getting sentimental and long-winded, and cut herself short.

Tyler had let her go on talking, and probably would have for as long as she wanted to continue. He paid attention, but didn't interrupt. Once she'd stopped, he nodded. "It sounds like it was good you were here."

This conversation had Janie thinking about the past she rarely revisited. She didn't mind so much. It was better to remember than to forget. "Yeah. I think so, too. Anyway, the answer to your question is no. No family around here. I have a close girlfriend in town, but she's got her hands full with a daughter who keeps her busy, as well as a husband, so we don't see each other as much as we used to. The people at the church are supportive, but . . ."

"You don't want to impose on them," he finished for her.

"Yeah." She let out a short laugh. "There's that, and I can't picture most of them helping me harvest my hay."

He smiled. "I'm thinking you're right. But you don't have to worry about that anymore. I'll handle it."

She still felt his generosity was too much. "I'm going to give you a percentage of whatever money that hay brings in."

"Janie. Stop."

"No, I'm serious."

"All right." He held up a hand to end her protest. "We'll revisit this subject later. Let's get it cut and sold before we debate any more about it. Okay?"

"Okay." That she would agree to.

She still wasn't sure that field was the gold mine Tyler predicted it would be. Then again, what did she know? Tom had always handled the finances, and as she'd told Tyler earlier, they'd never sold their hay before. It had always been for their own winter feedings.

"Anyway, not to eat and run, but I need to get out there and check on the machines. See what you've got and what I'll need to pick up."

"I'll show you where the equipment shed is." She pushed her chair back from the table. If he was really going to do her this enormous favor, she needed to at least help in any way she could.

"Stay and finish your meal. I'll find it on my own."

"No, don't be silly. I can show you where we keep the tools and oil. Maybe we've got everything you need already." Janie realized she was still saying *we* even though, as they'd just discussed, she was completely alone here. She moved past that thought. "Besides, I'm a grazer when it comes to eating. I'll probably wrap that back up for later."

After a moment's hesitation, he dipped his head. "All right. I'd appreciate a tour. Then, once I have the lay of the land, I won't need to bother you anymore. I can just start work when I get here."

"It would be no bother. Believe me."

What was funny was that she suspected she'd like nothing better than having Tyler come knocking to ask her something or another. Maybe she'd omit a few key places on her tour so he'd have to come and find her. As she led the way out the back door, she realized she'd most likely lost her mind. Or maybe she was just lonely.

Their conversation had only reinforced the truth

of her new reality. She had no close family and only one good friend who was as busy as a beaver. Janie would have to rectify that situation, because counting on this wild young cowboy as a substitute for the companionship missing in her life was sure to be a bad idea.

She supposed she could open one of those online dating accounts. That thought left her feeling as cold as Tyler made her hot. *Crap*.

Chapter Nine

Tyler had already put in a good bit of work at Janie's before he pulled into Rohn's driveway to start his day there. Slowing on the gravel drive, he saw Colton's truck was already parked by the feed shed.

It was no surprise that Colton had arrived first. Tyler had tried to get there on time, but it took him longer to finish up than he'd anticipated. Not to mention the time spent scrubbing his hands to get the grease off in the slop sink in her barn. He couldn't arrive at work looking as if he'd already been to work. Colton would be sure to notice and ask questions. Questions Tyler didn't feel like answering.

"Morning." Tyler nodded and moved toward the buckets Colton had already filled with horse feed.

"Hey." Colton returned his greeting. "Where were you last night?"

"What do you mean?" He had hoped that if he kept his head down and concentrated on work, there would be less time for chatter. He wasn't so lucky. Colton was the inquisitive type.

Tyler had woken way too damn early that morning. He was tired, and trying to come up with an excuse on the fly was beyond him at the moment. Stalling and playing dumb seemed the best option. He sure as hell didn't want Colton to know he'd been at Janie's house until after dark last night working in her equipment shed. Or that he'd been back there by sunrise this morning to finish the job.

"I called your cell and you didn't answer."

"You called me? Why? What's up?"

"Justin and I ended up going out."

"Good to hear. He must be feeling better." Another topic of conversation was exactly what Tyler needed to avoid answering Colton's question. "When's he coming back to work? He say?"

"He has to go to the medical center this week. If the doc clears him, he'll be back to work."

"Good." Still stalling and not answering Colton's original question, Tyler nodded. "That's real good. Three guys are surely better than two."

The three of them working at Rohn's place would mean Tyler could sneak over to Janie's earlier each day. Though how the hell he was going to get out from under Colton and Justin's scrutiny was still a mystery to him. They'd want to know where he was going, and he didn't want to tell.

This idea—helping her to spend time with her— belonged to him. He was helping Janie alone, without their assistance or their questions. She was the most interesting woman he'd met in a long time. Maybe because she was just that—a woman and not a girl. The girls his age he met at bars were starting to wear on him. Cookie-cutter women. Sure, sometimes there were a few distinguishing factors, such as a pissed-off fiancé who wanted to kill him. But besides a few instances like that, Tyler's dating life seemed to consist of a revolving door of almost interchangeable females.

Until Janie.

Tyler dumped the bucket of feed into the bowl, patting the gelding's flank after he did. "Good boy." He came out and secured the stall door, about to grab the next bucket when he saw Colton was watching him.

"You never answered me. What were you doing last night that you weren't answering your cell?" Colton's brows rose. "Or should I ask *who* were you doing?"

That particular question was easy to answer— Tyler didn't even have to lie—but Colton's insinuation was still pretty insulting. "I wasn't *doing* anyone. I was in bed by ten o'clock. *Alone* in bed."

"Then why didn't you answer your phone?"

"I didn't hear it, I guess. I forgot it in my truck." What he didn't add was that he'd left the cell in the console on purpose, but still, it wasn't a lie, either.

Over the years, he'd learned there were a few gray areas when it came to telling fibs. As a good churchgoing boy, Tyler had investigated, and become well versed, in pretty much all of them.

Feed bucket in hand, Colton paused in front of the stall where the stallion they still needed to saddle break was kicking the back wall. He glanced at Tyler. "Well, you missed a good time."

Thinking Colton would be better served paying attention to the horse and not Tyler's social life, he tipped his head toward the stallion. "We gonna work with him any today?"

"Yeah. That's the plan. God, I hate Arabians." Colton scowled at the sleek young horse. The whites of the horse's eyes were showing as he eyed Colton back. Against the midnight black of his coat, his wild eyes made the horse look a little bit crazy.

"Don't go condemning the whole breed because we have one high-strung, unbroken stallion. He'll be good once we work some with him." Tyler cocked a brow. "And maybe if you'd feed him instead of talking, he'd stop kicking the damn wall."

That comment earned him a scowl, too, but at least Colton slipped inside the stall. He dumped the feed into the bucket and the horse quieted. Backing out of the door, he secured it and shot Tyler a look. "Maybe you need to go out and get laid."

"What? Why would you say that?" While a little sex was always a nice thought, Tyler had to wonder what had brought that comment on.

"Because you're acting like a dick today, that's why."

He had been in a fine mood until Colton had started with his inquisition the moment he'd arrived. "You're pretty pissy yourself, which only leads me to guess there wasn't any action in the female department last night."

"Ha! Shows how much you know. There was plenty of action, and are you gonna be mad you missed it. So listen, Justin and I walk into the Thirsty Squirrel and there's a—get this—wet T-shirt contest. . . ."

Colton launched into a recap of the events of the night before as Tyler grinned.

The subject of what he'd been doing the prior night seemed to be forgotten, for the present, anyway. Tomorrow, and every day after until he was done working at Janie's place, would be another story, but he'd come up with something. He always did.

He picked up another bucket and moved down the row to the next animal waiting to be fed. The procedure was the same pretty much every day. Not a lot of thought required to get through this part of the day. For a man who was trying to secretly juggle two jobs, that was a good thing. On autopilot, he listened to Colton chatter on. Tyler dumped the feed in the bucket for the gelding, locked the stall door again, and headed for the next bucket.

After the horses had bolted down their morning meal, Tyler and Colton got busy with the rest of their morning chores. They turned the horses out to graze for the day, the geldings in one field and the mares in another.

The black stallion, the problem child among the animals, would go into his own paddock. Tyler put the halter on the Arabian and led him out since the animal and Colton seemed to have issues with each other. The gorgeous animal walked like a dream on the lead rope, but Tyler didn't let that fool him. Putting a saddle on the animal would be an entirely different story, but that was for later, after the horse had digested his feed.

Until then, there was manure waiting in the stalls that they needed to clean. Not to mention bedding to replace and water buckets to be scrubbed and refilled, just like every other morning. Tyler grabbed a pitchfork and joined Colton, who'd already done the same.

As they each worked separately, but only one stall apart, they could still talk while mucking. Luckily, Colton had a lot to report about the night before. All Tyler had to do was listen and make an appropriate response every now and again . . . and plan his escape to Janie's later on.

There was nothing more fun than sneaking around, even if it was only to harvest a field. Of course, the term *a roll in the hay* didn't come from nothing. His mind wandered as Colton chattered on. Thoughts of the hay harvest were followed closely by images of the lovely Janie and all the things he'd love to do to her in that hay.

Scooping manure and wet bedding out of the stalls wasn't fun, but his thoughts had him smiling through the work.

Tyler remained in a great mood, through Colton's tales, through driving the tractor out to the manure pile, through setting up the afternoon feed buckets for the horses. He even faced the whites of the Arabian stallion's eyes as he slipped the halter over its head in the round pen.

"Good boy. We've got an understanding, you and I. Right? You let me ride you, and I'll let you go back to that nice grass. Deal?" He rubbed the horse's flank.

The horse seemed to agree—at least he didn't bite Tyler or try to kick him. That was good enough. He hooked the lead rope through the metal ring in the halter under the horse's chin and gathered the slack in his hand. "Here we go. Into that nice ring. Nothing to worry about."

"So what's the plan?" Colton watched as Tyler led the horse into the practice ring.

"I'm getting on him." He unhooked the lead rope and backed out of the gate, securing it behind him.

"You sure about that?"

"Yup." Tyler ignored the doubt he heard in Colton's tone. He leaned his forearms on the saddle and blanket he'd rested on the railing.

"I think you need to start slow."

"He's already halter broke. It'll be fine." Tyler watched the horse, hoping they had an understanding—the animal and he.

The quicker they got their work done, the sooner both of them could get on to other things. The stallion could go back to grazing and Tyler could plow through the afternoon chores and then sneak over to Janie's.

"I don't know. I think we should put a blanket on him first and trot him around the ring on a lead for a while. If he takes to that, put a saddle on him so he gets familiar with the weight and the feel of the girth. Work with him on the lunge rope with the saddle on and the stirrups up, and then drop the stirrups. Do that for a few days before you put the bridle on him. Wait until he's used to everything before you get on." Colton shrugged. "That's how I'd do it, anyway."

Tyler threw a sideways glance at Colton. "I don't work that way. I like to jump right in."

"Yeah, so I noticed. Like you did at the bar the

other night with the chick and her bouncer fiancé. How'd that work out for you?"

"Ha ha." Tyler scowled.

"Seriously, Tyler. I'm pretty sure Rohn won't mind us taking our time with this one. He's going to be worth a pretty penny after he's saddle broke. When Justin breaks the horses, he takes a few days to let them get used to—"

"Justin's not here right now, is he?" Tyler shouldn't have to remind Colton that Justin, in fact, had gotten trampled pretty good in the saddle bronc competition a few weeks back. But it wasn't worth arguing about. Tyler let out a sigh. "All right. We'll do it your way to start, but I sure as hell don't think it will take as long as you laid out."

"How you figure?"

"I'll lunge him with the saddle on. Tire him out a bit. Then I'm getting on."

Colton cocked a brow. "A'ight. I guess we'll see."

"Yes, we will." Tyler climbed over the rail and turned to lift the blanket.

Piece of cake . . .

Chapter Ten

"Up, down, up, down. There you go. You have to feel the motion of the horse and post in time with her step."

"She's doing good, isn't she? I mean, I know I'm a mother and I tend to gush, but I really think she looks good out there."

Janie smiled. "She is doing well. In fact, she's doing great. We can have her cantering soon. Right after that, we can try jumping some ground poles."

"Really?"

"Sure. Why not?"

"She seems so young to start jumping."

Janie laughed at her friend, Rene Morris. "Now you sound like a mother. Do you remember some of the stuff we used to do? Jumping on bareback. Racing through the field to see who could get to the pond first."

"Pretending we were rodeo queens and trying to ride standing up in the saddle while holding the American flag." Rene groaned. "Oh, God, I do remember. We're lucky we didn't kill ourselves. Please, please never tell Khriste any of that."

"I won't. I promise." Janie smiled, her eyes on Khriste in the ring. She raised her voice to say, "Now reverse direction. And remember, you'll have to post in time with the other leg now. Right?"

Khriste, a model student, nodded. Rene settled a hand on Janie's arm. "You're a really good teacher."

"Thanks." At least that was one thing that hadn't changed in the last year. Janie could still give riding lessons.

"You doing okay? You know, with everything?" The concern was evident in her friend's question.

"Yeah, I'm fine." Her well-practiced, rote answer slipped out easily.

"You sure?" Rene wasn't easily deceived. They'd known each other too long for that.

Time for damage control. "Yeah. In fact, I'm thinking of expanding."

"Really? Can you handle that alone?"

Janie didn't like the doubt she heard in Rene's voice. "Sure. I'm not talking about getting back into cattle. I'm thinking about boarding horses. As long as I'm tending my own, I might as well take care of a few more and get paid for it."

If she ever got ahead of the bills and stockpiled enough money to hire someone to build more stalls in which to house more horses.

"Oh, that's a good idea. That will probably open up your lessons to a wider group, all the people who are boarding here."

"That's what I'm hoping."

There had been many things she didn't agree

with her father on while growing up, but that was one decision she couldn't argue with now—her father's insistence that if she was going to ride, she had to be trained in both Western and English styles.

Back then, her young self had been livid to have to sit through jumping lessons when all she'd wanted to do was learn to barrel race like the girls she'd seen competing in the rodeos her grandfather took her to.

In hindsight, it was a very good thing her father had forced her into things sometimes. He'd paid for her to go to college. He'd let her choose her own major, but when she'd told him she was joining the rodeo team, he'd made her take equine management classes and jump competitively, as well.

That she could advertise she was trained in both styles of riding, and the fact she had blue ribbons from taking first place in jumping competitions, only made her more marketable as a teacher. Little did she know back then that years later she'd have to survive off the money she made from teaching riding.

"Oh, before I forget. Here." Rene shoved a few folded bills at Janie.

She shook her head. "No. You don't have to pay me. You're a friend. I'm not going to take your money."

"Janie, we've gone through this ever since you started teaching Khriste. Just take the damn money."

"But—"

"Nope." Rene shook her head. "I told you before, if you don't let me pay you, I'll just find another teacher to give Khriste lessons and pay her. And you know whoever that teacher is can't possibly be as good with her as you are."

This was a losing battle they'd been through before. Janie sighed. She took the cash and shoved it into the front pocket of her jeans. "All right. But I'm warning you. I'm putting anything you pay me aside and I'm buying her the best birthday and Christmas gifts I can think of with it."

"You'd better not spoil my child. I'm the one who'll have to deal with her later."

"That's what being a godmother is all about. Spoiling your best friend's kid . . . and then sending her home to her parents." Janie grinned at the friend she'd known for almost as long as she could remember.

"You coming to church tomorrow?" Rene asked.

"Of course." Janie frowned at the sudden change of subject.

"Good."

Suspicious, Janie leveled her gaze at her friend. "Why good?"

Rene looked guilty as sin as she shrugged. "No reason. Just wondering."

Janie had missed church on Sunday morning exactly twice in the past ten years. Once when she'd had the flu and decided if she did manage to get herself out of bed to go, she'd only infect the entire congregation with her germs, which didn't seem like the Christian thing to do.

The other time was when there'd been a horrible ice storm and even taking the truck with its four-wheel drive into town would have been too dangerous. It turned out that the preacher had canceled services that day, anyway.

She'd even managed to attend through the worst of Tom's illness. He'd insisted she take the time for herself and go, knowing it would help her to get out and see people. He was right. It had.

The point was, it was a strange question from her best friend, who knew her habits better than anyone. Something was up with Rene, and Janie had a feeling she knew what.

"Rene . . ." She kept her voice low with warning and a good dose of suspicion.

"What?" Rene asked, the tone of innocence way over-the-top. She stared toward her daughter in the ring. "Hey, is Khriste posting correctly?"

Rene knew Janie well, but it worked both ways. Janie knew when her friend was trying—badly—to hide something from her. With one quick glance at the horse and rider she said, "She's posting fine. Now, answer my question. What are you up to? And it had better not be a setup. I told you, I don't want to be fixed up with any men."

"It's not a setup. He goes to church. You go to church. So what's the harm if you're at the same place at the same time and happen to both sit with me and Tim and Khriste?" Rene shrugged, as if it wasn't a big deal. "He's single. You're single. . . ."

The suggestion hung in the air, and Janie decided she needed to nip Rene's plan in the bud immediately. "First of all, I'm not *single*. I'm a widow."

"A technicality." Rene dismissed that protest with the flick of one wrist.

"It's not a technicality to me." Janie let out a huff

of air. If her best friend didn't understand how she felt, who could? "I'm not ready to be blindsided and thrown into some date. Especially not at Sunday-morning service."

Not now. Probably not ever.

Dating. Christ. Never in her wildest dreams had she thought she'd be forced back into the dating world. Her wedding day was supposed to be the end of that. And the start of her happily-ever-after. Forever, together. 'Til death did them part . . . and it had.

"It's been a year, Janie." Rene's voice softened. "Tom died. You didn't. You're allowed to live."

"I know that." The tears were too close to the surface to say more. Not tears of mourning, though she'd cried many of those. Of disbelief over how her life had altered so drastically, and her inability to prevent any of it. Tiredness, too. Bone-deep weariness that had her near tears all of the time it seemed.

Janie turned her gaze to Rene. "Just give me time. Please."

Rene pressed her lips tight before finally letting out a big breath. "Okay. No fix-ups. But be warned, I invited Clyde to sit with us tomorrow, so . . ."

Janie closed her eyes for a second and gathered herself. "Did you mention me to him?"

"No."

"Rene, swear to me."

"I swear." Her eyes widened. "I didn't. I thought there'd be less pressure if I didn't say anything first."

Thank goodness for that. Janie sighed. "All right.

Just don't bring me up. At all. I'll go to service, I'll sit with you like I usually do, but nothing more."

"Okay." Rene's pitch rose as she got defensive under the weight of Janie's glare.

"Promise me." Janie eyed her friend, trusting her in this particular matter about as far as she could throw her.

"I promise." Rene went so far as to make a cross over her heart with her finger.

Guessing she couldn't get any better than that, Janie gave up. "All right. Now, can I please concentrate on your daughter's lesson?"

"Go ahead." Rene folded her arms. "Who's stopping you?"

It was a good thing she loved this woman like a sister. Janie shook her head and brought her attention back to where it belonged—her student. "Okay, Khriste. Good job. Time to cool her down. Slow to a walk."

"You look great, honey." Back in mommy mode, Rene shaded her eyes and watched her daughter rein in the mare.

Maybe it was time Rene had another baby. That might give her something else to worry about other than Janie's social life—or lack of one. She was considering mentioning that when the sound of a vehicle on the gravel drive caught her attention.

She turned to see Tyler's truck and smothered a groan. Worlds colliding could be a bad thing. The twentysomething she'd been lusting over since first spotting him hiding in her truck and her best—not to mention nosiest—friend whom she'd known since they were little girls were about to meet.

Maybe she didn't have to worry about that fix-up tomorrow at church, because she was sure Rene would be grilling her about Tyler during the service instead. Then again, it wasn't like Rene to put off until tomorrow what she could do today, so more than likely the questions would come immediately and she'd still have to deal with what amounted to a blind date at church.

In essence, her troubles had just doubled, but Janie still got a little flutter from seeing Tyler's door swing wide and him stretch his long, lean leg toward the ground. She couldn't help but think that if Tyler was her biggest problem today, she was doing pretty damn good.

By the time the rest of his big body emerged from the cab, Rene was watching him as well. He'd parked close enough that his strong jawline and killer muscles beneath the taut cotton of his shirt were clearly visible from where they stood.

"Who the hell is that?" There was more than curiosity in her tone. Rene's comment also held a good dose of admiration.

Janie couldn't blame her. There was a lot about Tyler Jenkins to admire. She was doing just that—appreciating how good he looked as he stepped out of his truck—as she tried to pacify Rene with an answer that wouldn't raise more questions. "He's one of my neighbor's hired hands. He's going to be helping me with the hay harvest."

"Well, well, well. I think I could come up with a few things I'd like him to help me with, as well."

Janie frowned and turned to her friend. "What are you talking about? You're a married woman."

"Uh-huh." Rene nodded without taking her eyes off Tyler. "Doesn't mean I can't look, now does it? Gather a little fodder to get me warmed up for date night with the husband. There's nothing wrong with that."

"I guess not." Janie laughed, even though she wasn't sure Tim would agree with his wife picturing another man during their date night.

"Can you just imagine what he'd look like shirtless and sweaty and driving a tractor? Or unloading a hay truck? Damn." Rene was apparently deep into her fantasies about Tyler already.

Sad but true, Janie had thought some of the same things herself. Worse, chances were good one hot day she'd get to see all of those tantalizing scenes in real life. Then she'd have the actual sight of him to haunt her, rather than just her imaginings.

Janie yanked her gaze from her friend to glance back at the object of their conversation. She saw him walking toward them and noticed a pronounced hitch in what yesterday had been a smooth stride.

Frowning at his gait as he limped close enough to hear her, she asked, "What happened to you?"

Tyler shook his head. "Nothing. I'm fine."

Her brows rose as she noted how he was still favoring one leg. "You're not walking fine."

He brushed off her concern with the wave of a hand. "It's nothing. I just landed bad. I've had worse. Believe me."

"Landed badly from what?" She crossed her arms, beginning to see Tyler was one of those men who refused to admit when he was hurting, even when there was clearly no hiding it.

"There's this horse I'm saddle breaking over at Rohn's. I decided it was time for me to hop into the saddle. He had a different opinion on the matter. It's nothing. Really." By now he'd stopped his hobble and paused to stand, a bit crooked, in front of Janie. He angled his head toward Rene and tipped his hat. "Ma'am."

Janie realized Tyler had far more manners than she did. She'd rudely neglected to introduce him and he'd had to take matters into his own hands.

"I'm sorry. Tyler, this is my friend Rene."

"Aunt Janie. How long do I have to circle?" The small voice came from behind them.

Rene turned to smile. "That's my impatient daughter, Khriste."

"Goodness, I forgot all about her." Janie cringed as she turned toward the ring. "That's good, sweetie. You can stop. Wait there. I'll help you down and we'll unsaddle him."

When it rained, it poured. Janie spent more hours alone in a day than she could count, but now she was being bombarded by people and situations needing her attention. Khriste would need help with the horse. Tyler was still obviously injured, though not admitting the extent of it, and Rene still wore a far-too-interested expression.

First things first. "Tyler, you don't have to work today if you're hurt. Seriously."

"I'm not hurt—" He paused midway through his denial as Janie's brows rose high. "I'm not hurt so bad I can't lube up your harvester."

Rene's eyes went wide in reaction to his state-ment. Janie knew her friend's mind had taken a turn for the gutter. As Rene bit her lip, probably to hold in a laugh, Janie tried to concentrate on the situation with Tyler. "Are you sure?"

"I'm sure. I can unsaddle that horse for you, too. That way you can keep visiting with your friend."

"No, that's fine. I was going to hose her down."

"I can handle that." He turned toward the ring.

"No, Tyler. You don't have to—" Janie halted her protest since he'd already walked away from her.

Pausing by the horse, he put one hand on the bridle. "Hey. I'm Tyler."

The little girl glanced down at him and smiled. "Hi. I'm Khriste and this is Bella. Aunt Janie is letting me ride her twice a week. I've only had a few lessons so far."

"That's very cool of her. Do you know the proper way to get down?"

"Yes. Can you hold her, though, so she doesn't move?"

"Sure thing." Tyler gripped the bridle a bit tighter while Khriste kicked her feet out of the stirrups and swung both legs over until she was on her belly across the saddle, just the way Janie had showed her in their first lesson. She dropped to the ground on the left side of the horse and glanced up at Tyler. "Was that right?"

"Pretty good for a beginner." He nodded. "You want to help me hose Bella down after we take this saddle off her?"

"Can I?"

"Sure you can. That sun's pretty hot today and she looks a little sweaty. She'll enjoy a nice cool bath. Don't you think?"

"Yeah, I think so." Khriste nodded her blond head so hard, her helmet looked like it might fly off.

"All right. Let's get her back to the barn." Tyler turned the horse toward the building. "You want to lead her?"

"Yes." Kristie reached for the reins.

"Nuh-uh. Stand on her left side. Always. Remember?"

"Yeah. Aunt Janie told me that. I forgot." Khriste looked crestfallen over her mistake, but Tyler's smile revived her quickly enough.

"That's okay. I forget things sometimes, too."

Once Khriste had run to the other side of the horse, Tyler handed her the reins and the three of them—Khriste, Tyler, and the horse—walked slowly toward the barn.

"Jeez, would you look at that?" Rene watched the unlikely trio walk away. "It's so touching it could be a freaking Hallmark commercial."

Since Janie's chest felt so tight just from watching the scene she couldn't seem to look away from, she couldn't argue.

"No wonder you don't want me to fix you up with the guy at church," Rene continued.

"What?" She tore her eyes off Tyler as he helped Khriste hook the horse up to the crossties in the aisle outside the stalls. "No. Stop. There's nothing going on with Tyler."

"Nothing yet." Rene's tone dripped with suggestion.

"What are you talking about?" Janie frowned. "You're crazy."

"Janie, come on. A hot guy who's good with kids

and animals. There might not be anything going on yet, but there will be soon. Seriously, how do you keep your pants on when he's around?"

"Did you miss the fact he's like twenty years old?"

"He is not. He's probably closer to twenty-five."

"Yeah. And I'm thirty-six." Going on thirty-seven before the end of the year, a detail her best friend knew well.

"So?" Rene asked.

"What do you mean, so? That's more than ten years." As Janie's voice rose along with her agitation, she glanced toward the barn to make sure Tyler wasn't listening.

"I know. Who cares? You're not old enough to be his mother. In my book, that makes him fair game, and you should be chomping at the bit to play with him."

"You're insane."

"No, I'm not. Older women being with younger men is perfectly acceptable nowadays. All the big stars do it."

"Yeah, in Hollywood. In case you haven't noticed, this is Oklahoma."

"I know." Rene's eyes brightened. "You wouldn't find a man like him in Los Angeles. They only grow them like that around here."

Janie's frown deepened as she looked more closely at her friend. "Something's happened to you."

Rene nodded. "Yup, I'm an old married lady with a kid, so I have to live through you and by reading naughty romance novels." She looked in Tyler's direction once more. "God, imagine having that hard body naked and on top of you."

"Jesus, Rene!" What Janie didn't admit was the twisting low in her gut that image caused. "And why in the world would he want me when he can have countless girls his own age?"

"Young guys like an older, more experienced woman."

Not knowing where Rene was getting her information, Janie shook her head at the whole concept. "I'm not all that experienced, you know. I got married to Tom right out of college."

Rene waved away that concern. "You know what I mean. I'm sure all young guys have a Mrs. Robinson experience on their bucket list."

Having no desire to play Mrs. Robinson, Janie had no words for her obviously insane friend.

"Look, I'm not saying you should marry him, or even date him, but why can't you two have a little fun? You're available. He's available—he is, isn't he?"

"I don't know. See?" Janie lifted both hands. "I know next to nothing about him."

"You know he's got Khriste wrapped around his little finger already. You know he came here hurt when he should probably be at the doctor's office or at least home resting. Unless he's so desperate for money that he can't afford to take the day off, that proves he's got a good work ethic."

The guilt must have shown on Janie's face.

"What? Why do you look like that?"

"I'm not paying him."

Rene's eyes grew wide. "You're not paying—you mean he's working here for free?"

It sounded even worse hearing Rene say it. Janie scrambled to explain. "I offered to pay him. He won't take it. I'm still going to try to make him take a portion of the money I get from selling the hay."

"Janie. The man is working for you for free. What more proof do you need that he's interested in you?"

"No, I don't think so. He's just being nice." She shook her head and focused on the single white cloud in the sky rather than face her friend's scrutiny.

"You're the one who's crazy, Janie. Not me. Now come on. We're going over there to watch your hired hottie bathe that horse. If we were at one of those male strip clubs in Vegas, we'd have to pay a bunch of money for a show this good. We've got it here for free."

Janie couldn't help but laugh, even as she shook her head. "You are so bad."

Rene ignored the comment and started toward the barn. "Did you see how blue his eyes are?"

That Janie couldn't deny. "Yes. He has very nice eyes."

Blue and deep. The kind a woman could fall into and get lost in, which was exactly why Janie should steer clear of Tyler, no matter how incredibly adorable he looked squatting down next to Khriste as they sponged off the horse's legs.

They'd moved to within earshot, so Janie changed the subject to something safe. "Do you and Khriste want to stay for supper?"

"Thanks, but I have to get home."

"Oh. Okay." Janie knew she was going to make the same offer of dinner to Tyler. If he accepted it, she'd be here alone with him, only this time she'd have to deal with the images Rene had put in her head the whole time.

Her heart beat a little harder as she tried, too late, to avoid noticing how incredible his ass looked in his jeans. She was in big trouble.

Chapter Eleven

Inside the tack room, Tyler easily lifted the little girl's English saddle onto the rack. It probably only weighed about fifteen pounds, less than half of most Western saddles and far lighter than the one he used for roping.

They'd turned Bella out into the pasture to dry off, and then he'd sent Khriste back to her mother. The little girl could have handled the weight, but she would never have been able to reach the top rack.

He didn't mind taking care of putting everything away by himself. Of course, Janie might have a different opinion on that. Having Khriste clean up all the equipment they'd used for the riding lesson and for the bath could very well be part of her teaching.

Here he was, breaking the rules just like back in high school. That was one good reason he'd never teach riding or roping. Teachers had always made him twitch too much to ever want to be one himself.

Then again, he'd never had a teacher who looked like Janie, or who was nearly as sexy as she was.

He was just hanging up the bit and bridle when he heard the sounds of the women talking. Janie's voice filtered to him from outside. "You sure you don't want to stay? I made homemade macaroni and cheese and short ribs."

Tyler's attention was piqued at the mention of Janie's home cooking. After flipping the fleece saddle pad over a rack, he turned for the doorway. Ignoring the twinge in his ankle and the ache in his back from being thrown by the stallion at Rohn's, he walked out of the tack room and into the glare of the sun. Leaning against the wooden post supporting the overhang above him, he crossed his arms and watched the scene with interest.

"Thanks, but I'm sure. We gotta get home. Say thank you for your lesson," Rene instructed her daughter.

"Thank you, Aunt Janie."

"You're very welcome." Janie's smile for the little girl emitted a warmth he wished were for him.

"Bye, Tyler." Khriste turned to him and waved so fast her little hand looked like hummingbird wings.

He laughed at her enthusiasm. "Bye, Khriste. Thanks for helping me with Bella."

"You're welcome. See ya."

"See ya." He nodded.

As her friends got into their car, Janie turned back toward Tyler. "You're good with children."

"I'd better be good with kids. We've got a new little one who just joined my family."

"Oh." She frowned. "Um, I didn't realize you had a baby . . . or that you were married."

He laughed. "God, no. Not me. It's my brother's wife's sister who had the baby. I still haven't figured out exactly how or even if we're technically related, but in any case, I figure the little rug rat's gonna be visiting a lot, so . . ."

She smiled and frowned at the same time. "I'm not sure, either. I guess you can be an honorary uncle. Kind of like I'm an honorary aunt to Khriste."

"Well, that looks like a pretty good gig. I won't mind being that one bit." He couldn't help but notice she'd looked pretty shocked when she'd thought he was married, just like she looked pretty damn happy now she knew he wasn't. That encouragement was all it took for him to ask, "So, you going to invite me for supper or what?"

Janie's brows rose high. "Yes, as a matter of fact I was . . . if you'd given me a chance."

"A man can't take any chances when it comes to home-cooked mac and cheese and short ribs. I didn't want to risk it." Tyler grinned. "So, what time you planning on eating?"

"What time would you like to eat?" There was a smirk on her face that belied the mocking in her tone.

"Well, I was hoping to get a bit of work in on the machine before, if that's all right."

"Of course it's all right. You're doing me a favor. How much time do you need?"

A solid week alone with her wouldn't be enough to quench his thirst, but they were talking about her machinery, so he shrugged. "An hour, I guess. Maybe an hour and a half."

"Okay. You got it." She dropped her gaze down his body before bringing it back to his eyes. "You can wash up inside the house when you're done, if you like."

Janie was checking him out. At least, he sure hoped she was because there was nothing he'd like better than for this woman to be attracted to him the way he was attracted to her.

"I'll do that. Thank you."

"Sure." She hesitated almost as if she wanted to say more, or was thinking about it. "Um, I guess I'll let you get to work. I'll be inside, if you need me."

"All right." He nodded and finally she turned and headed for the house.

Smiling, Tyler folded his arms and leaned back against the post. His gaze dropped to the sway of her hips and her ass in those jeans. He knocked his hat back a notch to watch her better.

Yup. Best thing he'd ever done, volunteering to help her with the fence post and then with the hay harvest. Hell, maybe his good fortune had begun even earlier that fateful night, when one crazy woman had chosen to take him outside for a kiss and fondle to piss off her fiancé.

If he hadn't had to hide out in her truck, who knows when he would have met Janie. Funny how fate worked. He shook his head at the wonder of it all and headed for the machine shed.

Time seemed to fly. Tyler figured that was what happened when a man was trying to get two hours' worth of work done in an hour so he could get inside to the woman he was sweet on. Before he knew it, it was time for dinner, but it was all good. He'd gotten the equipment checked, tuned, and lubed. It was ready to start harvesting as soon as he could get away from Rohn's to do it.

Next dry, sunny afternoon he'd have to do just that, get away so he could cut Janie's fields, but now it was time to make hay in a different matter. By sweet-talking Janie. He loved turning her cheeks pink with something or another he said. He'd realized a simple compliment would make her blush. That was a total turn-on. He smiled at that thought all the way to the house.

Janie was in the kitchen and saw him standing there, but it was the polite thing to do, so he knocked on the back door even though he didn't need to. His mama would be proud.

Speaking of his mama, he'd have to text home and tell her he was eating out again tonight. Not that she'd care. Since Tuck had gotten married, it had been as if their middle-aged parents were on a honeymoon of their own. Going out all the time. Taking classes together. Acting like they were dating instead of married for forever.

That was all fine with Tyler. He had things of his own to do. "Hey. Sorry I took so long."

"Not at all. You're right on time."

He hooked a thumb toward the sink. "I'll just wash up."

"You can use the bathroom if you'd like. It's right off the hallway. There's nicer soap in there than that stuff I use for the dishes."

Tyler smiled. What kind of soap it was didn't

exactly matter to him. There'd been times he'd been happy to have any soap at all, but he didn't argue. "All right. I'll do that."

"Spare towels are inside the closet," she called after him.

"Thanks." He headed out of the kitchen door that led to a hall.

It felt strange walking through Janie's house alone. Seeing snippets of her life. Moving deeper into her private domain. He passed a doorway and peeked into a room that looked as if it was a guest room. There was a bed, a side table, a chair, and not much more. Tyler moved farther down the hallway and hit upon the bathroom.

The spare bedroom might have looked unused, but this bathroom had more life to it. A few old tin signs hung on the walls, which were covered in old-timey-looking wallpaper featuring horses. The bigger towels were a rich brown, while the smaller ones hanging with them were a pretty robin's-egg blue. The combination seemed both masculine and feminine at the same time.

Feeling extra curious, or maybe just nosy, Tyler opened the closet Janie had mentioned. More brown towels were stacked neatly on one shelf. Rolls of toilet paper and bars of soap rested on the other shelf. But it was the items on the third shelf that he found the most interesting. Band-Aids in sizes both large and small. Peroxide. Antibiotic ointment. Ace bandages. Gauze, in both pads and rolls. There was even a bottle of veterinary liniment and fly-repelling wound ointment.

That looked more like the supplies of the woman

he suspected Janie to be—the kind who took care of everybody and their injuries, whether man or beast. He smiled as he grabbed a towel and closed the door.

After taking off his hat, he pulled his T-shirt over his head. The shirt he tossed onto the closed toilet lid, and then rested his hat on top, before flipping on the hot water.

There was a day's worth of sweat and dirt to wash off his face, arms, and hands before he sat down to dinner with a lady. He cleaned up the best he could in the sink and dried off before putting his T-shirt and hat back on.

Once the porcelain and fixtures were wiped, clean and dry, he folded the towel and laid it on the edge of the sink for lack of a hamper. If he was a neat enough guest, maybe Janie would invite him again.

He flipped off the light and went back out into the hall, but he didn't head directly for the kitchen. The living room was off of the other side of the hallway and Tyler couldn't resist taking a look. Again, like the spare bedroom, the room looked lifeless. Almost unused. There were a few photos here and there, but otherwise, nothing personal distinguished it as hers. He couldn't picture Janie in here, seated on this stiff, formal furniture.

Nope. Not one bit. He turned for the kitchen, the room that fit her perfectly. Where she looked at ease even as she worked. She was at the stove when he arrived. Pausing in the doorway, he remained quiet as she opened the oven door and with pot holders pulled the rack out. The bubbling-hot macaroni and cheese casserole looked good, but damn, Janie's ass looked even better. And hotter.

She straightened and set the dish on the counter before she turned to smile at him. "Perfect timing."

"Yeah, it sure was." He pushed off the door frame he'd leaned against and meandered over to stand next to her under the pretense of checking out the food more closely. "Looks good. Can I help with anything?"

"Nope. Just have a seat."

"All right." He sat and let out a curse under his breath when he remembered he still hadn't told his mother about dinner yet.

Thank God she'd finally learned how to text a couple of years ago. He pulled out his phone and punched in the text. He hit SEND and moved to pocket the phone when he thought better of it. Tyler took the extra step of powering the phone off before he shoved it into the back pocket of his jeans. He didn't need Colton calling during dinner.

Glancing up, he saw Janie had noticed. "I'm sorry. This is rude, texting while you're serving me dinner."

She shook her head. "It's fine."

"No, it's not. The phone is off now. It's just that I had forgotten to call home. I didn't want my parents to expect me for supper."

Janie's brows rose. "Your parents?"

"Yeah. I, uh, still live at home." It had never bothered him before—hell, why should he pay rent when he could live at home for free—but saying it to Janie made him feel ashamed of his living arrangements for the first time. Admitting his mommy still cooked and cleaned for him, still washed his damn laundry, made him look like a kid. That was the last thing he wanted Janie to think about him.

"That's nice you're at home with your parents. I lived here with my grandfather for years, up until he died. I miss him being around." She transferred a huge amount of ribs to a plate next to a large scoop of macaroni and cheese. She pivoted and slid the dish onto the table in front of him.

He could see the sadness in her when she turned to face the counter again, but he remained quiet, hoping she'd talk more. The tidbits about herself and her past that she occasionally let slip out fascinated Tyler. He didn't want to miss even one of the things Janie might say, but as she picked up another plate, she put a much smaller portion on it for herself and didn't say more.

As enticing as the hot and creamy cheddar sauce looked, as amazing as the spice rub on the ribs smelled, he resisted. He waited for her to sit and start eating before he dug in. He'd been raised with manners. Some of them had actually stuck.

Finally, she sat and he lifted the fork full of food he'd been dying to try. Flavor assaulted his senses as the rich, sharp cheddar filled his mouth. His eyes drifted closed and a low rumble of appreciation came from his throat.

He opened his eyes again to see Janie watching and smiling. "I guess you like it."

"Oh, my God. This is the best I've ever eaten."

She rolled her eyes. "Thanks, but you don't have to flatter me, Tyler. I would have invited you to eat anyway. It's the least I can do in exchange for all you've done for me."

"Janie, there's one thing you should know about me." He set his fork down and leaned forward, his forearms braced on the table. "I never mess around when it comes to food. I'm not flattering you. This is amazing."

"Thanks." Her cheeks turned pink and he couldn't help but smile.

"You're welcome." Satisfied she believed he was sincere, he picked up the fork again and dug in for another bite. "What's the spice? It's not jalapeño."

"No." She shook her head. "It's a pinch of cayenne. I bought a cookbook the year I got married and I've been using the old recipes in it ever since. I know a lot of places use other spices and other cheeses, but I just do the same thing as I always did. Plain old sharp cheddar. Oh, and a little bit of mustard, too."

"That's what that other flavor is. Don't change a thing, whatever you do. I don't care what else other places are putting in their mac and cheese, you leave yours just as it is."

She laughed. "Okay. Since you feel that strongly about it, I promise."

He reached for a rib and prepared himself to be overwhelmed. He moaned at the pure pleasure in the first bite.

Janie laughed. "It's nice to cook for someone who appreciates it so much. I hate only cooking for myself."

"Well, you feel free to cook for me anytime you

feel like it." He bit into the rib again, and the tender meat fell apart in his mouth. Another rumble of appreciation emitted from deep within him.

Glancing up, he saw Janie smile as she picked at her own plate. If watching him eat gave her this much enjoyment, he'd be happy to do it often. This could be the beginning of a beautiful friendship, and hopefully, so much more.

Chapter Twelve

The sun was riding low over the horizon when Janie followed Tyler outside to his truck. "Thank you very much for all your help, but you really didn't have to wash my dishes."

"Sure I did." Tyler grinned, the charm oozing from his every pore.

Janie couldn't help but smile in response, even as she disagreed. "No, you didn't."

He leaned back against the open tailgate and crossed his arms. "I did if I want you to invite me again."

"Oh, that was your plan, was it?" She laughed as she turned and leaned next to him, hands braced on the metal of his bed.

"Yup." He shot her a sideways glance. "Did it work?"

"Yeah. I think it did."

"Good." He nodded. They both sat and stared toward the brilliant colors lighting the sky while the silence stretched between them, until Tyler broke it. "Do you ever hear from your dad?"

The question surprised her. "Not really. No."

"Did he come to your husband's funeral?"

"No. He called, but he was busy with work and couldn't get away."

The wound hadn't quite healed over. She still felt the emotional scars when she talked about her mother's death or her father's emotional abandonment.

This conversation brought a little closer to the surface the dull ache she usually kept buried. She didn't resent Tyler for asking, even if she was shocked he was interested. Most guys his age would be out with their friends, yet here he was, sitting on a tailgate at sunset talking to her about things much too serious for such a pretty evening. He was probably meeting his friends later and had to kill time until then. That scenario made sense.

She wondered where he went with his friends, and how the girls there reacted to the likes of Tyler and Colton walking into a bar. Given how good they both looked, they were probably swarmed the minute they got in the door.

"I'm sorry that all happened to you." He covered her hand with his and squeezed before letting go.

The touch hadn't lasted long, but long enough for her to know he meant what he said. That he was sincere in his empathy.

Janie should probably be getting used to Tyler doing the unexpected. She wasn't. Surprised yet again by this guy, she said, "Thanks."

The silence descended once more until he turned where he leaned and angled his body toward her. "So why are you only cooking for one?"

At the question, she turned her head to look at him. "Excuse me?"

"You said you don't like cooking for only yourself. Aren't you dating?"

That elicited a laugh she couldn't control. "No."

Dating. Who would she date? And where the hell would she meet him? Though thanks to Rene, she'd have to sit through church with a stranger her friend seemed intent on setting her up with. Maybe that was why she wasn't dating. Interfering friends.

"Why not?" he asked.

Her mouth dropped open at his bold question. She expected this kind of prying from Rene, but not Tyler. Still, she felt compelled to answer. "It really hasn't been that long since Tom . . ."

After a beat, Tyler asked, "How long has it been? I thought it was about a year."

"Yeah, about."

"So you're not ready?" His eyes pinned her. He obviously wasn't letting this go.

"I don't know. I haven't really thought about it. There's been so much else to think about."

"Like the hay harvest."

"Yeah, that, and the broken fence." *And the lessons. And the bills. And the animals.* She sighed. "Just everything."

"So if someone were to, say, take care of that harvest for you, and that fence was fixed so you had time to think about yourself, do you think you would be ready?"

"To date?"

"Yup." His intense blue eyes never leaving her face, Tyler dipped his head in a nod.

"I don't know." She shrugged. "I guess. Why are you so interested?"

"Because I'd like to ask you out, but only if you're ready for that."

Ask her out? She knew he could flirt with the best of them, and suspected he was a ladies' man, but that Tyler might want to go out with her was so far off her radar, she nearly fell off the truck's tailgate.

"So, what do you say?"

She didn't know what to say. Even if she were ready to start dating, which she wasn't, Janie had a feeling she'd never be prepared to be with a guy like Tyler. Too young. Too wild. Too tempting. "How old are you, Tyler?"

"I'll be twenty-five next month."

"So you're twenty-four." At least he was a couple of years older than she'd first assumed when she thought he was twenty. Still, he was too young. Or maybe she was just too old.

"Yeah. Technically, I'm twenty-four, for now. Why?" He shrugged. "Does it matter?"

She laughed. "Yes."

"Why?" His brow creased beneath the brim of his hat. He really didn't understand.

"Because I'm twelve years older than you."

"I know, and next month you'll only be eleven years older than me. You said you were thirty-six the night we met. So?"

She'd forgotten she'd mentioned her age that night. Maybe Rene was right. Maybe Tyler did have a Mrs. Robinson, older-woman sex fantasy. If so, she didn't think she was the one to fulfill it. "What do you mean, *so*? That's more than a decade."

"And?"

"And that's a big difference."

He blew out an exaggerated breath from between his lips. "No, it isn't. Janie, it doesn't matter to me. Why does it matter to you?"

"I don't know. It just does." She didn't want to tell him that being with him made her feel old. That her worst fear would be sitting in a restaurant with him and having the waitress assume she was his mother.

Tyler pushed off the tailgate and took a step so he was standing directly in front of her, so close that she was in the shadow of his hat.

"No. You're not getting away with that answer. Tell me. What's really wrong?" His voice had dropped low as he questioned her. It sounded husky, and even more sensual than usual.

With him standing so near, she could see the day's worth of stubble darkening his cheeks and chin. She might want to think of him as a kid—it would make it a hell of a lot easier to not succumb to him—but Tyler was a grown man. And a hell of a man he was. She couldn't deny that as she was eye level with the bulging muscles of his chest that stretched the cotton of his T-shirt.

Janie swallowed and tried to regain her focus. "You should be dating girls your own age."

That was one truth about her avoidance she would tell him. Twentysomething guys should date twentysomething girls.

"I have. I've gone out with plenty of them, but not a one of them was anything like you." His blue gaze pinned her even as she averted her eyes to avoid the intensity she saw in them.

Janie wasn't used to being the object of a man's attention anymore. At least, not like this. "So I'd be a novelty?"

"A novelty, no. But you are one of a kind, Janie Smithwick. Don't you ever forget it." He raised his hand to capture her chin between his thumb and forefinger before he lowered his head, close enough she could hear him breathing.

The brush of his lips against hers was so brief, so gentle, it was almost as if she'd imagined it. He pulled back, but his gaze grabbed and held hers.

"When you're ready to take a chance on me, you let me know." He released his hold on her and turned to walk toward the driver's door.

She was still speechless, but managed to have the good sense to get off his tailgate before he drove away.

With one hand braced on the top of the door, he glanced back at her. "I'll be back to hay that field as soon as I can."

Janie nodded and he climbed inside, slamming the door after him. She realized she'd yet to speak.

What could she have said? Her lips were as numb as the rest of her from the shock of Tyler's kiss. She watched him pull to the end of the driveway and stop before turning. He waved one arm out the window as he drove away, and only when he was out of sight did she remember to breathe again.

* * *

Tyler opened the kitchen door of his parents' house and stopped at the sight of his older brother. Tuck's six-foot frame was bent at the waist, his head hidden behind the door of the fridge.

"Hey." Tyler closed the outside door and moved farther into the room. "What are you doing here?"

Tuck straightened and closed the fridge with a sigh. "Starving, apparently. There's nothing in there but rabbit food. When the hell did Mom and Dad turn vegetarian?"

"It's not that bad . . . yet. They're not vegetarians, but she does have him on a strict diet as of last week." One reason, but not the main one, that eating at Janie's was extra appealing.

"Great. Perfect timing for a visit." He swung the door open again and emerged from the refrigerator with a bottle. "At least there's a beer."

"*My* beer."

"Thanks." Cracking open the lid, Tuck raised the bottle in a mock toast before pressing it to his lips.

Tyler scowled. "Yeah."

"So what's with the diet all of a sudden?" Tuck dragged a chair from under the kitchen table and dropped into it, stretching his legs out in front of him. "Is this Tara's doing?" he asked, mentioning their sister.

"No. Why would it be Tara's doing? You know as well as I do she's just about taken your hand off when you tried to steal the bone from her rib eye steak."

"Things change. Now she's got her sports medicine

degree, she might think she's some kind of doctor and want to get us all healthy and shit."

"Nah. Tara had nothing to do with it. She's hardly here anymore between work and Jace. She spends half her time on the road following the bull-riding circuit and the other half in Stillwater with her new beau."

Tuck blew out a derogatory-sounding breath. "Yeah, that's another thing. Tara and Jace not only dating, but actually lasting for what? Going on a year this fall? I never saw that one coming."

Tyler snorted. "I did."

"You did not." Tuck screwed his face up with doubt.

"No?" Tyler raised a brow in challenge. "I sure as hell did. Tuck, two people can't fight as hard and as long as Jace and Tara did and not be interested in each other on some level."

"Yeah, well, it shocked the shit out of me when they came back from her internship and announced they were going to go out."

Go out was clearly a euphemism Tuck needed to hang on to rather than think any more about their little sister's sex life. When Tara had come back from that internship, she and Tuck's best buddy Jace had the definite look of two people who were getting sweaty in the sheets together. Pure and simple.

Lucky for them, Tyler had been the one here that day she got back and Jace drove two hours like a madman to get to her, while Tuck had been blissfully ignorant back in Stillwater. Which raised Tyler's original question one more time.

"You never did tell me why you're here." He was pretty sure Tuck hadn't driven all those miles just to drink Tyler's last beer.

"Emma and Logan had to come to make plans for the baby's christening, so Becca decided we should come along and help them."

Tyler laughed. "You? Help plan the christening? Do you know how?"

"No. When Becca says *we*, she means she wants to do something and I'll keep my mouth shut and go along if I know what's good for me. You'll see when you're married."

"Um, yeah. Great. Thanks. Sounds real enticing."

Tuck tipped his head to the side. "There are fringe benefits to the deal."

Tyler knew exactly what Tuck was referring to. His brother always had been easily swayed by the promise of sex, one reason he'd ended up in a bad first marriage. At least he'd chosen better this second time around in marrying Becca.

"So, anyway," Tuck continued, "while Becca and Emma and Logan are meeting with the pastor tomorrow after the service at church and meeting with the manager at the restaurant to plan some brunch for after the thing, I'm free."

"Are you? You sure you don't have to go—oh, I don't know—sample christening cakes or choose party favors?"

"No, I already asked. I've been exempted from the party-planning stuff because I gave up fishing at the lake to come here with Becca instead."

It was funny seeing his big brother so totally and

completely whipped. "There's a rodeo tomorrow. Wanna come?"

Tuck's eyes widened. "Really?"

"Yup." Tyler dipped his head. "Rohn's supplying the bucking horses and bulls. One of the guys is still out hurt, so we're down a man. We're bringing a lot of animals and taking the big double-decker trailer. There's room in the cab for a third, and Colton and I wouldn't mind the company on the drive."

"A'ight. I'm in."

Tyler glanced at the cow clock on the wall of the kitchen. "You know, there's still time to call in if you wanna ride."

"You riding?"

"I am." Tyler nodded.

Tuck looked clearly tempted. "Nah. I better not."

"Why not?"

"I didn't bring my gear bag. I don't have my rope or any of my shit."

"So?" Tyler shrugged. "I've got spare chaps, spurs, a vest, a rope, and a glove. You can borrow it all."

"Yeah, but—"

"But what?" Tyler leaned back against the counter and crossed his arms over his chest, leveling his gaze on his brother. "Tuck, when I was little and you were just starting out riding pro, I remember times you couldn't afford what you needed. You'd ride with borrowed equipment all the time."

Tuck rolled his eyes. "It's not that."

"Oh, wait." Tyler held up one hand. "The wife thing, right? You didn't get permission."

The frown that creased Tuck's brow was so deep, it was comical. "I don't need permission."

Tyler wasn't sure he believed that. "Then what are you waiting for?" He pushed off the counter and dug into his pocket for his cell. He scrolled through the recent numbers until he found the one he needed. He thrust the phone at Tuck. "There you go. That's the call-in number."

Tuck hesitated for way longer than any bull rider should when presented with a chance to ride before he finally nodded. "A'ight." He punched the final button to connect the call and raised the cell to his ear, while eyeing Tyler. "If she pitches a fit over this—"

"I'll take the heat. Blame it all on me, the bad influence who twisted your arm and made you ride when you didn't want to." Tyler already took the blame for most things, anyway.

He could deal with his sister-in-law. He'd talked his way around pissed-off women before, and he was sure he'd do it again. With Emma, Logan, and their three-month old baby right next door as a distraction, Becca might not even notice Tuck was gone for the day.

As Tuck entered the event, Tyler could only hope, because Becca could be one tough chick. Finally, Tuck hit to disconnect the call and tossed the cell onto the kitchen table. Tyler walked over to retrieve it.

"So, how you been?" Tuck asked, taking another sip out of Tyler's last bottle of beer.

Tyler couldn't help but think that an ice-cold brew would have gone down real nice and smooth right about now after a long hot day of working at both Rohn's and Janie's places. He'd have to go out and buy more if he wanted one, but he wasn't sure it was worth the effort.

Tyler pulled out a kitchen chair and sat instead. "I'm good."

"You're home early for a Saturday night. No plans?"

Tyler raised a brow. "Why are you so interested? Living vicariously through me now that you're an old married man?"

He wasn't about to tell Tuck he was waiting for Janie to go out with him, and until she consented, he wasn't going to waste his time, or ruin his chances with her, by seeing anyone else.

"Hey, I might be married, but I'm not old."

"Don't sell yourself short, Tuck. You are very old. At least, you're older than me." Tyler grinned.

"Pfft, since you're twenty-four, that's not saying much." Tuck let out a snort. "And being your age is nothing I look back at and long for. I was young and dumb back then, just like you are now."

"Thanks a lot. Real nice way to talk to your only brother."

Tuck rolled his eyes. "You'll live."

"Yes, I will. Now excuse me. I need a shower."

"You're not eating?"

"I ate. Besides, you said there's only crap in the fridge."

"Yeah, I was just hoping you were going out and bringing something back."

Tyler shook his head at his brother's laziness. The man would run ten miles before breakfast, but he wanted Tyler to deliver dinner to him? Not gonna happen. "Where's your lovely wife? It's Becca's job to feed you. Not mine."

"Don't let her hear you saying that. And she's over next door with Emma doing christening shit. Invitations or something." Tuck waved the detail off.

"Then go get Logan. The two of you should hang out."

Tuck screwed up his mouth. "Logan's on baby-sitting duty while the girls work."

Tyler laughed at the image of Logan, a forty-year-old career army officer, being stuck home on baby-sitting duty. "You know, a real friend would be over there keeping him company."

"Then I guess I'm a failure in the friend department. When it's my baby, I'm sure I'll be fine, but the kid barfed all over Logan the other day and I swear, I nearly lost it myself just seeing it. Ugh, and the smell. I don't know what the hell they're feeding that boy, but damn, it reeked coming back up."

That image, combined with the expression on Tuck's face as he told the story, was enough to have Tyler laughing until his stomach hurt.

When he finally got himself together enough to talk, he said, "I'm sorry, bro, but you're on your own for food. I ate, I'm beat, and I need a shower. I'm fixin' to watch a little TV and then hit the sack early. We gotta leave for Rohn's at six to load the stock and then get on the road for Elk City."

"A'ight." Tucker sighed and stood. "Guess I might as well do the same. Ain't nothing better to do."

"Okay." It wasn't his job to entertain his brother, so Tyler started down the hall. He paused and turned back. "Don't forget to tell your wife you'll be gone all day tomorrow with me."

"Yeah, yeah. Don't worry about me."

"It's not you I'm worried about, bro. It's her." He didn't need Tuck getting phone calls all day and being in a piss-poor mood because he was hours from home with no wheels of his own and had an angry wife waiting for him. "Remember, 6 A.M."

"I heard you the first time. Don't worry about me. You know damn well I've usually run ten miles, showered, and eaten by 0600, so you worry about yourself." Tuck turned left down the hall toward the TV room while Tyler turned right toward his bedroom.

Just like old times, bickering with Tuck, Logan next door at his parents' house—if Tara came home this weekend, it would really be like the old days, and they weren't always the good old days, either. Things could get a little crowded around this house, not to mention hostile, when all the siblings were in residence. One more reason he didn't mind working late at Janie's. Not that Tyler needed another reason. She was enough inspiration.

He decided he was going to think about that inspiration the whole time he was in the shower. Maybe longer.

Chapter Thirteen

Janie's butt had barely hit the wood of the church pew when Rene whispered, "You're late."

"I know. Thanks for noticing," she answered even though she had to think her late arrival would have been less disruptive to the rest of the congregation if she and Rene weren't talking.

She only had a moment to listen to the preacher before Rene leaned in close again and hissed, "So that's him, sitting next to Tim."

Apparently this was not going to be a peaceful service. Janie played dumb and asked, "Him, who?"

"Clyde. The guy I told you about."

"You mean the man you promised you wouldn't force on me?"

"I'm not forcing him on you. I'm just going to introduce you."

"Mommy. Shh." Khriste, eyes open wide, leaned forward to shoot a frown at her mother.

Rene pressed her lips together into a tight, unhappy-looking line. On the other side of their daughter, Tim smiled.

Janie had to fight a smile herself. There was a modicum of satisfaction that Rene had gotten reprimanded by her nine-year-old daughter for talking in church. It didn't make up for her friend breaking her promise by trying to fix Janie up with some random single guy. That'd annoy her any day. On the day after Tyler's strange and enticing kiss, Rene's effort to fix her up had Janie even more agitated than it normally would have.

Khriste's shaming of her mother worked. Rene was quiet for the remainder of the service, much to Janie's relief. Of course, the one time she didn't want the sermon to end, the service seemed to fly by. Maybe it seemed to go so fast because Janie's mind kept wandering to the cowboy she shouldn't be thinking of.

More likely it was because she was dreading the end of this particular sermon because she knew what was coming—the big introduction when she'd have to formally meet Clyde.

When the preacher was done and everyone stood, Janie had to admit that, like it or not, church was over. Unable to avoid it, Janie stood, too, as the pews around her emptied. She was about to turn for the aisle to make a quick exit from the building when Rene grabbed her arm.

So close. Her friend knew she was about to run and hide, and now had a death grip on her arm.

"Janie, hang on for a second. Before you rush away, I wanted to introduce you to Clyde." Rene leaned back a bit to include the man standing on the other side of Khriste and Tim. "Clyde, this is my best friend in the world, Janie."

For the first time, Janie got a good look at her potential mate. At least that was what he'd be if Rene had her way. What the hell had her friend been thinking? This guy looked two decades older than Janie.

Or maybe it was his gray hair and pastel plaid button-down shirt and gray trousers pulled up much too high making him look more like a grandfather than dating material. The reality was, beneath the salt-and-pepper hair and old-man clothes, he might only be ten or so years her senior. He could have the same number of years on her that she had on Tyler.

That, in a nutshell, was why it was absolutely insane that thoughts of Tyler had kept her up half the night. Why she'd overslept and had to rush through the morning chores, all the while keeping one eye on the driveway in case he pulled in to do some work.

Outwardly, she forced a smile and gave a little wave in his direction, while inwardly, she cursed her friend. "Hi. Nice to meet you."

He smiled, his eyes lighting up as they dropped to take her in from head to toe. "It's a pleasure to meet you." His voice sounded low and held a familiarity in its tone that made her feel as uncomfortable as his intense stare.

"Sorry, I'm blocking us all in." She gestured to the pew; she was standing at the end and had them all trapped between the wooden benches. "I'm just going to head outside."

She turned before anyone could stop her. Rene followed her out, as Janie knew she would. There was really nowhere else to go but out the front door and down the steps onto the walkway. Her only hope was to claim she was busy and get to her truck.

"So, Janie . . ." Rene's voice quashed that plan. "You and Clyde have something in common."

Besides Rene's nosiness affecting both of them? Janie turned. "Oh? Do we?"

"You do. His daughter is at Northeastern Oklahoma and rides for the rodeo team."

Not quite getting the connection, and not really wanting to, Janie said, "I didn't go to NEO. I graduated from OSU."

"I know, but you were a barrel racer back in the day and you used to rodeo."

"Yes, that's true." Janie nodded, thinking Rene's connection was a bit thin, and also calculating that Clyde had to be older than she was if he had a daughter in college.

"She loves it. Myself, I never saw the use. Costs me a fortune in lessons and costumes and to board that horse of hers, and for what?" Clyde shrugged. "She'll never get anything out of it."

"It can get expensive." Janie shot Rene a wide-eyed glance that she hoped expressed everything she hadn't said. Her best friend had fixed her up with a man who thought horses were a waste of time and money, knowing that Janie lived and breathed horses.

Maybe Janie did ride for pleasure much less now than she had in the past, but riding and horses were a way of life, as well as her livelihood now that Tom was gone. Rene should have known better, and

Janie intended to tell her so as soon as she got her alone.

But first, Janie had to get herself away from this guy. "Well, on that note, I really have to get home and take care of some things for my own horses."

"You have horses on your property?" Clyde visibly perked up at that information. "Do you take in boarders? We should talk. Maybe I could bring my daughter's—"

"Um, no. Sorry." She cut him off, desperate to nip any further association with this man in the bud. "I don't board. I only keep my own."

"But you're planning to start taking in boarders, right? Didn't you tell me that?" Rene asked. She was apparently a little slow on the uptake if she didn't notice how unhappy Janie was with Clyde and this whole situation. How desperately Janie was trying to get out of this delicately.

"Uh, yeah, I did say that, but I don't think I can."

"Why not?" Rene continued questioning her, driving Janie deeper and deeper into the lie.

"Um, insurance and, uh, zoning issues." Janie came up with the only excuses she could think of on the fly. "Anyway, I'd better go. It was nice meeting you."

"You, too, Janie. I hope to see you again real soon." Clyde looked far more interested in Janie, and her curves as the breeze blew her dress around her, than she was in him.

It was an uncomfortable situation to be in, and she owed it all to Rene. Janie narrowed her eyes at her friend. "I'll talk to you later."

"Yes, ma'am." Rene's smile didn't reach her eyes.

She knew she was in trouble, and so she should. That gave Janie some satisfaction, at least.

Meanwhile, she noticed Tim had kept well out of the whole fix-up debacle, taking Khriste to the table where the kids were being served cookies. Good man. He knew when to stay out of her business and her love life. If only she could get Rene to do the same. Janie had enough on her plate already.

In her truck, she'd barely hit the road for home when her cell phone rang. No surprise there. She'd been expecting it to. So much so she'd put her hands-free earpiece in before she'd even pulled out of the church.

"Rene Marie Morris, if you ever, *ever* try to fix me up with a man again, I swear—"

"What's the matter? I think he's a handsome man."

"I don't care what he looks like. He's a . . . a . . . horse-hating letch." It was the best Janie could come up with for her rant, but it was pretty accurate, in her opinion.

"A what?" A hint of laughter colored Rene's question.

"He thinks his daughter's riding is ridiculous and a waste of money. What kind of a father is that?"

"He didn't say that. He's just tired of paying for boarding the horse. Which is why you should help him out—"

"Oh, no. No way." Janie shook her head, even if Rene couldn't see her doing it.

"Why not?"

"I don't have a good feeling about him, Rene. He kept looking me up and down as if he was picturing me without my clothes on. It made me feel, I don't know, dirty. Or like I wanted to hide myself from him." Didn't it figure the morning had been so warm that Janie hadn't taken a sweater and she'd chosen a cool cotton sundress that revealed her bare neck and arms.

"I didn't see him doing that. If it was true, and he was eyeballing you, I would have noticed. Besides, you should be flattered. He finds you attractive."

Some attention was flattering. Some was not. Tyler obviously found her attractive, too, judging by that kiss, but he didn't make her feel dirty. She didn't have the impulse to cover up when he looked at her.

"I don't want to date him, Rene. That's it. Case closed."

Though this really wasn't over and wouldn't be as long as Clyde continued to attend her church. She'd been going there since she was a child, when she used to go with her grandfather. She'd be damned if she would abandon it because of one man. Rene had to fix the mess she'd created. If Clyde asked about her, Rene would have to lie. Tell him Janie had a boyfriend or something. How Rene got her out of this was not Janie's problem. Making sure her friend knew how she felt so this never happened again, was.

"I'm serious, Rene. No. More. Men. Got it?"

Her sigh came through the earpiece. "All right. No more fix-ups. But I don't understand—"

"No. Stop." Janie cut off her friend, not believing for one moment Rene truly understood how adamant she was about this. "Look, I need you to be my friend—"

"I am your friend."

"And," Janie continued what she'd been about to say when Rene had interrupted, "I need to know that I can meet you out somewhere or come to your house for dinner without being blindsided by a single man who just *happens* to be there at the same time. It's too much stress. I need you and Tim and Khriste to be my safe place. The people I can turn to."

The moment of silence on the line meant either Rene was actually listening and absorbing what Janie was saying, or the call had dropped. Janie could only hope it was the first option.

Finally, Rene let out a breath. "All right. I get it. But you have to know, I'm always there for you."

"Yes, I do. But I need you to be there for me without a man you want me to date attached."

"Okay. From now on the only man I'll subject you to is Tim."

"That's fine." She smiled. "I like Tim and he's already married so, you know, that takes the pressure off and all."

Finally, Rene might actually have gotten it— understood what Janie was upset about. Only time would tell.

"So . . ."

Uh-oh. That didn't sound like a promising start to their new understanding. "What?" Janie imbued her tone with a good bit of attitude as fair warning to Rene not to mess anymore where her nose didn't belong.

"You've ruined my daughter, you know."

"What? How did I do that?"

"She hasn't stopped talking about that young cowboy of yours since yesterday."

That brought out a laugh Janie couldn't control. "Sorry about that. What exactly is she saying?"

"What isn't she saying is a better question. There's the rundown of exactly how he did every single thing with Bella, which I've heard so many times by now I've got it memorized. Then there are the questions. Will he be there for her next lesson? Can he come and watch her ride in her first competition? Ugh, it never ends. Now she's got Tim asking who the hell this guy is."

Apparently, she and Khriste had the same taste in men. Janie wasn't sure how she felt about that, given Khriste was in grade school. It kind of felt like a sign. The universe telling her that yes, indeed, she was way too old to be kissing Tyler on the tailgate like some teenager.

"So, will he?" Rene asked.

"Will he what?"

"Be there next lesson?"

"I don't know. He does have another job, you know. One that pays actual money. He's only helping me out in his spare time." Oh, how she wished haying season would last forever. Because once it ended, so would Tyler's visits, just when she was starting to get used to having him around.

That was a bad, bad thought. She couldn't get attached to this wild young cowboy, even if his kiss had been as soft as butterfly wings but had still heated her insides to the boiling point.

Janie dragged her mind away from that dangerously tempting memory. "So what do you and the family have planned for the rest of the day?"

Chapter Fourteen

Tyler bowed his head and murmured, "Amen." The word was echoed a hundredfold, from the crowd in the stands to the cowboys down on the dirt in the arena.

The service done, Tyler raised his chin, planted his cowboy hat back on his head, and turned to his brother with a grin. "Gotta love cowboy church."

"Why? Because it's quick?" Tuck cocked one brow.

"Yeah. That, and because the food vendors open right after it."

Tuck shook his head. "You and your stomach. I swear, you're always thinking about food."

Frowning, Tyler took offense at that remark. "Hey, that's pretty funny coming from you, since you were the one complaining just last night about Mom not having anything good to eat in the fridge."

"Yup, I was. Which reminds me, I'd better fill up here before we leave for home because I don't imagine that situation's changed overnight." Tuck glanced around at the selection of vendor stalls selling fast food and drinks.

"Unless you went food shopping, you're right. I wouldn't count on it."

"God, Becca and I have only been visiting for two days and already I'm dying for something besides all that healthy shit Mom's been feeding us." He pressed his palm against his stomach. "I'd kill for a fried bologna sandwich about now."

"I know there's the usual. Corn dogs, fries, sausages, but I don't know about bologna. But even if you could find it, you know it won't be the same as from that place in Drumright you love so much."

"Nope, it sure won't be as good as Joseph's smoked bologna, but desperate times call for desperate measures."

Tyler laughed at the gravity in Tuck's tone. "That they do, brother. That they do. So, you look at the day sheet? Do you know what bull you drew?"

"Yeah. I never heard of him."

"That's because you don't ride around these parts much anymore."

Tuck rolled his eyes. "Now you sound like Jace. He's always bitching I don't ride enough."

"Well, it's true. So tell me. What's the name of the bull? I probably know him."

"Fire in the Hole?"

Tyler nodded. "Yup. I'm familiar with him. Good strong bucker. Only been ridden a couple of times and the guys scored real high. Good bloodlines. He's the son of Hand Grenade."

"Hand Grenade?" Tuck shot Tyler a look. "The bull that broke my collarbone during the last round of the state finals."

Tyler smiled. "The very same."

"Great." Tuck rolled his eyes. The man had never batted an eye at jumping on the rankest bull on the circuit, but today, he didn't look happy about his draw.

"What's wrong, bro?" Tyler paused to look at his brother. In his entire life, Tyler had never known his brother to hesitate. Not while lowering his ass onto the back of a bull or, from what stories he'd heard, when running toward enemy fire while deployed in Afghanistan. "Are you afraid?"

"Afraid of getting on the bull? Uh, no."

Realization dawned. There was only one thing that made sense. Tyler took a guess at what was wrong. "You did tell your wife you were riding today, I hope."

"Of course I told her." Tuck's brow drew into an unhappy line above his eyes. "I don't keep things from my wife."

"Okay. So if she knows you're riding, then what are you so worried about?"

Tuck hesitated so long, Tyler had to wonder if he was going to answer or not. "Because I know if I come home broke up, I'll never hear the end of it. She doesn't love when I ride."

It wasn't a two-thousand-pound bull Tuck feared, but a 120-pound woman. Tyler laughed. "That's what you get for marrying a city girl."

"Yeah, whatever. When you get yourself a girl-friend who lasts longer than two weeks, you let me know. Then we'll talk relationships. But until that happens, little brother, you don't get to judge me or how I choose to handle my wife."

"All right. It's a deal, bro." Tyler nodded even

though he could clearly see that if there was any handling going on, it was Becca handling Tuck.

Tuck blew out a derogatory-sounding burst of air. "I just hope I live long enough to see you settle down. You think it'll be in this decade?"

Tyler's thoughts turned immediately to Janie, the one woman he definitely would like to spend a long time getting to know better. "Don't you look so damn cocky. It could happen a whole lot sooner than you think."

"I'll believe that when I see it." Tuck shook his head. "And buckle bunnies don't count, not that one ever held your interest for more than a couple of hours."

"There are more women in the world than buckle bunnies, Tuck. You know that."

"Yeah, I know that. Do *you* know?"

"Hey, Ty!" Colton caught Tyler's attention as he came toward them from behind the chutes. "You better start getting ready. The broncs are coming up right after the opening ceremony."

"You're riding broncs?" Tuck asked. "I thought you were entered in the bull riding."

"I am. I'm entered in three events."

"Three?" The crease between Tuck's brows deepened.

"Uh-huh. I'm competing in the bareback bronc, the calf roping, and the bull riding. Sometimes I enter the steer wrestling, too, but only when Justin's here since I use his horse for that." Tyler shot his brother a look. "Didn't you wonder why I brought my bareback riggin', a roping saddle, and my horse with me? Why the hell would I need all that if I was only riding bulls?"

"Hell, I don't know. I guess I didn't notice."

Not notice? Tuck's head really wasn't in the game any longer. Maybe Tyler had made a mistake bringing him here to ride. He was acting like a clueless city boy more than a veteran cowboy with his pro card.

Tyler shook his head. "Come on, big brother. Let me show you how it's done."

Colton nudged Tyler in the side. "You do remember your brother was a state champion. Right?"

"Uh-huh. But that was only in one event and it was a very long time ago."

"I heard that." Tuck's gaze cut sideways to them.

Tyler glared back as they all walked. "That's good, 'cause I meant you to hear, old man."

"Old man?" Tuck repeated. "I can still whup your ass in the bull riding."

"Oh, really." Tyler cocked a brow. "Willing to put a little wager on that?"

"Yeah, I think I am."

"Twenty bucks I score better than you." There was nothing Tyler liked better than a little friendly competition.

"How about fifty?"

Tyler laughed at Tucker's counteroffer. "Fine. Fifty it is."

Colton glanced from one to the other. "Oh, boy. This is gonna be good."

"Yes, it is." Tyler nodded. "Good to put some money in my pocket."

Of course, he wished they'd be putting a wager

on the roping, since that was his best sport. His horse was seasoned, well trained, and well rested. Together, they were nearly unbeatable. But Tyler was willing to take his brother on in the bull riding, even if it was Tuck's best, and only, event today. No problem.

They turned and walked toward the system of pens and gates the rough stock were run through to lead them into the bucking chutes.

"Broncs, tie-down roping, and bulls." Tuck shook his head, obviously still absorbing this new revelation about Tyler's upcoming events. "You know you're nuts, right?"

His brother should know him better than to be surprised that when he did something, he went all in.

"No, I'm just that good."

Although when riding a bucking animal that outweighed a man by ten times, being a little crazy didn't hurt.

Chapter Fifteen

"You should be riding with a helmet on." Tuck glanced at Tyler from where he balanced on the rails of the chute.

"I will when you do, bro." Tyler clamped his cowboy hat lower on his head and climbed to the top of the chute next to Tuck's.

"I told you, I didn't learn with one. You did."

"I did, and decided I didn't like it."

Colton stood by, shaking his head. "Why don't you two save all this energy for the bulls?"

Tyler tipped his head in Tuck's direction. "Tell the old guy in the chute next to me that. I'm young. I got plenty of energy, plus some to spare."

More than enough to expend some quality energy on female companionship after he rode, though not one of the girls hanging around the arena today had gotten Tyler's attention. The woman he wanted to spend time with was a long drive away. He wouldn't get to see her today, but there was always tomorrow, after he had his winnings in his pocket from this bet with Tuck.

Tyler reached into his pocket for his plastic mouth guard and slipped it between his teeth. He glanced over and noticed his brother still messing around in the chute. Tyler pulled his mouth guard out. "Come on, bro. Nod and get going."

Tuck didn't answer, but Tyler knew he'd heard him just by the stiffening of his spine. Smiling, Tyler shoved the guard back in his mouth and lowered himself onto the bull. He needed to take his wrap and be ready to leave the chute as soon as Tuck's ride was done and the arena was clear. The judges didn't take kindly to riders who weren't ready and took too long in the chutes.

As he got ready for his own ride, Tyler kept half an eye on his brother. Beneath Tuck, the bull was acting up, bucking in the chute and rearing. Colton hopped up on the rails. He gripped the back of Tuck's safety vest, poised to pull him out if necessary. One of the stock handlers balanced on the rails on the other side of the chute. When the bull quieted enough, he pulled the bull rope tight one more time and handed it to Tuck, who rewrapped it around his gloved hand.

Tyler heard Tuck's mumbled "Go!"

In response, the gateman yanked the rope that swung the gate open. It crashed against the rails with the clash of metal on metal, shaking the chute where Tyler waited. Torn between watching Tuck's ride and grabbing the tail end of the bull rope being handed to him, Tyler tried to do both, splitting his attention. Lucky for him, his bull didn't act up the way Tuck's had or there could have been a disaster.

Even though the stock handler helping him with his rope obscured the view of his brother, the cheering of the crowd at the sound of the buzzer told Tyler that Tuck had covered the ride.

Colton jumped up on the rails and leaned toward Tyler. "Damn, that was a good ride. You're in trouble with the bet, dude."

He frowned up at his supposed friend. "Thanks a lot." His response was so muffled by the mouth guard, Tyler could only hope Colton heard his sarcasm.

"Eighty-seven-point-five for Tucker Jenkins." The crowd cheered louder after the announcer's revelation of the score sounded through the arena.

It was a good score, and it was going to be hard to beat. But Tyler couldn't worry about that. He had to concentrate. Focus on his ride. Narrow his world down to nothing but him and the bull. Ultimately his battle was with the animal. Tuck and his score had nothing to do with it.

As he wrapped the bull rope tight around his gloved wrist, Tyler pictured the gate swinging wide. He envisioned the bull turning toward the left as the gate opened to that side. In his mind he saw the bull spinning into his hand, but that was as far as he went. Bulls were unpredictable creatures. This one could just as well back out of the chute as go forward. Turn away from his hand as turn into it. Given that, he counted on his reflexes to react to any change in the bull's movement.

Tyler laid the tail of the rope across the palm of his hand and closed his fingers. With his free hand, he pounded his fist tighter around the rosined rope. He flipped his chaps out of the way and moved his feet back and forth, ensuring that his spurs were clear of the bull rope so he wouldn't get a penalty.

That was it. With his feet in position and his weight centered, he figured he was as ready as he was going to get.

He nodded, forcing out past the mouth guard, "Buck 'em!"

As it had for Tucker's ride, the gate swung open with a clang and the bull took off into the arena. The animal burst out of the gate and spun to the left, just as Tyler had hoped. His free arm held back and high, his chest thrust forward, heels in, toes out, Tyler maintained the position he'd practiced so many times, whether on the drop barrel or a live bull.

The bull dropped low in the front and bucked high in the back, all while spinning to the left. Tyler's muscle memory took over. Reflexes reigned in a sport where the action moved faster than reasoning and thought could. He broke at the hips to absorb the force of every one of the bull's moves.

Cockiness took over. Tyler felt it—the score was going to be kick-ass. Higher than Tuck's. High enough to win this bet. . . . Then the bull bounced on his front legs, led with his head, and reversed direction.

Tyler compensated for the reversal as the bull's move threw him off center. But the damn animal wasn't really changing direction. After feinting to the right, he turned back to the left with one powerful move. The next thing Tyler knew, the ground was rushing toward his face. He clung to the end of the rope as he fell, all while the sound of the buzzer cut through the air.

He hit hard, landing square on his shoulder. One hoof struck the ground close enough to his head to knock his hat off. Tyler rolled clear of the still-bucking animal as the bullfighters ran to shield him while he was still down on the ground.

The pain in his shoulder made itself known when he pushed off the ground and ran for the rails.

Pain didn't matter. Whether he'd hung on for the eight seconds and gotten a score did. Tyler jumped up onto the rail and spun to try and see the scoreboard. Numbers started to appear—scores from each of the four judges—and Tyler couldn't suppress a grin.

He'd made eight, but the question remained, was his score good enough to beat Tuck? The total flashed on the screen at the same time the announcer said, "Eighty-seven points for Tyler Jenkins. Only half a point separate the Jenkins brothers, and they move into the top two spots in the bull riding with only two riders left to compete."

"Dammit." Tyler jumped down and felt the twinge in his ankle when he landed. He ignored it and stalked toward the out gate.

"Hey, Ty!"

Turning at the sound of his name, he saw one of the bullfighters walking toward him, carrying his hat and his rope.

"Jeez, Neal. I'm sorry." Tyler drew in a deep breath and shook his head at himself. "I'm not thinking. Half a fucking point cost me a bet against my brother."

The ride home with Tuck gloating the whole way was going to be painful.

Neal grinned. "No worries. I got a brother myself. I understand."

"Thanks, dude." Tyler grabbed his rope with one hand. After knocking the dust off his hat, he clamped it onto his head.

"Great ride, Ty." A stock handler slapped him on the back as he walked.

Tyler nodded. "Thanks."

It was still half a point shy of being good enough, and he was sure his brother wouldn't let him forget it. He braced himself for the gloating as Tuck met him at the out gate.

"Your shoulder okay?" Tuck's glance dropped to where Tyler hadn't realized he'd been holding his shoulder. The bull rope and attached cowbell dragged on the ground, dangling from his limp arm.

He forced his hand down. "Yeah. It's fine."

"It was a good ride, right up to the end. I haven't seen you on the back of a bull in quite a while. You've improved. You looked good out there."

Tyler frowned and tried to figure out what game his brother was playing. Tuck should be acting like an asshole. Instead, he was being nice and giving compliments. It was strange. He didn't like it.

Colton appeared and interrupted Tyler's obsessing. "Great ride, Ty. I didn't think you'd be able to hang on there at the end, but damned if you didn't.

You held on to that rope all the way until you hit the ground."

"Yeah, I guess I did." Which was exactly why his shoulder was hurting.

"You're both gonna finish in the money for bull riding." Colton glanced from Tuck to Tyler.

Tyler had finished in the top three for the tie-down roping and bareback bronc, too. Losing fifty bucks wasn't the issue—the sum was a pittance compared to what he'd won. His competitive streak and the ego attached to it was the problem.

He decided to just get it the hell over with and bring up the subject that Tuck seemed to be avoiding. "You won the bet, Tuck. You're just gonna have to wait for your money until we get back to the truck. I got my wallet locked in the glove compartment. Or I can give it to you out of my pay envelope."

"All right. Whenever. I'm not worried." Tuck shrugged. "Hey, how about I use it to get the three of us a decent meal on the drive home?"

Colton's eyes lit up. "Sounds damn good to me."

Tyler knew his older brother. Tuck was not going to win a bet—one that Tyler had made in a rash moment while he was feeling full of himself—and not gloat about it. It was coming, the gloating Tuck was somehow hiding. He felt it, the same way he felt the approach of a big storm blowing in on a summer's day. It was right on the horizon, and when it hit, he'd have to grin and bear it. That was the price for coming up short.

Tuck turned toward him. "Ty, what are you in the mood for? Steak? Barbecue?"

This magnanimous behavior put Tyler even more on edge. "Your choice, bro."

"Nope. Loser's choice. It wouldn't seem right for me to choose since I won and all. Besides, you're hurt and I'm not. You should get to pick. Go on. Anything you want." Tuck grinned.

And there it was, the dig he'd been expecting, but twofold. He was a loser and he was hurt, while Tuck was neither.

Tyler pursed his lips and nodded as a scheme began to form. "All right. I know a place right off the highway, halfway between here and home. We can stop there and eat."

"Really? What place?" Colton frowned.

"I don't think you know it." Tyler dismissed Colton's question with a warning glare before his friend went and ruined the plan.

Colton picked up that something was going on and nodded. "Oh, okay."

"Sounds good, little brother. Whatever you want. It's your money. Or at least it was until I won it." A satisfied smile tipped up the corners of Tuck's mouth.

"Yup. It'll be good all right." A slow grin spread across Tyler's face, but he squelched it before his brother got suspicious.

"Now, if you'll excuse me, I have to go see about collecting my other winnings. You know, from first place in bull riding. Not from that little bet against you." Tuck glanced at the scoreboard behind Tyler. "And look, Ty. You came in second. Right behind me."

Tuck smiled wider as he strutted toward the payout window, but in spite of that, Tyler felt okay.

He'd get the last laugh. Tuck wanted the loser to pick the restaurant? He'd pick the restaurant and it wouldn't sound so good to Tuck once they got there.

He'd see how his meat-loving brother who hated all flavors exotic felt about sushi.

Chapter Sixteen

Janie glanced out the window of the kitchen door and saw the sun hovering just over the barn roof. It was getting late. Her gaze moved to the digital readout of the clock on the stove.

That was probably the hundredth time since getting home from church she'd checked the time. When she wasn't doing that, she was checking the driveway, watching for Tyler's truck to turn in.

With a sigh she went back to washing the blueberries in the strainer in the sink. They'd been ripe for a while but she'd put off picking them until today, when she needed something to occupy her mind.

Waiting for him was crazy. He never said he'd come to work today. He'd simply said he'd be back soon. But he'd been here every day so far, so why the change now? Maybe he didn't work on Sundays? That was very possible, though ranchers generally couldn't take days off since the animals needed tending every day, including weekends and holidays.

Rohn employed a few hands. They could take turns covering the chores, she supposed. . . .

Obsessing over Tyler and his work schedule was self-destructive behavior. Knowing she thought entirely too much about that man, Janie shook the water off the berries while scowling. She was upset not only at herself for looking for him all day, but because these berries were about to go into a homemade crust to make a pie in case he came over, which he might not.

Her gut twisted with expectation, nerves, anxiety, and very possibly a good dose of lust that she was trying to ignore.

Yup. She was definitely crazy. That didn't stop her from flipping on the oven to preheat before she dumped the blueberries, sugar, and flour into the bottom crust.

Janie flung a handful of flour onto the counter and pounded the ball of dough for the top crust with the heel of her hand. The whole situation had her so crazy that it felt good to hit something.

Dealing with her attraction to him was bad enough, but the memory of that sweet kiss was impossible to forget. Not to mention his words, which swirled through her brain until she was exhausted.

When you're ready to take a chance on me, you let me know.

How could she give him a chance? She was too old. He was too young. She'd been married for too long to even think of these things. Yet it seemed it was all she could think of. She grabbed the rolling pin and slammed it against the lump of dough, using more vigor than she needed to flatten it.

"Crazy. Stupid. Insane." She spat each word in

time with the roll of the pin across the floured crust. When she lifted the dough, it was way too big and much too thin.

She was pitiful. Thoughts of him had her so crazy she couldn't even roll out a simple piecrust. She folded it in half and then in half again. This time she went back to rolling with less force and held back the running verbal commentary. Only crazy women talked out loud to no one.

She used to find the process of baking very soothing. Almost like yoga or meditation. The careful measuring. The mixing. The kneading. The quiet of the kitchen. The heat of the oven and the smells filling the air. They would all work to calm and relax Janie.

It seemed baking a pie for Tyler did the exact opposite. His energy replaced the peace and quiet in the kitchen, just as he'd shaken up her world and her life . . . and she'd never felt more alive since meeting him.

That was exactly the problem, because when he was no longer around, when he'd moved on, what would she feel? Janie feared she already knew the answer. She'd go back to her boring life, and the fire he'd lit inside her would fizzle and die, leaving her feeling burned out. Charred. A black hole.

With a sigh, she lifted the crust for the second time. Happier with its size and thickness this go, she laid it across the berries. Crimping the edges, she spun the pie plate, pinching until it was picture perfect.

It felt better working the dough with her hands than it had when she'd used the rolling pin. In this final step, there was no potential to let herself get carried away and beat the crust into submission. She was feeling a lot calmer by the time she bent and slid the pie onto the top shelf of the open oven, until the crunch of gravel on the drive had her heart leaping.

Slamming the oven shut, she whipped around, toward the door. She recognized the white car she saw creeping slowly toward the barn. Her afternoon student, the one she'd forgotten all about, had arrived.

She blew out a breath. "Get a grip, Janie."

There she was talking to herself again, but that was a worry for later. She had a student waiting for her. Janie grabbed her cell phone and scrolled through the apps. She found the clock utility and set the timer for the amount of time it would take for the pie to bake.

The pie could bake while she was out in the practice ring. It would be fine as long as she didn't forget to take it out. The loud and obnoxious alert on her phone should be enough to remind her, even in her distracted state.

With one more glance at the phone to make sure she'd actually turned the alarm on, she saw the little icon in the corner of the screen. That confirmed her pie would be safe. Confident, she headed out to the barn to meet her student, but not without another glance at the road to check for Tyler.

Dammit, she was a goner, and what the hell she was going to do about it, she had no clue.

* * *

Tyler's truck was parked by the barn when she pulled into Rohn's driveway late that afternoon.

Just the sight of it had Janie's heart beating fast, hard enough it seemed to vibrate against her rib cage. If his truck was here, he must be here, too. Probably in the barn finishing up his afternoon chores, which was why he wasn't at her house.

Feeling foolish that she'd obsessed over his not coming to her place today, when clearly he couldn't because he was working at Rohn's, she pulled her truck up next to Tyler's.

Since there was a pie riding shotgun next to her in the passenger seat, it would have made more sense to park by the house. That way she could take it right inside. Nothing she did lately made a whole lot of sense. Why should where she parked be any different?

Janie cut the engine and swung the driver's side door open. She'd find Tyler and then deliver the pie to Rohn's kitchen, where the guys could all enjoy it.

Happy with that plan, she slammed the truck door and headed for the barn.

A figure stepping out of the building had her pulse quickening. It only took a few seconds for her to realize he wasn't the cowboy she'd been looking for.

She smiled. "Hey, Rohn."

"Janie. Good to see you." Rohn strode forward and hugged her. "How you been?"

"Good."

His stare focused on her for a few seconds, making her think he was trying to decide if he believed her answer or not. "Glad to hear it. Everything going all right over at your place?"

"Yeah, actually, that's why I'm here. A couple of your guys did me a big favor the other day by telling me about my downed fence and then fixing it for me."

"So I heard." Rohn nodded. "They're good kids. A little on the wild side, that Tyler, but both he and Colton are good-hearted souls."

The offhand comment had Janie's mind spinning as she absorbed all Rohn had told her about Tyler in two short sentences.

Wild. She'd guessed that already. Good-hearted. She'd figured that out, too. That was why he was helping her at her place.

Rohn had really only confirmed what she'd already known about Tyler, except for where he was.

"Tyler and Colton around?" She realized that sounded strange, even with her decision to add Colton to her inquiry so it didn't sound like she was stalking Tyler. She scrambled to explain. "I baked them a pie. You know, as a thank-you. And a thanks to you, too, for letting them off work to come over to my place to help me."

"It's my pleasure, Janie. Anything I can do to help you, just ask. You know that."

"Thanks, Rohn."

"But to answer your question, no, they're not here."

She glanced at Tyler's truck. "Oh. I thought . . ."

"They took the trailer. They hauled a load of stock to a rodeo in Elk City for me."

"Oh. Okay." A rodeo. Of course. Breeding and

raising rough stock was a huge part of Rohn's business. "You didn't go?"

"Nah. The kids can handle it."

Kids. Rohn had reinforced her doubts about Tyler's age with that one word. Even so, she could see Tyler was cowboy to the bone, and born to handle animals. "I'm sure they can. So, let me grab that pie out of the truck and let you get back to what you were doing."

The pie she'd baked before she'd lost her mind from waiting for Tyler and decided to come find him. She suppressed her embarrassment at that knowledge, opened the passenger door, and grabbed the dish, still warm from the oven.

Rohn let out a groan when she turned and he saw the pie in her hands. "I haven't had home-baked pie since . . ." He let the sentence trail off but Janie knew what he'd left unsaid. Since his wife had died.

"Yeah, I figured you weren't over here baking. I also remember what it's like to have hungry farm hands around the place. Never enough to eat, so I figured it wouldn't go to waste here."

"It most definitely will not go to waste. I can promise you that." He reached out and took it from her. "You want to come in for a cup of coffee?"

"Thanks, but I better be getting back." To what, she didn't know. But home was her default. Her safe place to run and hide since Tom's death. Her comfort zone.

"All right. It was really good seeing you, Janie." He glanced down at the pie. "I'll return your plate as soon as I can."

"Sure. Whenever. No rush, really. I have a couple.

I've made lots of pies over the years." She realized she was babbling, and stopped herself. "Well, I better get going. Have a good night."

"You, too, Janie. And thanks again for the pie."

"You're welcome. Thanks for, uh, loaning me Colton and Tyler." She nearly groaned at how stupid that had sounded.

He laughed. "You're welcome."

She gave a little wave and got into her truck, feeling foolish and just a step down from a stalker. Tyler made her do crazy things. She knew that, but she couldn't seem to stop herself.

Chapter Seventeen

"Sushi." Tuck was still grumbling when they reached the last stretch of highway leading to the ranch. "Of all things."

"What?" Tyler asked, managing to sound innocent. "You like fish. You go fishing all the time."

"Fried catfish is not the same as frigging raw, slimy . . . ugh." A visible shudder ran through Tuck.

"Aw, come on. It's good for you. All that raw fish and rice and vegetables is very healthy." Tyler grinned while at the same time bracing himself, because at any moment, Tuck was likely to haul off and crack him one.

"Both of you shut the hell up. Jesus. For hours you've been fighting." Colton shook his head. "Here's the sign for the exit. Thank God we're almost home. I couldn't take you two another mile, I swear."

Tyler grinned wider. Pissing off Tuck had been his main goal, but annoying Colton sure was a nice bonus. "What's the matter, Colton? Don't you have a brother you fight with?"

"I've got two brothers, but we sure as shit don't act like you two. My da would've tanned my hide when I was coming up if I talked to either of my brothers the way you two do to each other."

"Hmm." Tyler pressed his lips together and considered that scenario. "Sounds pretty boring to me."

"It figures you would think that." Tuck shot Tyler a look and then leaned forward to address Colton. "I can tell you, after being his brother for twenty-four years, your house sounds pretty damn nice to me. Quiet. Peaceful."

"Yup." Tyler nodded. "Like I said. Boring."

"A little boring would be real nice right about now." Colton let out a deep sigh and flipped on the blinker for the turn off the highway.

As they passed the beginning of the fence that marked the start of Janie's property, Tyler decided that a visit to her place would be a great end to a pretty good day, and seeing her sure as hell wouldn't be boring.

Colton steered the big trailer rig into Rohn's driveway, pulling slowly up the gravel drive. When Tyler saw his truck parked there, it reminded him that there'd be no stopping by Janie's this evening. He had Tuck with him, and they'd driven over together in one truck. He'd have to unload the stock and then hit the road for home with his brother. Poor planning on his part, he supposed. He smothered a sigh.

There was always tomorrow. Besides his desire to see her, there was actual work to do there. He'd have to get his normal work done and then sneak over in the afternoon to get at least one field mowed. The weather was supposed to be nice.

Make hay while the sun shines, they always said. Whoever *they* were. That went for more than just hay. He'd have to make his move on Janie soon, too, and ask her out for real. Not just hint about it. He wanted to take her out on a date and prove to her he was serious before some other man scooped her up.

A woman like her wouldn't be single long. Before the line formed, he intended to let his intentions be known. When she was in the mind-set to move on, he wanted her plans to include him.

Colton pulled the truck to the back pasture. They had the broncs in the top compartment of the trailer, the bulls in the bottom half, and in a small compartment separate from the bucking stock was Tyler's roping horse.

It took a little while to get the animals back to their proper places. They had to move the truck twice. Finally, Colton parked the trailer where it would remain until the next time they needed it as Tyler led his horse to the barn. One nice benefit of working for Rohn was being able to board his horse here for free. This was a good job all around. Even better now that he'd met the neighbor.

Tyler slid the bolt home on the stall door and turned to see Tucker. "Almost done. I just want to throw him a flake of hay, and then we can go."

"A'ight. I unloaded your saddle and the rest of your gear before Colton parked the trailer."

Surprised at his brother helping without being asked, Tyler said, "Thanks."

Tuck took a step closer. "He's a nice-looking horse. Where'd you get him?"

"At auction. He was pretty green and not all that well behaved under the saddle, so he went for cheap." Tyler was good at finding a diamond in the rough.

The same thing was true of his truck. It had cost him only eight hundred dollars because it had looked like a piece of crap when he'd bought it used, but some tender loving care and he had himself a great vehicle that he could take pride in because he'd fixed it up himself.

Tuck leaned a forearm on the door, looking in at the chestnut quarter horse. "So you trained him?"

"I sure did." Pride swelled inside Tyler. "Worked with him every day for over a year. Didn't take long to see that once properly trained, he could be more than just a pleasure horse. He must have cutting horse in his bloodlines. He took to it like a champ."

"He is a champ." Tuck scratched beneath the horse's forelock and got a snort and nuzzle in response. He glanced at Tyler. "You won the tie-down roping today."

"Yeah, I did." That his brother had admitted that out loud was pretty huge to Tyler.

It was almost a compliment, which was more than he'd ever expected. Tuck was certainly an enigma. At the arena after the bull riding, he'd been concerned and then went right to gloating. After the drive he'd gone from being cranky to giving compliments.

Tyler didn't know what to expect from him next, but after a long day on the road, and a fall that had his shoulder aching, he was in the mood for a bit of peace. "Hey, wanna stop at Big Daddy's for a burger on the way home? I'll buy."

Tuck's eyes widened. "Oh, my God. I would love a Big Daddy burger."

"All right. You got it." Tyler grinned at Tuck's enthusiasm. His brother was so easily bought. Just a big old hunk of beef could make the man happy. After tossing hay into the stall, Tyler brushed his hands together. "That's it. Let's head out."

Outside the door of the barn, they found Colton. "Trailer's parked. Just gotta check in with the boss and we're done."

Being done sounded good to Tyler. He turned toward the house and saw Rohn was already heading their way.

"Hey, boys. How'd it go today?"

"Good," Colton answered. "That new bull bucked better than I've ever seen him."

"Hmm, good to hear. He might earn his keep after all. How'd the horses do?"

Tyler fielded this question. "The roan was off. Second competition in a row he didn't buck well. I don't know if we're gonna get the rest of the season out of him."

Rohn blew out a breath. "All right. We'll put him in the practice ring next week. I wanna see him before I make any decisions."

"I'm up for it." Tyler nodded. He'd take any chance he got to practice his riding. If it helped his boss at the same time, all the better.

"Well, thanks again for handling today. My hip is acting up pretty bad. All those hours in the truck would've done me in. And thanks for the hand, Tuck. I appreciate it."

"My pleasure. I got to see my little brother ride, and I got to take some of his money as well as the purse in bull riding." Cocky Tuck was obviously back.

Tyler rolled his eyes as Rohn said, "Congrats."

"Thanks much." Tuck grinned.

Rohn shot Tyler a glance, as if he knew it was killing him to have his brother tease him here on his own turf. "You boys head home. I'll see you in the morning."

"That you will." Colton adjusted the angle of his hat. "Ty, see you tomorrow. Tuck, thanks for helping."

"Sure thing." Tuck dipped his head in a nod.

The good-byes done, Colton headed for his truck.

"Ready?" Tyler glanced at Tuck.

"For burgers, more than ready."

"All right. Let's go." Tyler spun on a boot heel, about to head toward his own vehicle.

Rohn's voice came from behind him. "Oh, I almost forgot. Get here in time for coffee in the morning. Janie Smithwick dropped off a home-made blueberry pie today."

Hearing her name alone stopped Tyler dead in his tracks. The fact she'd been here had him regretting he'd missed her as he spun back to Rohn. "Janie was here?"

"Yup. Looking for you and Colton. She brought over the pie to thank you for helping with the fence."

She'd thanked them for that. She'd made them coffee and fed him dinner. Twice. And if she'd come here today, it was because she was looking for him. At least that was what he hoped was her motivation.

The information had Tyler ready to crawl out of his skin. He wanted to get into his truck and drive directly to her ranch, but he had Tuck with him, and he'd promised him burgers.

Wrestling his eagerness to a manageable level, Tyler forced himself to sound only moderately interested in Rohn's news. "Sounds good. I'll be here for pie and coffee in the morning. Even if your coffee sucks, the pie will still be good."

"Yeah, yeah. I keep telling you, you don't like mine, you can make the damn coffee yourself. Funny how you never take me up on it."

"One day, Rohn. One day." Tyler turned and waved a hand, heading for his truck even as his mind spun, trying to come up with some way he could get to see Janie tonight.

"Damn, now I'm craving blueberry pie." Tuck laughed as he climbed into the passenger seat.

"Sorry. I don't think you can get homemade blueberry pie at Big Daddy's." Ty slid the key into the ignition as an idea began to form. "Hey, you mind if we get those burgers to go instead of eating there?"

"Not at all. I've been gone all day. I should be getting home to Becca anyway."

"Yup, that's what I figured." The thought that he could sneak back out and over to Janie's without Tuck even noticing had him smiling.

She'd come looking for him and she'd brought pie. That deserved a thank-you in person. Tyler emerged from his thoughts about Janie to find Tuck frowning at him. "You're fixin' to dump me at the house and go back out, aren't you. What? Some buckle bunny text you for a booty call?"

"There's no buckle bunny. Did you see me even talking to any girls today?"

"No, I didn't, but that don't mean you haven't got a few put away in reserve."

Tyler probably had half a dozen girls' numbers he could call if a tumble was what he wanted. But he didn't want to call any of them. A quickie with some girl who was interchangeable with any other wasn't what he was after.

Maybe it had been in the past, but not now. Not since Janie and her serious eyes and worried little frown and adorable pink cheeks had come into his life. She opened him up to the possibility of something deeper. To the existence of a woman capable of more than drunken flirting.

He'd be damned if he would tell his brother any of that. It sounded sappy in his own head. Out loud it would sound even hokier, and Tuck would surely mock him for it.

"You're right, bro. Heading out for a booty call. Jealous?" Tyler glanced sideways. "You better not let Becca know that."

"No, I'm not jealous, you ass. I just can't believe after leaving the house at the crack of dawn, working and riding—and wrecking—you're going back out to get laid."

Tyler let out a short laugh. Little did Tuck know it was worse. That Tyler was going out to see a woman without the hope of getting any sex out of it.

He was going just because he wanted to see her. "Well, you know me. I'm just a horndog at heart."

"Yup." Tuck let out a very judgmental-sounding sigh, like he'd given up on his wayward brother and his wicked ways.

This conversation was starting to suck the joy out of Tyler. He focused on the reality of seeing Janie again, not on Tuck's perverted, overactive imaginings about what his love life was like.

Let Tuck judge all he wanted. Janie had come looking for him at Rohn's. That was all that mattered.

Chapter Eighteen

After an early dinner, Janie lay in bed in her pajamas, flipping through channels and finding nothing to watch. Finally she turned off the television and grabbed the paperback that had sat on her nightstand for months. Most nights she was too tired to read. Tonight, it seemed she couldn't settle her brain to sleep, so she might as well give the book another try.

She'd just thumbed to the point where she'd left off when a sound caught her attention. Was that someone out in the drive? She sat up, torn between fear and excitement. At the soft knock on the back door, her hope grew.

As she hurried down the stairs, she ran through the possible scenarios. It probably wasn't a burglar. They wouldn't knock. But it could be Tyler. He would have had enough time to drive home from a rodeo, unload the stock, and get here.

She slowed once she reached the kitchen and saw the dark form at the door. The light she'd gotten used to leaving on outside all night illuminated exactly the man she wanted to see.

Trotting to the entry, she flipped the light switch and the locks and pulled open the door. "Hi."

"Hey." A wide smile spread across his face. "Cute jammies. Can I come in?"

"Um, sure."

What were the odds that the one night she was in pajamas hours earlier than usual, Tyler would show up? Actually, the chances were pretty good since he'd been there every night for days. She'd just figured since he'd been away at a rodeo, she wouldn't see him. She'd been very wrong.

"So, I heard you were at Rohn's today." He moved to the counter and leaned back.

"I was. I dropped off a pie."

"That the only reason you went over? To drop off a pie?" A sly smirk settled on his face and remained as he waited for her answer.

"Why else would I go over?"

"I don't know." He shrugged. "I thought maybe you might have come looking for me." He pushed off the counter and moved closer to her as he spoke, until he was so near she had to tilt her head to look up to talk to him.

Her mouth dropped open but she wasn't sure what to say. Deny it? That would be a lie. Admit it and be embarrassed? She couldn't do that either. "Um . . ."

His smile widened. She was so damn transparent. Of course he knew she'd gone in hopes of seeing him.

"I was sorry I'd missed your visit, so I decided to

come over." Tyler's gaze dropped to take in her T-shirt and boxer shorts. "I didn't realize I'd be so overdressed."

"Um, yeah. I was going to go to bed early and maybe read for a little bit."

"Reading. Wow. Not sure I know many girls who do that."

Her brows rose. "Then you're hanging out with the wrong girls."

"No doubt. I most definitely have been . . . in the past, but I've raised my standards a bit recently." His gaze was so intense, she felt her cheeks heat. Tyler shook his head. "Damn, it makes me crazy when you blush like that."

Janie raised her hands to her face. He took a step back, grabbing a chair from the table and sitting.

She guessed he was staying for a bit. Dressed properly to receive company or not, it seemed she had a guest. A hot cowboy with a smile that made her heart speed, and she was in her nightclothes. Janie pulled out the chair opposite and sat anyway.

"So, Rohn is holding the pie hostage until tomorrow. We're having it with coffee in the morning."

"I made extra."

His eyes widened. "You did?"

"I did." She didn't tell him it was because she hoped he'd be over the next day working and she wanted to be able to offer it to him. "Want a piece?"

"Heck, yeah."

Janie laughed and stood. It didn't matter what she wore. Apparently, all she needed to impress Tyler was food. She slid a knife out of the block on the counter and cut him a good-sized piece. After grabbing a fork out of the drawer, she put the slice on a plate and delivered it to him at the table. "There you go."

"Thank you much." He had the first bite in his mouth before she'd even sat again. She smiled as his eyes rolled back in his head. "Oh, man. Janie, you keep feeding me like this and I'll never leave."

If only that were true. "I'm glad you like it."

"More than like it." He stabbed another piece and shoveled it into his mouth. After swallowing, he glanced up. "So, have you thought more on what we talked about?"

"And what was that again?" Watching him eat made it hard to think of anything else except kissing those tempting lips.

"About if you're ready to go out yet, on a real date." The fork laden with pie remained poised in the air as he leveled his gaze on her. "With me." He shoved the pie into his mouth and chewed, but didn't stop staring at her.

She rolled her eyes. "If we went out and anyone saw us, they'd think I was your mother or something."

"You look nothing like my mother, and I think that's a pretty poor excuse." He put his fork down and pushed his chair back. "But if that's really your concern, I can fix it."

"How?"

"We'll have our date but we won't go out."

"So you mean we'll stay in, and like have coffee together, or eat chili, or mac and cheese, or pie. . . ."

"I know what you're getting at and no, I'm not talking about that. If a date in public is the problem,

then we'll have our first one in private. Come on."
He grabbed her hand and pulled her up and out
of her chair.

"Where are we going?"

"Outside."

"You said we were staying in."

"Stop being so literal." He glanced down at her
feet and her flip-flops. "Good. You have shoes on."

"Not exactly shoes."

"Good enough." He led her out the door, flipping off the kitchen light as they went. She scrambled to keep up with him as he set a fast pace to his
truck. He opened the passenger door. "Get on in."

Her feet stayed planted on solid ground. "I'm not
dressed and you said we weren't going out."

"Trust me. We'll never leave the property. I
promise."

For some inexplicable reason, she did trust him
and pulled herself up into the truck. He ran around
to the other side, started the engine, and swung the
truck into a wide turn. Soon they were headed
across her field toward the pond. He pulled up
close to the fence and cut the engine.

She smiled as he trotted around and opened her
door for her. The night air was perfect. Not too cool
or too hot. The only sounds were the peepers and
crickets and the occasional bellow of one of the
herd. As he handed her out of the truck, she said,
"All right. I'll give you credit for creativity. This is a
really pretty spot."

"You ain't seen nothing yet. Come on." He led
her around to the back of the truck and said, "Stay
right there for a sec."

He ran back to the passenger door and returned with a blanket. He spread it out in the bed of the truck. Before she knew what was happening, his hands were around her waist and he'd lifted her so she was sitting on the open tailgate.

He hopped up into the bed behind her and dragged a cooler forward. "Let's see what we have left here. Coke, water, beer, and energy drinks. All still cold. What's your pleasure?" He glanced at her, waiting.

Janie shrugged. "I don't know. Water is good."

"All right." He took a bottle out for her and one for himself, and then closed the lid on the cooler before he settled next to her on the tailgate.

She smiled at his impromptu cowboy date. "You done?"

"Well, there's some beef jerky in the cab, but I'm not going to insult you by offering you that after you've fed me such good food. But there is one more thing." He lifted his chin toward the tree line. "Look."

She turned to look where he'd indicated and saw it, the top edge of the full moon rising above the trees. Huge and bright, it was larger than life, a big brilliant orb hanging low in the sky. "Wow."

"Yeah. I saw it on the drive over. It's pretty cool, huh?"

As the moon rose before her very eyes, the first beams hit the pond, sending sparkles of light bouncing off the water. "It's beautiful."

"So are you." His voice seemed to brush across her, like soft, smooth silk.

"Thank you." Embarrassed and feeling shy, she

forced herself to just accept the compliment rather than tell him what she really thought—that she felt far from beautiful.

He reached out and smiled as he stroked his thumb across her cheek. "I bet you're blushing again because I said that. It's too dark, but I sure do wish I could see it." He let his hand drop. "So, this isn't so bad. Right? Maybe next time we can get inside the truck and, I don't know, drive somewhere off the property. What do you think?"

"Tyler, I don't—"

"Janie, I'm not giving up."

She smiled. "I'm starting to see that."

"Then you might as well get over it and say yes."

She didn't say yes, but she did say, "Thank you."

"For what?" He looked genuinely confused when he asked the question.

"For getting me out of my rut." She'd thought she'd been happy stuck in her nice safe box. It took a push—or two—from Tyler to get her out of it. But now that she was out here, what was she going to do?

"You're welcome." He grinned. "So you'll go out with me?"

She could not date a twenty-four-year-old, even if he was about to turn twenty-five. "No."

He nodded and drew in a breath. "All right. I'll keep trying."

She smiled, her guard dropping by the minute thanks to his never-failing charm. "I hope you do."

His brows rose as he looked surprised. "Janie."

"Yeah?"

"I made myself a promise that I wouldn't touch

you, not even to kiss you, until you went on a bona fide date with me. Once I set my mind to something, I usually stick to it, but . . ." He sighed and shook his head.

"But what?" She wanted nothing more than for him to finish that sentence.

"But, dammit, with you looking so perfect tonight, and us talking here in the dark, all I can think about is what you would do if I kissed you right now?"

She swallowed hard before being able to say, "I'd let you."

After his question and her answer, she'd figured he'd lean over from where he sat and kiss her. Instead, he hopped down off the tailgate and moved to stand between her bare legs, one hand on each of her thighs. She should have known Tyler didn't do anything halfway. It seemed he was a full-body kisser.

The heat of his touch against her skin only served to ramp up her need as he leaned in, watching her eyes the whole time. His hands moved up to her face as he closed the distance between them and her nerves got the better of her.

What the hell was she doing? This was real. Not some fantasy. "We probably shouldn't—"

"Blame it on the moonlight." He spoke the words close and then his mouth covered hers.

With the warmth of his palms against her cheeks and the pressure of his lips pressed to hers, Janie had to think the full moon was as good an excuse as any for losing her mind and letting Tyler kiss her.

This kiss was nothing like that first peck. True,

she'd barely been able to think of anything else since, but now she realized that kiss had been nothing compared to this one.

Tonight, she sensed the barely controlled passion in Tyler. Felt him holding back even as he surged ahead, leaning forward, kissing her harder.

He moved his hands down her body to her hips and pulled her closer to him. She felt the rough denim of his jeans poke into her through the thin fabric of her shorts. She felt something else too—the physical evidence that left no doubt in her mind Tyler wanted her.

Without breaking the lip lock, he took his hat off and laid it next to them. Tipping his head to one side, he took the kiss to the next level and slid his tongue between her lips.

Need twisted deep and low inside her. It twined through her body like kudzu vines growing out of control, taking over and smothering what little good sense she had left.

She welcomed his tongue into her mouth with her own, feeling the intimacy of the connection through to her core. She wanted this man. Needed him, and more than just this. Having all of him all night long might not be enough to quench her thirst, but it would be a start.

Janie wrapped her arms around his waist and held tight, half-afraid he'd leave. More scared he wouldn't and she'd do something she'd live to regret. If not in the morning, then a little farther down the road when he finally moved on and she was left here, right back where she'd started. Alone. Lonely.

The way she was feeling, she'd do anything this man asked of her, and to hell with the consequences. That response was so unlike her usual cautious self, it was as if someone else inhabited her body. Someone reckless who didn't worry about tomorrow.

There wasn't much hope of rational thought because both sides of her, the usually sensible self as well as the impulsive persona who seemed to have taken over, liked very much what Tyler was making her body feel.

He broke the kiss and brought his hands back up to her face. Leaning his forehead against hers, he sighed. His lips were upon hers again, but for much too short a time before he pulled away and took a step back even as she leaned forward to follow him.

Planting his hat back on his head, he sat on the tailgate next to her and cracked open his bottle of water. She'd long ago forgotten about her own.

He stared up at the sky for a second before shooting her a sly sideways glance. "Not such a bad first date, is it?"

"No." Her voice sounded so husky, she reached for her water, opened it, and took a sip.

"So do you think that maybe next time we can leave your property?"

"Tyler, I don't think—" She stopped midsentence at his loud exhale.

"Janie, you keep avoiding going out in public with me and you're gonna give me a complex. It's like you're embarrassed to be seen with me or something." He'd said it lightly, as a joke, but she had to wonder if it was what he really thought deep down.

"No, not at all. It's not you. It's me."

That elicited a laugh. "I've said that to a few girls myself. Now I know how it feels to hear it."

"It's true. It's not you. I just wouldn't feel right out in public."

"Because it's so soon after your husband . . ."

She nodded, not adding it was just as much because she felt too old to be out on a date with a man Tyler's age.

"All right. I get it." He tipped his head. "That doesn't mean I'm gonna stop trying, though."

"That's okay."

"It also doesn't mean I'm going to stop doing this." This time he did stay put when he leaned close and pressed his mouth to hers. His arm wrapped around her shoulder, cradling her head in the crook of his elbow as he kissed her deeper.

Somehow they ended up horizontal. She suspected it might have been her leaning backward that took them there, but Tyler didn't fight it. He followed her down, his arm cushioning her head when they landed.

One long, muscular leg moved over her. His weight on top of her only ramped up her need. It was crazy. She couldn't care less that they were in a truck bed instead of a real one.

The hat came off again and she took advantage of the opportunity. She ran her fingers through his hair, tugging his head next to her and holding him close as his mouth worked hers.

His tongue slipped between her lips, shooting the fire of desire through her whole body. Her hips lifted to press up, closer to him. He wasn't unaffected and moved farther over her, covering her body with his.

Parked by the pond in the moonlight, they made out like two teenagers in the back of his truck until she was a breathless bundle of need. She had no idea how long they kissed. All she knew was it didn't last nearly long enough as Tyler groaned and broke the kiss.

He let out a short laugh. "I can't believe I'm going to say this, but I think I'm gonna go."

She was ready to tear off that big buckle of his and explore what hid behind it, and he was leaving? "Um, okay."

"Believe me, Janie, there's nothing I'd rather do than stay."

Then stay. The words that echoed so loudly in her head never made it out of her mouth.

He pushed himself up and ran both hands over his face and hair before grabbing his hat and hopping down to the ground. He turned and extended one hand to help her up. He led her to the passenger door, and she followed, a little wobbly as her head still spun from his kisses.

He glanced at her from the driver's seat as he started the truck and maneuvered it over the grass toward the house. "I'll be here tomorrow afternoon to start on the small field."

He'd moved back to their business arrangements. Janie struggled to keep up. "I don't know how to thank you for that."

"I do. I wouldn't be opposed to having dinner with you after I'm done working." He held up a hand.

"And before you say no, dinner here at the house is fine, if you don't want to go out."

"Okay."

"Good." He threw the truck in park by her back door and got out to run around to open her door. When she'd stepped down, he dropped a much-too-quick kiss on her lips. His gaze dropped down her body and he drew in a deep breath while shaking his head. "I really gotta go. See you tomorrow."

"Tomorrow. Good night."

"'Night, Janie." He tipped his hat and got into the truck, but Janie didn't miss how he'd tried to inconspicuously adjust himself inside his jeans before climbing inside.

At least she knew a part of him hadn't wanted to leave. She'd have to live with that consolation. Right now, alone and needy, it wasn't nearly enough.

Chapter Nineteen

The alarm on his cell phone hadn't even gone off when Tyler was awake and out of his bed. He liked sleep as much as the next guy, but today he had inspiration to get up and out. Janie's pie awaited him at Rohn's house. Since she'd dropped it off yesterday, who knew how much Rohn had already eaten? He wanted to make sure he got a piece before Colton and Rohn made pigs of themselves and devoured whatever was left.

More than the pie, Tyler needed to finish today's work early so he could get to Janie's and mow that field. There was an optimum time to harvest hay, right before it bloomed. He wasn't about to sacrifice the quality of Janie's crop because he didn't cut it in time.

Dressed, his teeth brushed, and his hat and boots on, he was ready for the day ahead of schedule. At least he had been, until he reached the kitchen.

Tuck turned from the counter, brow raised. "You're awake earlier than I expected."

"Why do you say that? Unlike you, who seem to

be able to set your own hours—how, I don't know—
I have a boss who's counting on me to be there at a
certain time."

"You know we're between semesters at the univer-
sity. Usually I'm up well before the sun, working out
with the ROTC cadets."

"Yeah, whatever." Tyler's brother always acted like
the army was the only career where a man had to
get up and work early. He'd obviously forgotten his
cowboy roots. Most days, ranchers were up and out
earlier than anybody.

"Judging from your piss-poor mood and your
rising so early, I'm going to take a wild guess that
your booty call was less than you'd hoped for." Tuck
smirked behind the coffee mug as he took a sip.

The comment drew Tyler's brows low. "You don't
know half of what you think you do, big brother."

Last night with Janie had gone even better than
he'd planned. The memory of Janie's kisses was
enough to keep him warm the whole drive home
and straight through until when he finally passed
out. Their time together gave him some bright hopes
for the future.

Soon enough, she'd get over her hesitation about
giving their dating a shot. And in the meantime, he
was just as happy with their current relationship. He
sure as hell couldn't complain about the little make-
out session they'd had in the bed of his truck, even
if it had left him feeling pretty damn needy.

He had neither the time nor the inclination to
debate with Tuck. He had places to be and things to
do. "I gotta get going."

"Um, one of these days are you going to stick

around long enough to at least say hello to my wife? It would be nice if you could see Emma and Logan and the baby before we go back to Stillwater. Or is this girl of yours, whoever she is, going to continue to keep you so busy you barely come home long enough to change your clothes?"

Playing the family card was low, but not beneath Tuck, apparently. Tyler scowled. "I'll see them all, but not right now. I gotta get to Rohn's."

"Then how about dinner tonight?"

"All right, yeah, fine. Dinner tonight."

"A'ight. I'll hold you to that."

"Okay. Now I really gotta go. I'll see you later."

"Later."

Tyler left Tuck and his judgmental expression behind and strode for his truck. He didn't need the guilt trip. Usually he was a damn good son, brother, and neighbor. Didn't he help Logan's dad out at their family store when the old man had a stroke? Didn't he build that wheelchair ramp for him, too? Didn't he rebuild Tara's piece-of-shit car when it crapped out and she needed transportation for school and work?

The answer to all of that was yes, he did. Yet he was still feeling like shit because of Tuck's insinuation that he wasn't around when he should be. Inside the truck Tyler fired up the engine and sighed. He needed Janie to get over her aversion to public dating. Then he could bring her home to meet his parents. Maybe have her over for a family dinner. Bring her to meet the new baby over at Logan's house. Show Tuck that he wasn't only interested in booty calls. He could be serious when the woman was the right one for getting serious about. But Tuck would never believe Tyler could attract more than buckle bunnies until he saw it with his own eyes.

Then again, he kind of wanted to keep Janie to himself for a little while. She was too skittish as it was about dating him. He didn't need his crazy family scaring her off.

Too many things to consider for so early in the morning, and before coffee, too. Besides, it was all a moot point until he got Janie to agree to go on a real date with him. But every kiss brought him one step closer to that. He was sure of it.

Rohn's place wasn't far, and before he knew it, Tyler was swinging the truck into the driveway. The tires crunched on the gravel beneath him as he crept to the barn and parked in his usual spot.

Janie's homemade blueberry creation awaited him, so Tyler wasted no time jumping out of the truck and striding toward the house. He found Rohn and Colton already settled at the kitchen table with plates of pie and mugs of coffee in front of them.

"Morning." His gaze swept to the counter. He let himself relax when he saw half the pie was still there. He wouldn't have been above stealing Colton's plate if there hadn't been any left.

"Morning. Grab yourself a piece." Rohn waved his fork toward the counter.

"Oh, I intend to." Ty reached for the knife, cutting a generous-sized slice that didn't leave a whole lot for anyone else. He didn't feel at all guilty about it, either.

"So, I've been thinking—"

Tyler snorted out a laugh at Colton's words. "Uh-oh. That's dangerous."

"Shut up, Ty."

Grinning, Tyler poured a mug of coffee for himself. One glance at the table told him the milk and sugar were already out, so he carried his mug, fork, and plate over and sat.

He was just stirring in some sugar when Colton continued, "You and Janie Smithwick should go out."

Did Colton know he'd been sneaking over to Janie's? That he had hopes she'd go out with him? Tyler's head whipped up, but he could see Colton wasn't talking to him. He was clearly directing his suggestion about dating Janie to Rohn.

What the hell?

"Ah, I don't know about that. She does make a hell of a pie, though. Is that why you have this sudden interest in me going out with her?" Rohn's graying brows rose.

Colton smiled. "The pie sure is good. Her coffee is even better, but no. That's not why. I was just thinking. You're alone. She's alone. You're not that far apart in age."

"Yeah, they are. She's only thirty-six." Tyler had to nip this little plan in the bud, and right quick.

"Hey." Rohn frowned at Tyler. "How old do you think I am?"

"Way older than thirty-six." Tyler snorted.

"Weren't you the one, just the other day as a matter of fact, telling me I'm only as old as I feel and how I should go out drinking with you and Colton at the Two-Step?"

"Yup. You should come out with Colton and me. But you and Janie?" Tyler shook his head. "That's not a good idea."

Colton frowned. "Why the hell not?"

"Didn't you ever hear the expression don't shit where you eat? They're neighbors. They knew each other's spouses."

"Exactly my point." Colton's eyes widened. "That's why it's perfect. They have a lot in common."

"No. It would be . . . weird." Tyler couldn't come up with a better objection. He'd gone cold with fear that Rohn would actually ask her out.

Silently, he willed Colton to shut the hell up before this started to sound like a good idea to Rohn. Tyler glanced at Rohn and tried to gauge his interest. Rohn could ask her out. She could say yes. He knew the fact that her husband had only been gone a year wasn't her only objection to dating him. Tyler realized his age was a big issue for her.

There was nothing he could do to make himself older. He could only make her understand that his age, and hers, didn't matter. But Rohn didn't have that hurdle. He was free and clear of the age issue that had Janie so worried.

Rohn let out a sigh. "I don't know."

Good. He was hesitant. Maybe he'd never ask her out and Tyler's concern would all be for nothing.

"Just think about it. Okay?" Colton pushed the point and made Tyler want to lodge his size eleven boot in the man's mouth.

Rohn sighed. "A'ight. I'll think about it."

With that, Tyler lost his appetite even for Janie's delicious blueberry pie. Not about to waste something made by her hands, he shoveled the last bite into his mouth, washed it down with the remainder of his coffee, and stood. "I'm gonna get started on work."

Mouth full, Colton glanced up. He swallowed and said, "Um, okay. I'll be outside in a sec."

"No rush." He turned and headed out the door. The rest of the day couldn't pass quickly enough for Tyler's liking.

He got through his work, but being sociable was more than he could handle. The good thing was, he was such a miserable bastard that when the work was done and he said he was leaving, Colton didn't question why or ask if he wanted to hang out and grab a bite or a beer. Score one point for being antisocial.

It was early afternoon when he headed for Janie's house with new determination, not to get the field cut, but to cement in her mind that he was the one she should be with. Not Rohn. Not anybody else. Him and him alone. And once Tyler set his mind to something, he didn't give up until he got it.

When he'd woken that morning, he'd had every intention of going to Janie's, heading directly to the equipment shed, and getting to work. That was before Colton had put that shit about her dating Rohn out there. It had festered in Tyler's brain all the damn day.

He found himself driving not to the shed, but instead to the back door of the house, right to the spot where he'd parked the night before. To where he'd kissed her that first time. Where he'd made the decision to walk away last night and not push her too far, too fast.

In hindsight, that had been foolish. His leaving before sealing the deal left the field wide open for Rohn to step in and ask her out, and what reason would Janie have to say no? Tyler wouldn't make that mistake again.

Determination fueled him. He cut the truck engine and pocketed the keys. Hand on the door handle, he stopped and eyed the glove box. He flipped open the compartment and pulled out a strip of condoms. He didn't know what was or wasn't going to happen, but it was better to have them and not need them than the opposite. He folded the strip and shoved it in his back pocket as the reality hit him that this might actually happen. Today. With Janie.

Pulse racing with that thought, Tyler hopped down from the truck and slammed the door behind him. Boots crunching on the gravel, he strode to the kitchen door.

It was afternoon, so there'd be no chance of finding Janie looking soft and adorable in her little shorts and T-shirt again. More likely she'd be in her barn clothes—jeans and boots. That was perfectly all right. She looked smoking hot dressed like that, too.

She was in the kitchen, standing at the counter doing something, probably cooking dinner. Maybe making another pie. He didn't know, and at the moment, he didn't care. He knocked and saw through the window when Janie turned toward him and smiled.

That was all it took. He didn't wait for her to invite him inside. He reached down. The knob turned in his hand and he pushed the door open. Stepping inside, he gave a shove and it shut behind him and moved toward Janie.

"Tyler." Her eyes widened. "Hi."

Her expression of surprise increased as he backed her up against the counter. Bringing his hands up to cradle her face, he crashed his lips against hers. She kissed him back with equal enthusiasm. He took that as a good sign.

He pulled back from her lips just far enough to be able to say, "I walked away from you last night."

Her green gaze met his. "Yeah, you did."

"I'm not making that mistake again." He shook his head. "Believe me."

"Okay."

Judging by the look in her eyes, even if Rohn did ask Janie out, there was no way she'd ever say yes. She wanted him. If Tyler could only get her to agree to a real date, he'd be golden. Then there'd be no doubt in anyone's mind. Not his or hers. Not Colton's or Rohn's. Then Tyler would be one happy man.

The phone in his pocket rang. He was intent on ignoring it as he leaned in toward Janie. He'd waited too damn long for this already. He'd almost closed in on her lips when she said, "Your phone is ringing."

"Ignore it." Thrusting his hands into her hair, he took her mouth, just as a sequence of beeps from the phone signaled he had a voice mail.

Whoever had the incredible bad timing of calling him at a moment like this had left a message. He'd get back to them later. Much later.

Another, different chime sounded and Tyler knew he also had a text message. Beginning to hate his cell and every one of its many alerts, all of which it seemed he'd heard in the last thirty seconds, he pulled back from the incredible feel of Janie's lips.

He sighed deeply as she smiled. "It's okay. You should check that."

"I know." Taking a step back from the warmth of her soft body so he could check his phone sucked. This was no time for interruptions. In future, he'd remember to keep the damn thing turned off. Or at least have it set on silent.

Family dinner in an hour. Get home!

Tyler barely managed to bite back the cuss he almost let fly when he saw the text message from Tuck. He'd completely forgotten that he'd promised to have dinner at home tonight with everyone.

"Everything all right?" Janie watched his face.

"Yeah. It's just . . . dammit." He shook his head and shoved the phone back in his pocket. Tuck could wait for a response. "I promised to have dinner at home with the family tonight. My brother and his wife are visiting."

"Tyler, don't look so upset. It's okay. You should see your brother while he's in town."

A wonderful idea struck. One that would kill two birds with one stone. Maybe even three. "Come with me."

"What?" She laughed.

"Sure. Why not?" Tyler liked the idea more with each passing moment.

He'd get to spend the evening with Janie while fulfilling his obligations. And as a bonus, her having dinner with his family might bring him one step closer to her agreeing to go out with him in public on a real date. That would lead, hopefully, eventually, to her agreeing to give a serious relationship a try. It was perfect.

"No."

Her answer took him off guard. "No? Why not?"

"For one, your family's not expecting me. It's rude to show up uninvited."

"No, it's not. My mother cooks enough for an army. Our friends and neighbors are always stopping by to eat. Jace. Colton. Logan. And you're not uninvited. I'm inviting you."

She shook her head. "No."

"Janie." He took a step closer, settling his hands on the curve of her waist. "You like me. I know you do."

"You're right. I do. That doesn't mean it's proper for me to go to dinner at your parents' home."

"It's my home, too."

She pursed her lips and shook her head and he knew arguing the point wasn't working. Maybe he could use his lips in a more persuasive way than flapping them at her with words she'd stopped listening to. He leaned low and pressed a kiss to her mouth . . . and felt her smile beneath his lips.

Curious as to what could be funny about his kissing her, he pulled back and asked, "What?"

"If your plan is to kiss me until I agree to go to dinner with you, it's not going to work." When she saw his frown, she laughed. "Did I guess right?"

He refused to admit it and let out a burst of air instead. "All right. I'll give you a pass today. You don't have to come with me, but there'll be no family dinner tomorrow." He glanced at the counter, where she'd already started to prepare supper. "I'm sorry about bailing on you today."

"It's fine. I understand. It'll all keep for a day."

"Good. I'll be back to start on that field tomorrow, as early as I can get away from Rohn's."

"Okay. Thank you."

His eyes narrowed as he leaned in again and took a kiss that wasn't half as long or deep as he wanted it to be. "Mmm, you're very welcome. And I'll be around for some more thanks after I'm done mowing."

Janie smiled. "Am I paying you for your work in kisses now?"

"No. You're paying me with good home cooking and blueberry pie. The kisses are just a bonus." He grinned.

She laughed even as her cheeks grew pink. "Okay. It's a deal."

"You sure you won't come with me to supper tonight?"

"I'm sure."

He waited, but he knew she wouldn't change her mind. Not tonight. He'd change it for her, though. One day. Very soon. Hopefully.

Damn, he'd never had so much trouble getting a woman to do what he wanted in the past. Maybe that was what made Janie so special.

Tyler drew in a deep breath. "Okay. I'd better get going. Tomorrow, I'll be back."

"I have no doubt."

He cocked a brow. "Am I that predictable?"

"Yeah." She dipped her head. "But I think I like it."

"Good." He couldn't go without one more kiss, one that he had to physically drag himself away from. It was very hard leaving her, but he had to. "Damn. Okay, I'm really going."

"Okay." A smile tipped up the corner of her tempting lips.

He shook his head and turned toward the door, forcing himself to go directly to the truck without turning back. It would be so easy to say to hell with the family dinner and stay, but in the long run, it would be easier to go, get it over with, and make Tuck and his parents happy.

But tomorrow—tomorrow would be another matter entirely.

Chapter Twenty

Rene blew out a slow whistle as she stared across the field. "Oh. My. God. That man riding on that big old John Deere might be the hottest thing I've seen in a real long time."

Janie followed Rene's stare to where Tyler was cutting the hayfield. She would admit, the view was nice, but she had to think the hottest thing she'd seen lately was the heat in Tyler's eyes as he came busting into her kitchen, intent on kissing her, and more, if he hadn't gotten that text from home.

Although even hotter was the dream that had woken her just before midnight. It was hard enough to fall to sleep with Tyler and his visit in her memory, never mind being tantalized by him in her sleep.

In her dreams, he didn't kiss her and leave her wanting the way he had for three nights straight. He stayed, and damn, things got hot. Molten. Just like her insides when he was around. In her dreams, he took her on a midnight ride that had her waking sweaty, her body still clenching around his, even though he'd only been there in her mind.

Rene was probably expecting some kind of response, so Janie wrestled her attention back to the present. "He is a good-looking guy."

"Good-looking doesn't even begin to cover it." Rene shook her head. "Jesus, Janie. I don't know how you get anything done with him here and looking so fine."

"He's not around all that often." Janie had to think how that was a shame.

Rene sighed. "I guess that's a good thing."

Janie glanced at her friend. "You mean because of times like right now when we're both ignoring your daughter, my student, because we're too busy watching Tyler drive my tractor?"

"Eh, she's only cooling down the horse." Rene waved off Janie's concern with a hand. "She'll be fine."

Shaking her head, Janie forced herself to turn back to face the ring. "That's good, Khriste. You can bring her back to the barn. I'll help you unsaddle her and then we'll hose her down. Okay?"

"Can't Tyler help me, like he did the last time?"

"We'd all love to have Tyler come and help like the last time, sweetie." Rene shot Janie a knowing glance. "But it looks like he's busy working right now."

"I wish I could ride in the tractor with him. It looks like fun."

"It sure does. Doesn't it, Aunt Janie?" Rene's words were heavy with suggestion. "Wouldn't riding with Tyler be fun?"

Out of the mouths of babes . . .

"I'm sure." Janie shot her friend a glance. "But your mother's right, Khriste. Tyler is very busy right now and we have to let him get his work done. Come on. I'll help you. Let's get Bella unsaddled."

Rene was right about one thing—Tyler sure was a distraction. Janie had been working with horses for as long as she could remember, but just knowing he was on the property—in her line of sight every time she turned around—had her concentrating twice as hard to complete even the simplest tasks. It had her marking his progress across the hayfield, anticipating when he'd be done.

It was truly horrible, and she should be ashamed of herself, but she hoped Rene and Khriste would be gone by the time he was finished for the day so she could be alone with him. Khriste was her goddaughter. Rene, her best friend since childhood. Janie loved them both, but they'd always been in her life, and she knew they always would be. Tyler, she wasn't so sure of. His continuing presence was iffy at best. That made her want to absorb every second with him she could.

"Okay, Janie. I get it."

She glanced up at Rene. "Get what?"

"Why you didn't want me fixing you up with the guy at church."

"Um, first of all, I don't want you fixing me up with anyone. But in particular not that guy. He's kind of creepy and he hates horses. What in the world possessed you to think—"

"It's way more than all of that, and you know it." Rene's gaze focused past Janie. "Oh, so much more."

As the memories of the handful of kisses she'd shared with Tyler had her cheeks heating, Janie had to hope Rene wouldn't notice. Offense seemed the best defense here. She was about to lay into Rene, tell her to mind her own business when it came to her love life, when Khriste dropped the sponge she'd been using to wash Bella back into the bucket.

"Tyler! You missed my lesson. You wanna help me finish giving Bella her bath?" The girl took off running and Janie didn't need to look to know where or why. That much was obvious.

Janie turned in time to see Tyler grin down at the little girl before he scooped her up and slung her onto his hip.

"Hey there, darlin'. That's exactly what I'm fixin' to do. Help you with Bella."

"I already washed most of her with the sponge, but now I have to hose her off, then dry her, then put her back."

"Okay. We can do that. It's a hot one today. I might join her under the hose." He carried Khriste toward them and then swung her down. He set her on the ground next to the horse and turned toward Janie and Rene. "Afternoon, ladies."

The raw charm of his smile and the easy tip of his hat during that greeting was enough to melt any woman's heart, but especially Janie's as she remembered the feel of those lips against hers. How he'd ditched his hat to kiss her in the truck.

"Tyler." Rene smiled wide. "Very nice to see you again."

"Sorry I didn't come right over when I got here. I saw you were in a lesson, so rather than bothering you, I just hopped on the tractor and started mowing. I hope you don't mind." He directed the last to Janie, forcing her to find words.

"That's fine. I don't mind at all. You're helping me. You do what you want to do, whenever you want." That had come out sounding kind of suggestive. "Um, anyway, thank you again."

Her face felt hot just from talking to him. Or maybe it was how she could almost feel the heat in his eyes. Knowing Rene was watching her like a hawk—watching both of them—didn't help, either.

He waved away her thanks. "It's nothing, Janie. I wanna help."

"It is something. And I appreciate it."

His gaze grew more intense as it focused on her. "It's my pleasure. Anything for you."

Janie looked over at her friend, afraid of what reaction she'd find. Brows raised, eyes cutting between her and Tyler, Rene cleared her throat and said, "Well, we should probably get going. Khriste, time for us to head home."

It seemed Rene was still playing matchmaker, only this time her goal was to leave Tyler and Janie alone.

"But, Mom, we're not done with Bella yet."

"Then hurry and finish up. Aunt Janie has other things she needs to do."

Tyler grabbed the bucket and moved it out of the way. "I'll get Bella all settled, but then I'll have to get moving myself."

That caught Janie's attention. Was he in a rush to finish and go? Why? "If you have to leave, I'll finish with the horse."

"I meant get back to work." His eyes cut to Janie. "I've got about another two hours to finish the first field. But I should be done by suppertime." He smiled as he dropped that reminder about her promising to cook him dinner.

Tyler bent to pick up the hose and Janie's eyes followed the move, watching the denim tighten across his ass in the process and feeling even more grateful he wasn't in any rush to leave. Out of the corner of her eye she saw Rene watching him, too. That was one way to get Rene's focus off her— parade Tyler's fine butt in front of her.

Khriste seemed to be the only one who wasn't ogling Tyler and his assets, and that was because she was only nine, but even at that tender age she'd fallen prey to his charm and his smile. That much was obvious from the way her eyes lit up when he came around.

It seemed no female, young or old, was immune to Tyler's charm. That scared the hell out of Janie, as it should, but not enough to make her stop wanting him.

Chapter Twenty-One

It was a hot, dirty, sweaty job, but that wasn't the reason he was in such a rush to get the field finished. Janie, back at the house cooking him dinner, was.

Swath by swath, the hay fell to the blades of the mower he towed behind the tractor. It was mind-numbingly repetitive work, but he didn't mind, because he had a lot to think about. The agony of being torn between trying to keep things slow with Janie and wanting to push their relationship along kept him plenty occupied.

Not that Tyler had the final say in the matter. Janie said yes, and no, according to her own free will.

What was unsettling was that she was willing to spend time with him, but at the same time refused to let him take her out on a proper date. It was the opposite of what he assumed women wanted, which reinforced what he knew already—Janie was nothing like the girls he'd known.

The riddle that was Janie occupied his mind and made the hours go faster. Before he realized how much time had passed, he glanced up to find he had only two passes left to reach the fence line and be done. At least with this field. There was another one he'd have to tackle tomorrow, which meant he had a good excuse to come back. Not to mention he'd have to come back and rake the hay and bale it up for her once it was dry.

Yup, plenty of reasons to spend lots of time here, though all he really needed was one, and she was in the kitchen expecting him for supper. Her there, him here, it felt so domestic. So natural, and so different from anything he'd ever had with anyone before. He liked the idea of finishing up a day's work and having a woman he wanted to see, who wanted to see him, waiting for him. It felt good.

No wonder so many of the men he knew were pairing off and getting married. For the first time ever, Tyler got it. Hell, he more than understood it. He could see himself doing it. But Janie was still fighting their relationship and he had yet to change her mind.

No problem. He liked a challenge, and it sure would be fun convincing her.

The thought of the varied and creative ways he could convince her had him grinning as he finished the field.

The delay killed him, but he couldn't jump right off the tractor and sprint to the house, much as he wanted to. He had to put the machines away and take the time to at least hose his face and arms off.

Haying was a dirty job. He pulled off his shirt and bent over to grab the hose they'd used to rinse off Bella. The sun had warmed the standing water in the black rubber hose until it was almost too hot on his skin. He made quick work of rinsing off the dust and sweat, then turned off the water. Using his shirt, he dried his face and torso.

Bare-chested, he headed for his truck to change into the fresh T-shirt he had inside. He'd parked by the kitchen door when he'd arrived. Wishful thinking on his part that he'd be ending the night in her house and leaving past dark, so he'd want the truck close. The notion, and the desire to get inside, quickened his step.

He glanced at the house as he walked by and saw Janie standing in the kitchen doorway, watching him walk, her eyes pinned to his bare skin. She was checking him out without his shirt. Damn. That had him heating to the boiling point. So much so he nearly said to hell with it, forgot about putting on the shirt, and headed directly for her. But he needed to play it cool with this woman. Building a relationship with her would be more like a marathon than a sprint.

He slowed his last few steps to the truck. Opening the door, he tossed the dirty shirt inside and reached in for the fresh one folded on the passenger seat. He made sure he moved from behind the door so she'd have a good view as he stretched and then pulled the T-shirt over his head.

Out of the corner of his eye, he saw she hadn't budged an inch. She was still standing in the shadow of the doorway, watching, probably thinking he couldn't see her or how her eyes were pinned to him. He saw her, all right. And oh, yeah, her stare totally made all the hours of manual labor that kept him in shape worthwhile.

Impatient to get inside, he swapped the old straw hat he'd worn to work in the field for his good one, slammed the truck door, and turned toward the kitchen.

When he saw Janie wasn't standing there any longer, a smile tickled his lips. She'd probably ducked back inside because she didn't want him to see she'd been watching.

Too late. He'd seen and he was so turned on, any thought of food had totally fled his mind as another, more pressing hunger took over.

He pushed through the door and directly across the room to where Janie was concentrating overly hard on the vegetables on the cutting board. It was the stance he'd become used to seeing her in, but he'd never get used to the way his heart pounded the nearer he got to her.

At the sound of the door closing, she'd turned. She put the knife in her hand down as he strode toward her. Smart move, since he had no intention of slowing down, even if the blade was frighteningly long.

"Done for the day?" The casual question didn't match her heated expression.

"I am. Done, washed up, fresh T-shirt . . . but you know that already." He grinned as her cheeks turned pink. He reached out and reeled her in to him. "Come here and kiss me."

"Okay."

"You let me kiss you, but you won't let me take you out on a date." He shook his head. "Maybe I'm going about this the wrong way. Maybe I need to convince you that you can't live without me."

She raised her brows. "How are you going to do that?"

"I'll show you." He pressed closer as his hands roamed down her body. "But it might take all night. That okay with you?"

"I've got nowhere else to be."

He groaned at that response and leaned low to close the small distance between them. "Good."

The kiss he'd started out controlling soon took control of him, fueled by the feel of her hands on his hips holding him close, the knowledge she'd been watching him strip outside, her tongue battling with his. . . . It all combined to take hold of him, and he gave in.

At the pace they were going, there was only one way this night could end. He pulled back just far enough to say, "You have to tell me if you want me to stop, because if you don't, I'm not going to."

Her eyes were heavily lidded as she shook her head. "I don't want you to stop."

The breath he dragged in after hearing her answer made his chest feel even tighter than it had before. His hands cradling her face, he leaned in, intent on taking her mouth again when she said, "Do you want to go upstairs?"

That stopped his motion. Heart pounding, he went still, holding on to the last vestige of his control as best he could. His answer was a definite *hell yes*, but Janie was not just any woman. She was a widow, and even without his asking her, there was no doubt in his mind she hadn't been with another man since losing her husband.

As much as he wanted her, he needed to make certain she was ready. "You sure?"

"Yes." She nodded.

The last of his restraint broke and he hauled her against him, lifting her feet off the ground. With an adorable squeal, she wrapped her arms and legs around him as he turned toward the doorway leading to the staircase.

"Tyler, what are you doing?"

"Taking you up to the bedroom."

"You can't carry me up the stairs."

"Watch me."

Janie had all the curves a woman should, but she was a head shorter than he and he was used to throwing bales of hay and lifting sacks of feed all day at the ranch. Carrying one woman up a flight of stairs would barely present a challenge, and he was certainly motivated to get the job done.

She looked honestly concerned as he moved to the staircase and planted one boot on the first step. "Tyler—"

"You hush up, woman. I'm not going to drop you."

"I'm more worried we'll both fall down the stairs and break our necks."

"That's not happening, either." He could tell her the calf he'd picked up in the tie-down competition he'd won had weighed over two hundred pounds, but even in his frenzied state to get her to the bedroom, he realized no woman would appreciate being compared to a cow.

The best course of action was to show her he could easily carry her. He took the flight of stairs fast with her wrapped around him. The effort had left him breathless by the time he reached the top, but that was nothing. Just the thought of being with Janie took his breath away.

In the upstairs hallway, the sight of her flushed cheeks and soft lips got to him. He braced her against the wall and kissed her, hard and thorough, claiming her mouth as his. She unwrapped her legs from around him, and he set her feet down on the ground. That freed his hands so he could run them over her bottom before he hauled her hips tight against his.

This close, there was no doubt in his mind that she'd feel his arousal. He wanted her to know what she did to him. To know how much he needed her. The pressure of her body pressed to his only made the situation more urgent.

"Bedroom?"

"First door." Her answer sounded as breathless and as needy as his question.

Taking Janie's hand in his as she led the way to her bedroom, he was shaking like a virgin. It was ridiculous because that couldn't be further from the truth. He'd been with more women in more places than he could remember, and Janie had been a married woman. It was far from the first time for either of them, but this would be his first time with her. For once, that mattered to him. It felt different and he knew why. It was because he felt different about her.

Inside the bedroom, Tyler closed the door and turned toward her. He was aware of the room—

how it felt like her. Unlike the formal living room or the sparse guest bedroom downstairs, her touch was obvious in this room. Books stacked on the nightstand made him envision her in her night-clothes, snuggling against the masses of pillows on the bed and reading until she fell asleep. Cut daisies in a vase on the dresser had him imagining her picking them out in the field where he'd noticed the flowers growing along the fence line.

The room only got a quick glance before he focused solely on Janie. While still holding her with one hand, he palmed the crown of his hat with the other. After lifting the hat off his head, he set it on the dresser next to the flowers.

That was the last thing he was completely con-scious of doing before the jumble of movement that ended with him and Janie, lips locked, falling onto the mattress. Lying next to her, he laced his fingers through hers and moved from her mouth to kissing her fingers. They smelled clean, like fresh vegetables.

"You smell like . . . green peppers." He spoke as he kissed up her arm to her face before he moved to her ear, where he nipped at her lobe.

"I was cutting them. I'm making"—she drew in a stuttering breath in the middle of her explanation as he dragged his tongue down her neck—"fajitas."

He lifted his head. "I'm invited, right?"

"Yes." Her answer was spoken on a sigh.

"Good." He loved fajitas, but he loved the way a tremor ran through Janie when he kissed her neck even more.

Tyler pulled the skin of her throat into his mouth and she moaned. The sound shot a bolt of pleasure straight through him. It was enough to make him suck harder. He came to his senses and stopped himself before he marked her neck.

That he had any sense or rational thought left at a time like this was astounding. It wasn't due to a lack of desire on his part. More an instinct to protect Janie as strong as his urge to possess her. The desire to have her, all of her, was strong. He raised the bottom of her T-shirt and exposed her stomach. Leaning low, he kissed the bare skin he'd uncovered. The soft curve of her belly rose and fell beneath his lips with each of her breaths.

They both had too many clothes on. He wanted more of her, not to mention he was still wearing the boots he'd worked in all day. They shouldn't be on top of Janie's clean bed, but Tyler wouldn't mind one bit if his boots spent many nights underneath while he was in it with her.

The thought twisted still tighter the need that had settled low in his gut. It was as if a fire had been ignited within him and it could only be put out by having her.

He pushed her shirt all the way up and tugged it over her head, exposing her bra. He liked the soft, feminine look of the white lace. It made a sexy-as-hell contrast with the faded denim jeans she still wore. He moved his hands down to the button at her waist.

The whole process of his undressing her seemed to be moving far too slowly given his current lack of patience, but at the same time, he didn't want to rush even one step of it. He wanted to commit every second to memory so he could relive it over and over, every hour they were apart.

He was overdressed himself. As tempting as he found unwrapping the gift that was Janie, he had to get out of his own clothes. Sitting on the edge of the bed, he yanked off first one boot, then the other, dropping them to the floor.

As an afterthought, he glanced down at the carpet, hoping he hadn't dragged in mud. He hadn't exactly taken the time to wipe his boots before he'd busted into the kitchen and attacked Janie. He'd clean up whatever mess he made, later. Now he had far more important things to do.

Tyler stood and yanked his T-shirt over his head, dropping it to the floor. Reaching for his buckle, he made quick work of his belt and the fly on his jeans. He wasted no time shoving them down his legs.

In nothing but his underwear, he straightened and found Janie's eyes on him. Her gaze roamed over him from head to toe and all the important parts in between. She realized he was watching her watch him and yanked her focus up to his face.

Pure male pride filled him and had him on the bed in seconds, kneeling next to Janie to divest her of the last of her clothes.

She wanted him. He knew that. He felt it, both last night and now. Hell, she'd invited him up to her bedroom while the sun was still up, and it wasn't because she needed him to kill a spider or something. It was because she wanted this as much as he did. Because she couldn't wait any longer either.

In spite of all that evidence, and knowing down to his very soul she wanted him, he still feared she'd change her mind. At any second she could ask him to stop. Could tell him she wasn't ready for this. If she asked, he'd stop. Put his pants back on, go downstairs, and maybe start cutting the other field, like he should be doing. But damn, how he hoped she wouldn't.

He trailed one finger down between her breasts before he leaned over and followed the path with his lips. When he pulled back and glanced up, he saw the color rise in her cheeks. It made him smile. "You okay?"

"Yeah. It's just . . . it's daytime."

"So?"

"I've never—" She swallowed. "Um, done this in the daytime."

He tried not to let his surprise show. If he was married to this woman, he was sure they'd be at it day and night. But as unexpected as her revelation was, he was happy with it. He liked that he was the first to get her to loosen up enough to let go, even while the sun was bright.

"Get used to it." He moved up her body, bringing his hand to her face as he pressed a kiss to her lips.

Coming inside from the heat of the workday to have the A/C blow cool air across their heated skin as the sunlight filtered through the curtains, sending shadows across her body—it couldn't be any more perfect.

He'd thought it didn't get any better than this until she ran her hands over his back and he felt her palms, warm and soft on his bare skin as she pulled him on top of her. Then he realized it could get a whole lot better.

Chapter Twenty-Two

He was hard as a rock, and she wasn't just talking about that one part of him that she felt pressing against her thigh. He was cut. Ripped. Whatever those bodybuilders called it when a man's body was all muscle and no fat, that was what Tyler was.

She finally understood the term *washboard abs*. It was impossible not to after running her hands up Tyler's torso and feeling them for herself. And his arms, and his legs, and God, the perfection that was his back—he was all solid muscle. Hard as granite. She'd never had her hands on any man like him, much less had him undressed and in her bed.

And the tattoos—they were another thing she had no experience with, but damn, they were hot. Until today when he'd taken off his shirt, she'd never known what art was hidden beneath. Both of his shoulders, his back, and even one thigh sported designs she could happily study for hours.

It was hard to get a close look with him lying on top of her, not that she was complaining. She could catch up on her tour of Tyler's tattoos later.

Right now, she was having trouble concentrating on anything except what she was feeling. What he was making her feel.

The combined heat of his mouth and his hands was enough to quiet the nagging voice in her head. The one that kept telling her she was crazy to do this. It had been so damn long since a man had touched her, and it felt so good.

While his big, rough hands traveled over the bare skin of her hips, he trailed his mouth across her chest. The difference of rough and soft was enticing. Tyler moved his hands around her back and Janie felt her bra release.

Her eyes widened. "How did you do that?" She hadn't even felt him touch the clasp.

"Talent." He smiled and peeled the lace down. He drew her nipple between his lips and scraped his teeth over the sensitive flesh.

His groan vibrated through her breast, and a shudder ran through her. Thinking was nearly impossible. All she could do was feel. That was a good thing. She'd done entirely too much thinking lately.

Tyler slid his hand downward, and she drew in a shaky breath. He snaked his fingers beneath the waistband of her underwear, and then lower. Janie stilled, waiting for what she knew was to come. She might keep focusing on his age, or lack of it, but Tyler was all man, and he knew his way around her body. He connected with a spot that had her hips rising off the bed. It had been so long since she'd been touched like this, she felt as if she'd shatter from the sensations rocketing through her.

The heat of Tyler's breath against her ear as his

weight pressed her into the mattress, combined with the touch of his hands, drove her insane. Her breath began to come faster. He groaned above her.

"Yes, Janie." His words, spoken softly against her hair while his hand continued to work her, were enough to push her over the edge.

The orgasm broke through her and, God help her, she couldn't control her cries as they filled the small room. She didn't recognize the sound of her own voice. It seemed too loud, too wild. It wasn't until he'd eased his touch that she could think again, and they were only beginning. There was a lot left to explore.

The thought had her feeling needy all over again. She reached between them and ran her hand over his thick, hard length. Every part of this man was impressive. She should be embarrassed to think it, but this part in particular was exceptionally so.

With eyes that seemed unfocused, he watched her touch him through the cotton of his briefs. Then he reached down and there were no more briefs between them. He pulled them off and, leaning over the edge of the bed, he dropped them to the floor. He reached down for his jeans, and then he was back and holding a strip of condoms. She stared at what was in his hand as he separated a single packet from the strip and ripped into it.

He rolled the latex over himself and moved to crawl over her. He glanced up, saw her watching him, and stilled in midmotion. "You okay?"

Rather than slowing as she came down from her orgasm, her heart rate sped at the realization of what was to come next. "Yeah. I'm fine."

"Good." His relief at her answer was clear as he rolled to settle between her legs and ran his palms up each of her thighs.

Lifting her hips, Tyler was inside her with one sure thrust.

Janie's eyes closed as she pressed her head back against the pillow. She forced her lids open again so she could see him over her. Since she was actually going through with this craziness, she didn't want to miss one moment of it.

A frown formed a deep crease between his brows and his eyes were squeezed tightly closed in concentration. Then he opened those eyes and she was drawn into the depths of his deep blue gaze.

Tyler was handsome on any given day. Unbelievably, he was even more so now, as he moved above her—inside her—all while he held her captive in his stare.

Leaning low, he kissed her, taking her mouth softly at first and then deeper as he thrust his tongue between her lips, and the motion of his hips increased.

He leaned back, rising above her as he ran his hands down her legs. He lifted her knees and thrust deeper, and she welcomed every one of his strokes.

Each plunge of his body inside hers made her want more. Tyler gave her what she wanted, what she needed, until it became impossible not to close her eyes and grasp at the sheets beneath her as she was consumed by the pleasure gripping her body.

Janie had no idea how long she lost herself in the moment. It could have been mere minutes, or as long as half an hour, before Tyler finished in a frenzy of motion that left them both breathless and sweaty, clutching each other like life preservers on a sinking ship.

It was by no means a brief encounter. Still, she didn't want it to end. Of course it had to, but maybe that didn't matter. She spied the rest of the condoms he'd tossed onto the bed. He'd come prepared for more than just one time.

Finally, Tyler rolled to his side, but his arms remained wrapped around her, pulling her with him so they lay facing one another. He brushed his fingers down the side of her face, and the intimacy of being his sole focus hit her again. She wasn't used to really being seen. Studied.

It had been a long time since she'd worried too much about how she looked. With Tyler, she feared her hair was a mess, and God only knew what he thought of the few extra pounds she was carrying.

Self-conscious, she redirected her focus and ran her fingers over the black ink of the American flag and eagle decorating Tyler's shoulder.

He glanced down. "I got that one last year."

It hit her that she didn't know much about this man or his past. Had he served in the military? Did he just get out? She knew the taste of his skin, and the feel of his muscles beneath her hands, and so many other things, but his history was probably something she should have learned before she invited him to her bed.

"It's um, very patriotic."

He smiled. "Yeah, it is. My brother was missing in Afghanistan. It was driving me crazy to just sit there, waiting days for the army to tell us if he was dead or alive. So I got in the truck, drove to my tattoo guy, and told him to do this. I knew it couldn't help Tuck any, but doing something—anything— felt better than doing nothing."

Janie's stomach twisted at his words. He'd talked about his brother visiting, but did he have more than one? "But he was okay, right?"

"Yeah. He came back safe and sound. He's the one I had dinner with last night."

Janie exhaled in relief and tried to calm herself. "Good. I'm glad."

"Yeah. Me too. He can be annoying, but he's my only brother and I love him."

His stomach growled, a deep, loud, disgruntled sound that lightened the heavy moment. After all the times he'd teased her for blushing or some other thing that amused him, this time it was her turn to smile. "Hungry?"

"Little bit." He pressed his lips together. "All right, I'm starving. I guess I just hadn't noticed that when I had more important things on my mind."

His heated gaze settled on her face and confirmed her suspicion that the important item on his mind had been her. The whole situation seemed surreal.

Not sure how to act around him now, she needed a diversion. Cooking seemed the perfect thing.

"I'll go finish supper." She sat up as best she could with Tyler half on top of her. He groaned in protest and didn't move the leg thrown over hers, pinning her lower half in place. She laughed. "You're hungry. You'll have to let me up so I can cook."

He sighed. "Okay. As much as it kills me to do it, I'll let you get out of bed."

Tyler rolled onto his back and crossed his arms behind his head. He watched as she pulled shorts and a T-shirt out of a drawer. She might as well dress comfortably. He'd already seen all of her and he looked pretty comfortable himself, lounging naked as the day he was born on her bed while she dressed.

She wasn't about to complain. Tyler had a really nice body. The kind of body that made the words *really nice* seem much too weak to refer to both him and how she felt looking at him. She'd need a thesaurus and probably a week to paw through it to come up with just the right words to describe him.

He wasn't perfect. There were calluses on his hands and a scar on his upper lip. His second toe on each foot was too long to be in proportion with the rest, and when he smiled it was a little bit crooked. It was his imperfections that seemed to make him more perfect, which made no sense.

Janie yanked her eyes off him, but that was easier than getting him out of her mind. "I'm gonna head down."

Finally, he sat up and swung his legs over the side of the mattress. He hooked a thumb toward the bathroom door. "Can I jump in your shower real fast? Then I'll come right down and help you."

"Sure, but no rush. Take your time."

"Nah, I'm quick . . . when I want to be, that is." His grin told her he was very pleased with himself when his innuendo made her blush. He was probably pretty pleased with what they'd done together and how long that had lasted, as well.

She couldn't help laughing even as she shook her head, but she didn't play into his hand and respond. All she said was, "I'll be downstairs."

"Okay." He headed for the bathroom, whistling as he went.

If she didn't feel in grave danger of getting too attached to this man, she might have been inspired to whistle a happy tune herself.

Chapter Twenty-Three

He couldn't get enough of Janie. Even after controlling himself long enough for them to cook and eat dinner last night, and tumbling her into bed right after the dirty dishes were dumped into the sink, he still woke up next to her dreading having to leave.

It wasn't just sex, either. He wanted to be near her. It didn't matter what they were doing. Eating. Sleeping. Tending the horses. He was content as long as he was by her side. That, coupled with a physical need so powerful his body craved her like a drug, was almost frightening.

It was still dark outside, but he was awake, hard and needy once more. With his arms around her as she slept on her side, her back to him, he felt Janie breathing, deep and steady. He should let her sleep, but dammit, he couldn't resist pressing closer against her.

A low grumble vibrated through Janie. "What time is it?"

"Don't know." He moved her hair and kissed her

neck. "Don't care. As long as it's still dark, I know I don't have to leave for work yet."

He moved his hand down to her thigh and pulled her leg over his, giving clear access for his persistent morning hard-on.

"You are insatiable."

"Is that a complaint?" he asked with a smile.

"No."

"Good." He reached for a condom on the table and made quick work of that necessity before sinking into Janie. A shudder ran through him. Even after being with her twice last night, he was still amazed at how perfectly matched they were. "I gotta warn you. Mornings take me a while."

She laughed. "Longer than usual?"

"Yup." He moved his hand across her belly, all the way to connect with the spot that had her drawing in a sharp breath. "This okay?"

She let out a shaky exhale. "Mmm-hmm."

Her answer, tinged with a moan, had him smiling. "Good."

Moving his fingers in a slow circle that had Janie letting out a sound that cut straight through to his core, he hoped the sun never rose.

Tyler hadn't been lying when he'd issued the warning that things could take a while. He'd loved her until the morning light streamed through the window blinds and he knew he was going to be late. It had killed him to leave her, looking all sleepy and satisfied in her bed. He ended up running out of her place much later than he should have.

There was no time to go home and change. He'd showered at her house the night before, so he slapped some of her girly deodorant under his arms and took off for Rohn's place.

Thank God she lived right next door to his job, so he didn't have far to travel. As it was, he arrived after Colton. And after Justin, who finally had been cleared by the doc to come back. That was a good thing, not only for Justin, but for Tyler, too. His return after being out healing for weeks would take some of the attention off Tyler sliding in way after the others.

"Here he finally is." Justin took a step forward to greet him, and Tyler couldn't help but notice he still had a limp.

Colton's brow shot up. "Better late than never, I guess."

Ignoring that, Tyler clasped Justin's hand and pounded him on the back with the other. "How you doing, bro?"

"Good enough to convince the doc to let me work." Justin grinned as he pulled back.

"And ride?" Tyler asked.

"Not yet, but I'm working on it."

Tyler laughed. "You're following doctor's orders for once? What's up with that?"

"I was wondering that my own damn self." Colton laughed.

Justin shrugged. "Kind of have to. My mom begged me not to ride until I was completely healed."

Tyler dipped his head in a nod. "Understood, bro."

Unlike Tyler's family, who'd had the life scared out of them when Tuck went missing but ultimately got him back, the Skaggs family hadn't been so lucky. Justin's brother didn't make it home alive from his deployment.

"Gotta keep Mom happy." Colton slapped Justin on the back. "But I'm glad to have you back here. Working alone with only this sorry ass for help for all those weeks sucked balls."

Tyler rolled his eyes. "Yeah, yeah. Like you're so wonderful to work with."

"At least I don't wander in late, rush through the day, and leave early."

"Oh, really? Rolling in late—and looking like you didn't get a whole hell of a lot of sleep—and sneaking out early?" Justin's brows rose as he scrutinized Tyler a bit too closely for his liking. "Sounds like little Tyler's got himself a girl."

"Ah, shut up." Tyler tried to act like it was a ridiculous notion, hoping the truth didn't show all over his face.

Colton turned to Tyler with the look of a man who'd just had a lightbulb turned on over his head. "Oh, my God. Do you? And you didn't tell me? What the hell?"

"So what?" Tyler shrugged, trying to figure a way out of this mess. "If I did, maybe, have a girl, and I'm not saying I do, what's it matter?"

"It matters because we're supposed to be friends. But besides that, I'm the one who had to wait around here after work for the blacksmith to come yesterday because you cut out early. And one of the horses he shoed was yours." Colton's eyes widened to drive home the point.

"Shit. Sorry, man. I totally forgot about him coming."

"Because you snuck out without telling me, or I would have reminded you. So where were you going?" Colton folded his arms across his chest and glared at Tyler, clearly waiting for an answer.

Sometimes a man had to throw in a little bit of the truth to cover up a bigger lie.

"A'ight. I'll tell you. I'm helping Janie Smithwick with her hayfields. She was going to try to do it herself, even though she's got no experience. So I offered to step in."

"Why didn't you just say that in the first place? Jeez. She's got no hired hands, so of course you should help out." Colton let out a snort and turned to Justin. "You knew Tom Smithwick, right?"

While Tyler breathed in relief that Colton was satisfied with his story, Justin nodded. "Yup. Not well, but I knew him."

Colton let out a slow whistle. "Let me tell you, his widow is a hell of a looker. I'm trying to convince Rohn to ask her out."

"And what's Rohn got to say about that?" Justin's eyes cut to Tyler even as he addressed Colton.

"He's dragging his feet, like he usually does when it comes to any new idea." Colton shook his head.

"He's not gonna ask her out." Tyler screwed up his mouth. "They were friends with each other's dead spouses. They can't date now."

"You're nuts." Colton scowled at Tyler. "They're perfect for each other."

"No, you're nuts." Tyler frowned.

"Whatever. I'm going in for coffee before we get

to work." Colton let out a snort and stalked toward the house.

Colton needed to get off this matchmaking kick before Rohn actually took his advice and asked Janie out, only to be shot down when she said no. There was no way in hell that Janie would say yes to a date with Rohn after the night—and morning— they'd had together.

Tyler glanced up to see Justin smirking. "What's up with you?"

Justin shrugged. "Nothing. Just thinking how Colton missed asking the most important question."

"What the hell you talking about?"

"He asked where you went when you left here yesterday. What I wanna know is where'd you come from this morning? Because I'd be willing to bet this week's paycheck that it's the same place."

"What? No." Tyler nearly choked on his denial.

"Mmm-hmm. Okay. If you say so." Justin grinned. "By the way, I've met Janie. I don't blame you one bit."

"I'm not—"

"Don't worry. I won't tell Colton if you don't want him to know." Justin's gaze dropped to Tyler's throat. "You might want to try and hide that bite mark on your neck, though."

With a grin, Justin turned toward the house while Tyler flashed to the memory of Janie's mouth on him during their second time together. How amazing it had been when she'd come so hard with him inside her that she'd latched onto his neck. How he never even considered stopping her because he'd liked it. A lot.

He didn't want Colton to know he was sleeping with Janie. Hell, he didn't want anyone to know yet. Once they were a couple, fine, but not now. He knew he didn't have the best reputation with the guys when it came to women, but Janie was different. He was different with her. And he didn't want his past to cast a shadow on her reputation. She shouldn't be judged because of him and what they did together. She didn't deserve that. But if he didn't tell Colton, the idiot would keep pushing Rohn toward Janie.

Damn. Justin was more observant than Tyler had given him credit for. This was way more complicated than he'd thought it would be.

The sick part was, even with Justin guessing, Tyler wouldn't exchange his time with Janie for anything in the world. And as soon as he got out of there, he was going right back over for more.

Chapter Twenty-Four

Janie was cooking dinner at two in the afternoon.

She couldn't settle herself long enough to concentrate on anything, so she figured she might as well start the beef Stroganoff. It was her grandmother's recipe, and to be fair, it was best if it cooked for a few hours. At this rate, it would be done at five, a little on the early side for a late-spring evening when it stayed light so long that Tyler would have sunlight to work until late.

That Janie was planning supper around Tyler even though she hadn't talked to him all day and hadn't even invited him to eat over yet wasn't lost on her. Making assumptions was bad.

Assuming anything at all about a man like Tyler was worse than bad. It was a recipe for disaster and a good way to get her heart broken. That was exactly why she needed to keep her heart out of this, which wasn't easy to do, especially since her body was all in.

The lust. The insecurity. The excitement. It was

like being a teenager all over again and a totally ridiculous way to feel at her age.

Completely distracted, she realized it was past time to flip the first batch of meat chunks browning in the pan.

She'd run in and out of the grocery store that morning as quickly as she could so she wouldn't miss Tyler in case he came early. She'd come home with enough cubed beef to feed a family of six. So much, she had to brown it in two batches because there was too much to do in one.

Yup. She was nuts. Crazy for a cowboy. Insane enough to have sex with him. Three times. Three incredible, unforgettable—

"Knock, knock."

The voice startled Janie out of her sexual remembrances as the back door swung wide and Rene walked in while announcing herself.

"What are you doing here? Cripes. Did I forget a lesson with Khriste?" Janie frowned and pawed through her memory to see if she'd screwed up her schedule.

"No. Relax. There's no lesson. I just dropped her off at her friend's house nearby, so I thought I'd pop in." Rene pulled out a kitchen chair. "Not that you look all that happy to see me."

"Sorry. I am. Really." Janie spun to glance into the pan as the beef started to smoke. She flipped the heat down to low.

She was too frazzled to be multitasking right now. Talking while cooking could result in burnt meat, if not worse. In her state, she could probably burn the whole damn house down.

Turning back to Rene, she said, "You want something to drink? Wine, maybe?"

Rene's brows rose. Her eyes cut to the time displayed on the microwave. "Uh, sure. I could have one glass. But no more. I have to drive and pick up Khriste in a couple of hours."

"Okay." Janie nodded.

Thank goodness she wouldn't be going anywhere. Just in case her worst fears came true and Tyler didn't show up and she was left with a vat of Stroganoff, she could finish off the bottle. She might need to drown her sorrows if she never heard from him again after foolishly giving herself to a cowboy a decade her junior.

Drawing in a bracing breath, she reached into the cabinet and pulled out a bottle. She uncorked it and poured two glasses. She put Rene's on the table.

"Thanks."

Janie carried her own to the counter. "You're welcome."

Rene sniffed the air. "Smells good. What are you making?"

"My grandma's Stroganoff." She spoke while taking out round one of the browned meat.

"Mmm. I always loved that meal."

"Me too." The pan sizzled as Janie dumped in the other half of the raw meat.

"Who are you cooking for? You're making a lot."

"Nobody. Just me. The family-sized package of

beef was on sale. The leftovers will freeze." She remained facing the counter, turning the meat as it browned faster than the first batch now that the cast-iron pan was good and hot.

As she turned to the fridge to grab the Worcestershire sauce, she hoped Rene wouldn't see the lie in her face.

"So what are you going to do with your newfound freedom until you have to pick up Khriste?" She took extra time adding the remainder of the ingredients to the pan rather than turn back to her friend and risk more questions about why she was cooking so much.

"Hmm. For starters, I think I'm going to get to the bottom of what has you acting so weird. Spill."

"There's nothing—"

"Janie, I've known you since you were that skinny little girl with the buck teeth and pigtails who used to spend summers with her grandparents. I know you better than anyone else in the world, including Tom, rest his soul. So tell me what's up." Rene took a gulp of wine and eyed Janie's glass. "Drink up and then out with it."

She covered the pan with a lid and had no more excuses to avoid Rene's stare. Picking up the wineglass she turned, dragged in a breath, and blurted out the truth. "I had sex with Tyler."

Rene's eyes widened as her mouth dropped open, but no words came out.

Janie shook her head. "Well, it was totally worth telling you the truth if it means you're speechless."

"Oh. My. God. You slept with Tyler?" Rene pressed her hand to her chest and drew in a breath.

Truth be told, there hadn't been a whole lot of sleeping. Janie didn't reveal that. Instead, she said, "It was stupid, right? Go on and say it."

"I will not. I'm happy for you. Jeez, I'm light-headed just thinking about it and it wasn't even me." She leaned forward, pushing her wineglass to the side. "So tell me how it was, as if I have to ask. It was amazing, right?"

"Yes, it was amazing." Janie covered her face with her hands. "And now what do I do?"

"What do you mean, now what? Do it again. That's what."

"What if he doesn't want to do it again? And besides that, I shouldn't want to." Janie took a sip of wine to drown her sorrows.

"Why not?"

"Rene, it feels like a betrayal."

"Of Tom? Do you really think he would want you to spend the next half of your life alone?"

When her friend put it that way, there was only one answer. "No."

"Then stop feeling bad."

Easier said than done.

Thank God she'd moved into the bigger bedroom upstairs last year after Tom had died. Having sex with Tyler in a different room than she'd shared with her late husband made it feel a tiny bit less like she'd betrayed his memory.

That room upstairs had been her grandfather's for as long as she could remember. It was his when she and Tom married, so of course they used the bedroom on the first floor where Janie had always slept. After her grandfather died, she and Tom had never bothered to move. They'd been settled in their room on the first floor for so long, it seemed silly to switch.

"In all seriousness, Janie, it's all right. It's horrible that Tom died, but you were there and you were his rock right up to the very end. That's all over now. He's gone and you're alive, so live. Don't you deserve that?"

"I guess." To her horror, her eyes began to mist.

Rene reached out and squeezed her hand. "Let yourself be happy."

Janie let out a huff. "I can't. He's too young. He's too good-looking."

"And these are problems, why?"

"He probably has to fight off the women."

"And still he chose to be with you."

"What if all he was after was sex? What if he wanted to check off the Mrs. Robinson fantasy on his bucket list? Now that we did it, that could be it."

"Do you really believe that?" Rene leveled her gaze at Janie.

"Maybe." Not really. He was too attentive in so many ways. And harvesting her hay was a hell of a lot of work to go to just for a night of sex.

A truck pulling into the drive caught Janie's gaze and her heart thundered.

"What's wrong?" Rene spun to look behind her and then laughed. "Hmm, it seems Tyler's here. So, what's your next issue, because it looks like that last worry of yours—about never seeing him again—has been taken off the table."

A totally new worry gripped Janie. "Rene, you

cannot let him know I told you anything about what happened."

"To be truthful, you haven't. I asked for details and all I got was you blabbering about how you shouldn't have done it." Rene cocked a brow.

"I can't give you details."

Rene crossed her arms over her chest. "Then I can't promise you I won't accidentally let it slip that I know everything."

Tyler was already out of his truck and heading toward the kitchen door. Panicked, Janie gave in. "All right. I'll tell you anything you want to know when he's gone. Just keep your mouth shut in front of him. Okay?"

"All right, but I'm gonna hold you to that." Looking satisfied, Rene smiled.

Blackmail was the only word Janie could come up with for what her supposed friend was doing to her, but there was no time to deal with that now because Tyler was at the back door.

As was becoming his habit, he didn't wait for her to get up or open the door, he knocked and then immediately pushed it open himself. He strode into the kitchen, his trademark smile making him look even better than usual.

"Hey. You two kicking back with some drinks already? I like it. You're my kinda girls." He grinned wide, but not quite as wide as Rene did.

"Tyler, it's good to see you again." Rene had a look about her. A look that said she knew something and it was in danger of spilling out.

"Did you need something from me?" Janie asked.

When Tyler's smile beamed at her question she realized how suggestive it had sounded and added, "The tractor and, um, hay—they're all right?"

"Yes, as far as I know everything is just fine." There seemed a secret message in his expression meant just for her.

She imagined she could see it in his gaze. She definitely felt it. Like a pull between them. As if they both wanted to move closer, but held back because they weren't alone. If Rene hadn't been in the room when Tyler arrived, Janie could venture an educated guess as to where they'd be now. What they'd be doing. He'd have her pressed up against the counter, kissing her; that was, if he didn't just scoop her up and carry her directly upstairs.

Janie swallowed hard and tried to get her voice to function. "That's good."

Still smiling, Tyler tipped his head toward the door. "I'm gonna get to work. I should be able to get that last field done today."

"Oh, great. Thanks." Her gaze cut to Rene, who'd sat by uncharacteristically silent throughout her interaction with Tyler. She hated to ask it in front of Rene, but she saw no way around it. She sucked it up and said, "I hope you can stay for dinner. I got a big pot of beef Stroganoff on the stove."

"I'd love to." His eyes met hers before he moved his focus to Rene. "Nice seeing you again."

After a tip of the slightly battered straw hat that still made him look hot as hell, he was out the door.

Janie let out a breath she hadn't realized she'd been holding and looked toward Rene, dreading the interrogation about Tyler she was sure would follow.

"Holy cow." Rene blew out a long, slow whistle and pressed a hand to her chest. "That man is enough to give a girl heart palpitations."

Didn't Janie know it. "I know, but what am I doing? This thing between us can't go anywhere."

"Sweetie, why does it have to go anywhere besides the bedroom? You always were too serious, marrying the first guy you had sex with."

"I did not. I had sex before Tom . . . once."

Rene shook her head. "I'm still not so sure that first time counted. I mean, the guy kind of has to get his dick inside you before he comes all over you for it to count."

Janie blushed. This was what she got for telling Rene about that first awkward and embarrassing encounter. She was still bringing it up almost twenty years later.

"Listen," Rene continued. "Just have fun with him. I sure as hell would if I were you. Relax. Enjoy it while it lasts."

Enjoying it wasn't the problem. Her fear of how bad she'd feel after it ended was.

"So, I need to know everything." Rene leaned forward.

"I don't know what you want to hear."

"How about you start with those incredible chest muscles of his and move down from there."

Face burning, Janie reached for her wine. She was going to need some liquid courage to have this conversation. A thesaurus might not hurt, either.

Chapter Twenty-Five

"Did you have a nice visit with your friend?" Even as he asked the question, Tyler looked relieved Rene was gone and they were alone as he strode across the kitchen and wrapped his arms around Janie.

"Yes." She felt her cheeks heat at the memory and dammit, he noticed.

He eyed her with a smile. "Oh, my God. You told her about us, didn't you?"

She drew in a breath, about to deny it, but she couldn't lie to him. "Yes. I'm so sorry. She knows me too well. She could see something was going on."

"That's okay. I don't mind if she knows, as long as you don't." His smile widened. "You know what this means?"

"No, what?"

"Now you have no excuse for us not to go out on a real date, since your friend already knows."

Janie shook her head. "Tyler, I don't think we—"

"So you'll have sex with me, but you still won't date me?" His brows rose.

"I'm sorry."

"It's okay. You'll change your mind. I'll just have to work a little harder to help you change it. Supper smells good, but I'm hungry for something else." He hoisted her onto the counter and stepped between her legs. He leaned in and took her mouth in a deep kiss. Pulling back, he said, "Just so you know, I ran home and packed an overnight bag. It's out in the truck."

"Oh."

The surprise must have shown on her face. He laughed and shook his head. "Janie. We both know chances are good that I'm staying the night. And we know as much as I intended on having time to run home before Rohn's this morning, it didn't exactly work out that way."

Remembering how he'd woken her this morning, and what followed, heated her insides to the boiling point. She really couldn't argue with him. "Okay."

He must have been remembering the same thing. His eyes narrowed. Cupping her face, he pressed his mouth to hers, slipping his tongue between her lips in a kiss that stole her breath away.

He drew back and glanced at the pot on the stove. "Will the food hold for a little bit?"

The need showed clearly in his eyes. If they did what she assumed he wanted to do, and went upstairs, she knew they'd be there for a while. "Yeah. The burner's on low. It can slow cook for another hour or two."

"Good."

In the blink of an eye, he'd planted her feet back

on the floor, grabbed her hand, and they were on the way upstairs, as she'd anticipated.

His seduction wasn't as precise and deliberate as yesterday. This time, there was a chaotic urgency in Tyler's movements.

"I couldn't get my mind off you all day." He spoke as he yanked her shirt over her head, right where she stood. Once that was gone, he moved his hands down to unfasten her jeans. He pushed them and her underwear to the floor in one motion. "I mowed that whole damn hayfield with a hard-on because of you."

As he unfastened her bra and tossed it to the floor, she didn't know quite what to say to that. Thank him? Apologize? It seemed he wasn't looking for a response because he picked her up and tossed her onto the bed.

Still standing, he started to strip, and the sight of him would have made it impossible for her to form sentences anyway.

"Does Rene approve of me?" He glanced at her as he pulled open the drawer next to the bed where he'd stashed the three leftover condoms.

It struck her how he already had made himself at home both in her bedroom and in her life. "Yes."

"I'm glad. That'll make things easier." Packets in hand, he crawled, naked, onto the mattress.

"What things?" She watched as Tyler moved to kneel between her feet.

"You and I going out," he said, tossing the condoms to the bed next to them before running his palms over her bare skin.

"We're not going out."

"We'll see about that." With a hand on each of her ankles, he spread her legs. "I just have to convince you, is all."

His eyes held hers as he leaned low over the juncture between her thighs. Then she couldn't see his face any longer as he dipped his head, and his effort to change her mind began in earnest.

As she felt the heat of his mouth all the way to her core, she had to admit, even if only to herself, that Tyler could be very convincing when he put his mind to it.

Janie woke up in bed alone, a little stiff, and sore in places that sent her mind directly to memories of the night with Tyler. As consciousness fought back sleep, she glanced at the empty side of the bed, then farther away to the rest of the room. His boots were on the floor by the wall where he'd tossed them and his hat was on the top of the dresser.

If she knew one thing for sure, it was that if his hat and boots were here, the cowboy himself hadn't gone too far. She stretched, wondering exactly where he'd got to, until an aroma good enough to inspire her to get out of bed, tired or not, hit her.

Bacon.

Now that she knew where he was and what he was doing, Janie flipped back the covers. If Tyler was in the kitchen cooking, she had time to use the bathroom and make herself look halfway presentable before seeing him.

She stood and padded barefoot to the doorway and paused. Tyler might be downstairs, but reminders of him were all over her bathroom. His overnight bag sat on the tile floor, but most of the contents were out of it. She moved to the sink and stood for a moment, slowly absorbing the evidence of the presence of a man in her life again.

His things littered the space around the sink. She picked up the deodorant sitting next to his toothbrush, pulled off the top, and sniffed. It smelled like him—a nice warm, spicy scent. Janie should know his scent by now. She'd spent enough time pressed up against his chest while they made love that she knew his smell intimately. She'd also spent plenty of time tucked under his arm in bed trying to fall asleep over the past two nights.

He slept like the dead. Her? Not so much, but that was nothing new. She had to admit that not sleeping while pressed up against his hard, warm body was very nice compared to not sleeping while alone in bed.

There was also a razor and shaving cream out. Seeing it sent her mind back to the feel of his stubble—against her face while they kissed, between her thighs while he did other things. The memory sent a flutter through her.

Janie resisted the urge to tidy up behind him, the way she had for so many years as a wife. Yes, it was her house, but these weren't her things, and putting them all back into the small leather travel case resting on the back of the toilet tank felt like an invasion of his privacy. Funny, though, how she did lean in to try and take a peek at what else was in his bag.

She spotted the white plastic dental floss and a

bottle of generic-brand pain relievers within the dark recesses of his bag easily enough, and beneath those things was another strip of condoms. Her face heated. She pushed past the knowledge that he obviously didn't want to run out of those and moved on in her visual invasion of his privacy.

There was a small wooden bristle brush inside the bag. From where she stood, she could see it wasn't a hairbrush, but rather a hat brush.

Just looking at Tyler's traveling case revealed so many personal things about him. He traveled with a super-sized bottle of the cheap brand of ibuprofen, but he owned what appeared to be a top-of-the-line hat brush.

Typical cowboy—practiced at cutting costs, almost always in pain, but still worried about his hat looking good. She smiled and turned back to the sink. She had to brush her teeth and make herself look at least a little bit presentable before going downstairs. Tyler and bacon were waiting.

She put on a bra because she felt really naked without one, but she didn't get fully dressed for the day. Jeans and boots would come later, but shorts and a T-shirt would do for breakfast.

When she reached the bottom of the stairs, she could hear the telltale sounds of cooking. The water running in the sink, before it turned off and a drawer opened and closed. By the sound of things, this guy, whom she'd only met a few days ago, was making himself at home in her kitchen, and it didn't feel at all as strange as it probably should.

Knowing from experience that she was going to feel the emptiness twofold in every room he'd occupied in her home once he was gone, she still had let him into her life. She was clearly a glutton for punishment. That didn't stop her from pausing in the doorway to watch and admire him from behind.

Barefoot and in jeans, he faced away from her. His back muscles moved beneath the tight cotton of his T-shirt as he reached into the cabinet and took down two plates.

He turned and put one at each place on the kitchen table, which was already set with napkins and forks. He caught sight of her hovering in the doorway and smiled. "Mornin'."

"Good morning." She took a step forward as he did the same. He met her where she stood and reeled her in by one arm for a quick kiss.

He groaned and pulled away. "Don't get me started or the eggs will be overdone." With a grin, he released his hold on her waist and moved to the stove. Grabbing the spatula, he glanced at her over his shoulder. "I'm sorry, but you'll have to make the coffee. I was going to give it a try, but I think I'd need a degree in engineering to operate that thing."

"It's okay. I know it's a little scary." She moved to the maker and hit the POWER button followed by the BREW button.

Tyler tracked her movements. "That's it? Two buttons. Well, dang, now I feel like an idiot. I could have done that."

She laughed. "You didn't know. I cleaned out the old grinds, ground fresh beans, set the number of cups, and filled the water compartment yesterday."

His brows rose. "A'ight. I feel a little better now. And seriously, my parents' and Rohn's makers have one button. You can turn the thing on or off. I wasn't real sure what to do with those five buttons."

"I know, I know. A twenty-dollar maker from the hardware store would work just as well."

"No, it wouldn't. Remember, I've had your fine coffee. If it takes five buttons and grinding beans and all that other stuff you do, then I reckon I'll just have to learn to do it."

"Okay." Her heart gave a little skip that Tyler was, by all evidence, planning to be around long enough he'd want to learn to make coffee.

"Now sit down. Breakfast is ready."

Janie did as told while Tyler carried the frying pan to the table and divided the scrambled eggs between their two plates. He put the pan in the sink and reached to grab the plate of bacon. That he slid onto the table. She stared at the feast before her and didn't have the heart to tell him she usually survived on coffee alone in the mornings nowadays.

Luckily, coffee was on the horizon as well. As the aroma of the fresh pot filled the kitchen, Tyler moved to the cabinet that held the mugs. He took down two, which he filled and carried over to the table before he went back to the counter to grab the sugar and then a spoon. After his trip to the fridge, she had the half-and-half in front of her.

Only then, after he'd set out everything she could possibly need or want, did he sit down himself. He grabbed his fork and eyed her. "Go on. Dig in while it's hot."

She'd been so flabbergasted at being waited on by him, she hadn't even lifted her fork yet. "Okay."

This morning was pretty surreal. Then again, her whole experience with Tyler so far had seemed that way. She pushed the odd feeling away, grabbed a piece of bacon off the plate, and then took her first bite of the eggs. Unexpected flavor filled her mouth; these were more than just plain scrambled eggs.

"Wow. These are really good."

He glanced up from his plate and smiled. "Thanks."

Janie took another bite and tried to decipher all she tasted. Cheddar cheese, possibly. She did have a block in the fridge. Had Tyler gone to the trouble of grating cheese for the eggs? She supposed it shouldn't surprise her. He did love to eat. With his passion for food, it made sense he'd be good at cooking it.

She remembered last night and realized he was pretty damn good at doing the other things he loved doing, as well. As a distraction, she reached for her mug and concentrated on stirring in sugar and cream. She took a long sip and hot coffee burned a path down her already heated insides.

Feeling the need to say something, even though he seemed fine just shoveling the food into his mouth in silence, she said, "So you found everything you needed all right?"

"Oh, yeah. There's not much that gets between me and food." He grinned. Having known him even a short time, she'd seen enough to believe his words. He glanced at her barely touched plate. "Everything okay?"

"Yeah, it's incredible. I'm just not real used to eating such a big breakfast."

His brows rose. "Well, get used to it. Breakfast is the most important meal of the day. I never miss it—unless somebody makes me so late I don't have time to eat, like you did yesterday."

"Sorry." She took another bite of eggs to try to hide her embarrassment, but still her face heated at the memory.

He smiled. "Oh, don't apologize. Well worth it. Besides, Rohn had one of those boxed store-bought crumb cakes, so I grabbed a piece of that before work."

"You're not going to be late today, are you?"

"Nah. We're good." His plate empty, he sent her a smoldering look. "Of course, I'd be fine with it if you wanted to make me late."

Her eyes widened. "Tyler."

"What?" He laughed and pushed his chair back from the table. "Come here."

It seemed she couldn't say no to the man when it came to sex. She did exactly as he wanted. Got up and went around the table. He pulled her toward him until she sat facing him, straddling his lap. "You need a dog."

"Why?" She knew he was right, of course. A woman living alone should probably own a dog for security. And most every ranch around had more than one to help with the stock, but Janie was curious to know Tyler's reasoning. Not to mention why he'd choose to bring up the subject now, while his hands were palming her ass.

"To warn us if someone drives in while we're having sex in the kitchen."

She laughed. "We're not having sex in the kitchen."

"Sure we are." He snaked his hand down the front of her shorts. "No underwear. Nice."

She didn't have time to explain she'd been planning to get dressed for the day later. His finger had already zeroed right in on her center and had begun to work her.

"Tyler . . ."

"Mmm-hmm." His other had moved up to settle on the back of her neck. He pulled her down to kiss him. He always was good at ending a conversation he didn't want to have.

She pulled back from his lips. "We shouldn't do this here."

"I disagree." He wrapped his hands around her and stood, lifting her with him, before he put her feet down on the ground. He spun her to face the table, and standing behind her, pulled her shorts down her legs.

"Oh, my God. We really shouldn't do this here."

"That's what will make it all the more fun." The metallic click of him unfastening his belt buckle told her what was happening behind her, even before she felt him nudging between her legs. "I put a condom in my pocket, just in case."

Good thing he'd thought about their current lack of birth control, because she hadn't even considered it.

There were some forces of nature impossible to fight. For Janie, sex with Tyler was one of those things. Kicking the shorts off one foot, she gave up fighting and widened her stance.

As she braced her palms flat on the table, his empty plate between them, he pushed inside her with a groan. Arms wrapped around her, he plunged inside her, sending the coffee sloshing inside the mugs.

Some time soon, she was going to have to sit down and think on this, all of it, before she lived to regret it. But not right now.

"I'm competing in a rodeo tomorrow afternoon. Come watch me." He never missed a stroke as he issued that invitation, his mouth close to her ear, his breath warm against her.

"What?" She was more surprised at his timing than confused by the question.

"It's a local event. I want you there." He began to sound out of breath. "Just think about it."

It was a good thing he left it at that, because he reached around and began to work her with his hand even as he hit the sweet spot inside her from behind. Elbows bent, Janie leaned lower over the table, closed her eyes, and let him make her feel things she'd never thought she'd ever feel—at least not inside her kitchen.

Unbelievably, considering everything, she felt the orgasm build and break over her, right there while she was bent over the kitchen table. She heard him groan behind her.

Tyler pulled out and grabbed for the paper napkin next to her. He tossed the napkin and the used condom in the trash before he braced one arm against the table and leaned against her back, panting. "So, will you come watch me?"

A laugh burst from her. This competition was obviously still uppermost in his mind if he continued to talk about it through all they'd just done. "Okay."

"You will?" Tyler took a step back and spun her to face him, leaving his hands on her waist. She could see the excitement in his expression.

"Yeah, if you really want me to, then I'll come."

"Thank you." Looking as excited as a kid on Christmas morning, he pulled her close and planted a big kiss on her mouth.

She'd promised herself she wouldn't let it happen. Yet here she was, standing in her kitchen in nothing but a T-shirt, letting herself get in deeper and deeper with a man who'd move on one day and break her heart.

He leaned his forehead against hers and sighed. "I want nothing more than to stay, but I need to get moving. I have to clean up breakfast and get to work."

"I'll clean up. You go before you're late."

He glanced at the clock. "Already too late to worry about that."

"Tyler!" She frowned. "Why didn't you leave before?"

"Janie, do you really need to ask me that?" He pulled her tight against him and grinned.

"Please, go now so I don't have to feel any more guilty that you'll get in trouble. I'll see you later."

"That's the thing. I can't come over later. I've got something I have to do, so I won't be able to see you until tomorrow."

And there they were. The doubts she'd managed

to hold at bay while she and Tyler were together began to rise to the surface and make her imagine what—or who—Tyler would be occupied with later that he wouldn't be able to come over to see her.

A guy like Tyler, as nice and sweet as he was, wouldn't be satisfied killing time with her for long. Maybe not today, or tomorrow, but one day, he'd meet a girl his own age. They'd fall in love. He'd want to get married and have babies and grow old with her. It was inevitable, a natural course of events that she couldn't fight.

She held her insecurities in check long enough to say, "Okay. I'll see you tomorrow, then."

"A'ight. I gotta run upstairs and grab my stuff."

She nodded and forced a fake smile as the small bit of breakfast she'd eaten sat like a lead weight in her stomach.

Chapter Twenty-Six

"Wow, look at that. Quitting time and you actually stayed and worked for the full day. That's a nice change."

Justin smirked at Colton's smart-ass comment, while Tyler shook his head. "Ha ha. I finished mowing the last of the hay yesterday."

"Yeah, but you'll have to go back and rake it, and then bale it all. There's still lots of time left for you to put in over at the Smithwick place." Justin shot Tyler a knowing look.

The innuendo pissed him off, just as he was sure Justin had intended, but he couldn't let himself rise to the goading. "Yup. Lots more to do."

Colton shook his head. "You're nicer than me, man. I mean, I know she's a widow and all, but that's a hell of a lot of work. What's she paying you?"

He hated to say it because it was sure to raise questions, but Tyler couldn't lie. "Nothing. I'm doing her a favor."

"Jesus, Tyler. You're nuts. Hell, even if she was paying top dollar, I'm not sure I'd wanna spend all day here and then go work until dark there."

"Some things are more important than money, Colton . . . like being neighborly. Right, Ty?" Justin grinned as Tyler shot him a look that clearly said *shut the hell up.*

"Yup." He gritted the one word out between clenched teeth and willed Justin to quit talking.

Colton might not be as observant as Justin, but he wasn't stupid. If Justin kept hinting, Colton was going to guess something was up. The last thing Tyler needed was anyone else getting too interested in what was going on at Janie Smithwick's place after the haying was done for the day.

"So you wanna go out tonight? It's ladies' night at the Two-Step again. It should be exciting." Colton grinned wide.

Judging by Justin's snort of a laugh, he'd already been clued in about the last fateful time Tyler had set foot in the front door of the Two-Step.

"Yeah, no thanks. I've got work tonight anyway."

"What the hell? You just said you were done with the mowing." Sometimes Colton could whine like a little girl.

Tyler shook his head. "Not at Janie's. I'm working at the Hunts' store tonight."

"You're still doing that shit?" Colton asked. "I thought Mr. Hunt had recovered."

"He's better, but not back to 100 percent. I try to

work one night a week to give him a break." Tyler shrugged. "It isn't so bad."

Justin's brows rose. "More charity work. Damn, boy. You're gonna be up for freaking sainthood, you keep at it."

"Yeah, yeah." Tyler rolled his eyes at his friend's teasing. "When my neighbor had the stroke, I promised I'd help out at his shop. Besides, I'm not working totally for free. I get a kick-ass discount on anything I buy at the store and he lets me sell my leatherwork there. Half the time I can work on my own stuff in the back. I only come out if there's a customer."

"Tyler Jenkins. A damn shopkeeper." Justin swung his head from side to side. "Never thought I'd see that day."

It seemed Justin was on a roll today. He was enjoying having so much fodder to tease Tyler with.

"Yup." Tyler nodded, humoring him. "It's real hard work, too, let me tell you. A few weeks ago these two girls came in and I had to give them my opinion on which jeans made their butts look better. Tough job, that was."

Colton laughed. "In that case, maybe I'll stop by for a visit."

"You do that." Tyler reached up to tilt his own hat a bit farther down over his brow. "A'ight, boys. It's been fun, but I gotta get going."

He'd had enough sparring for one afternoon. There were places to go. People to see. Leather to emboss. And somewhere in there, he wanted to look into getting a puppy as a gift for Janie.

Just imagining the look on her face when he handed it to her put a smile on his. Tyler's good mood continued as he walked into Hunt's for his shift and found Logan and the baby there.

"Logan. Good to see you, bro." Tyler slapped his friend and neighbor on the back and reached a finger out to tickle the baby's cheek. "And how are you, little man?"

"He's still not sleeping through the night, but that seems to be harder on me and Emma than on this little guy here."

"That's not a surprise. Old folks like you need their sleep." Tyler laughed off the look Logan leveled at him for the *old* comment and asked, "Where is the little woman, anyway?"

"She's shopping with Becca. They're looking for a christening outfit for the baby, so I offered to take him. Bad enough the poor kid has to wear whatever they come up with, and look at pictures of it for the rest of his life. I didn't want him to have to get dragged through Lord knows how many stores looking for it. I figured we could come down here and hang out with Dad for a little bit."

He glanced around the shop but didn't see Logan's father. "Is your dad here?"

"Nah. I told him to take off about half an hour ago and that I'd wait for you. He gets tired so easily still."

Guilt hit him. He'd been shooting the shit with the guys at Rohn's. Then he'd stopped at home to shower, change, and eat—all while Mr. Hunt was exhausted from trying to hold down the fort at the shop and recuperate from the stroke that had nearly killed him last summer.

Pissed at his own selfish behavior, Tyler dropped his chin. "I'm sorry. I'll get here earlier from now on."

Logan waved off the apology. "No, Tyler. We're grateful enough you help out after working a full day at the ranch. Besides, Dad will never admit to you he gets tired. He'll tell you he's fine, but I see it in him."

"Yeah, your dad's a stubborn one when he wants to be."

"No kidding." Logan sighed.

Tyler had had to physically wrestle a box way too heavy for him out of the man's hands one day. Then there was the time he'd caught him standing on a step stool, struggling to get a saddle up on the wall display.

He kept all that to himself. It would do Logan no good to know it. Not while he still lived in Stillwater for his job and could only visit on occasion. Tyler knew this family well. He had for his whole life, and he knew Logan was already torn between work and family. Until Logan could resolve that issue, Tyler had no problem helping out.

"I'll keep an eye on him for you."

"Thanks, Ty."

"My pleasure. You've got enough to keep you busy with this little guy."

Logan blew out a burst of a laugh. "Very true. I'm told once the colic stops, the teething starts. That should be fun."

Tyler couldn't help but laugh. "God bless ya, but better you than me."

"Oh, come on, Ty. Don't you want a little guy of your own running around one day?" Logan set the three-month-old on top of a saddle display, supporting him with his hands.

Like he was born to be there, the baby kicked his feet and grabbed onto the saddle horn with both hands . . . and then leaned down and tried to suck on it. Tyler cringed, but Logan was on top of things. He pulled the baby upright before he had a chance to slobber on the leather, not to mention get a mouthful of probably toxic leather polish at the same time.

"A'ight, I'll admit it. He is cute as a button. But, dude, who'd he get this red hair from? I mean, you're dark haired. Emma's blond." Tyler let the implications hang in the air.

Logan shot Tyler a warning glance. "First off, stop with the insinuations before I hit you. Second, my great-grandmother was born with bright red hair, and every once in a while, someone in my family pops out a redhead, right out of the blue."

Tyler squatted down to be eye level with the baby and ruffled his ginger-colored downy tufts. "Well, I like it. I'm gonna call you Red. Red Hunt. That name will look real good up on the leader boards."

Logan shook his head. "I hesitate to say this because I bet Emma will hate it, but I kinda like the name Red for him. It'll be less confusing when both he and my dad are in the room."

"See, I can be helpful sometimes. I'm going to enjoy teaching him to ride and to rope. And who's gonna put you on top of your first sheep, Red? That'll be your Uncle Tyler." He glanced over the baby's head at Logan. "Yes, I know. Technically, I'm not his uncle, but I don't care. I want the title, and Tuck and Becca don't seem to be cooperating and giving it to me legitimately."

Logan laughed. "Give them some time. Until then, I'm happy for you to be an honorary uncle. The mutton bustin', though, we might have to discuss."

Tyler frowned. "That city girl wife of yours is going to fight me on it, isn't she?"

"Good chance." Logan dipped his head in a nod.

"Humph. We'll see. Won't we?" The baby laughed at the face Tyler made at him. Maybe he wouldn't mind having one of these of his own. It would sure be fun working to make one. Remembering that morning in the kitchen, he glanced at Logan. "Hey, did your dad leave today's newspaper around? I needed to look at the classifieds."

"I think it's in back." Logan frowned. "What are you looking for in the classifieds? You moving out of your parents' house?"

"No. Not as long as I'm living with Mom and Dad rent free, I'm not. I'm looking for a puppy."

"For you?" Logan's brows shot up high. "You better talk to your parents about that first, or you *will* be looking for an apartment to rent."

"The dog's not for me. It's for a friend."

"A female friend?" Logan asked.

"Yes." And hopefully, his soon-to-be girlfriend.

"Really? You're serious enough about a girl that you're ready to be a doggy daddy?" Logan looked surprised by that.

Tyler laughed. "I guess I am."

Chapter Twenty-Seven

The book sat in Janie's lap, open but unread as thoughts of where Tyler could be and what he might be doing swirled through her mind.

It was exactly one week since she'd found him, pants undone, hiding in her truck. Was he in town right now, jeans open wide, but with someone else? And why?

None of the different scenarios she could come up with gave her any solace, nor would they as long as she was still in the dark.

This was why she shouldn't have begun anything with him. This crazy, illogical insecurity and feeling of dread as she waited for the day this thing with him—whatever it was—would be over.

Stupid Rene. Telling her she could just have fun with him. Janie should have known better. She wasn't wired to *just have fun* with a man. The fact that she'd married right out of college proved that.

The idea of enjoying a sweet, good-looking, hard-bodied cowboy for a fling might sound like fun when being thrown around over some wine between girlfriends. The reality was far different.

In fact, she was going to tell Rene that, right now. She grabbed her cell phone and punched in a text.

The phone rang barely a minute after she'd hit SEND. Janie answered and heard her friend ask, "I clearly must have missed something, but what is my fault and why do I have to go to a rodeo because of it?"

"You encouraged me. It's your fault I let myself fool around with Tyler." Janie lowered her voice for the last part. She was alone in the house, but who knew if Tim or even Khriste could be close enough to Rene to hear her through the phone.

"Mmm, mmm. You should be thanking me for that."

"Well, I'm not because now I'm like a crazy woman." She was lucky she hadn't given in to one crazy thought she had and gone driving around town looking for his truck and stalking him.

"Just relax."

"I can't relax, and now I promised to go to the rodeo he's riding in tomorrow. You know what that means, don't you?"

"Oh, yeah. I do. I haven't been in a while but I surely do remember all those hot cowboy butts. Rodeos are like a Wrangler-and-chaps buffet."

Janie sighed. That was exactly her fear. That there would be a thousand females of all ages there and, unless they were blind or crazy, they'd be after Tyler. True though it was, that wasn't what she'd been getting at. "It means you have to come with me."

She shouldn't have agreed to go in the first place. It felt too much like she was his girlfriend going to watch him ride. More than that, she knew rodeos and how things worked. The number of pretty young things throwing their boobs at the riders, trying to get their attention, would be frightening. She couldn't handle being there alone. She needed her friend for support.

"Okay."

Rene's answer halted Janie's panic. "You'll really go?"

"Sure. It's about time I took Khriste to her first rodeo. I can't believe I haven't before. She'll love seeing the barrel racing, and once I tell her Tyler's riding, there won't be any keeping her away."

Janie blew out a breath in relief. "Thank you. I appreciate it."

"Jeez, it's not like you asked me for a kidney or something. It's a rodeo. You really need to learn to chill out."

"Yeah, okay." Janie rolled her eyes. "I'll work on it."

She didn't see that happening as long as she was sleeping with a man eleven years her junior or while she still had a mountain of bills to pay, or two fields full of cut hay yet to be baled and sold.

"So we good? Can I go now before Tim commandeers the remote and changes to the Hunting Channel?"

"Yes, you can go." She smiled. "Say hello to your man for me."

Rene let out a laugh. "Yeah, you say hello to yours, too."

Janie disconnected the call without comment.

Besides his not being there, Tyler was by no means her man. Janie's curiosity about where he was returned.

A knock on the back door sent her heart racing. She tossed the book aside, hopped off the bed, and let herself hope.

That soft knock, barely loud enough for her to hear it from upstairs in the bedroom, seemed so typically Tyler, she felt to her core that it had to be him. It was his considerate way of saying he wanted to see her while being reluctant to wake her if she was already asleep.

She reached the darkened kitchen and saw his shadow through the glass, the cowboy hat so familiar to her now. She flipped on the lights and got a better look at his hopeful yet contrite expression. No wonder she was powerless against this man. Who could possibly resist him when he was as beautiful on the inside as he was on the outside?

She unlocked the door and pulled it open. "Hi."

"Hey, there." His smile made her want to forget everything—her doubts, her worry. Tamping down her excitement, she waited to hear whether he'd tell her where he'd been. "I know it's late, too late to just show up, but I didn't want to call the house and wake you. And I don't have your cell number or I would have texted first to make sure you weren't already asleep."

"I wasn't sleeping."

"Good. I couldn't stand not seeing you. I spent the whole time I was working at the store thinking about you."

"You work at a store?" Janie frowned. As confusing

as his confession was, his revelation had her spirits lifting. He hadn't been out with the guys, or out with a girl. He had been working. "What store?"

"I fill in here and there at my neighbor's shop. He had a stroke last year and needed help—"

He never got to finish. She let out a laugh even as she fought tears. Warmth filled her chest, chasing away the cold fear as cautious hope and pure joy overwhelmed her. The relief she felt couldn't be contained. It bubbled to the surface as she jumped him.

Janie threw her arms around his neck and crashed her mouth against his.

Tyler pushed the door shut before he wrapped his hands around her waist. Kissing her as they moved, he backed them farther into the room.

"Not that I'm complaining . . ." He kissed her again and then broke away to continue, "But what did I do to deserve this very nice reception?"

"Just you being you. Come upstairs."

"Gladly." Smiling, he grabbed her hand and pulled her toward the door leading out of the kitchen and toward the staircase.

She tugged to stop him. He glanced back. "What's wrong?"

"I have to lock the door and turn off the lights."

His smile widened. She guessed he knew exactly what she was thinking. That once they got upstairs, neither one of them would be coming back down again until morning.

Just to make sure they were really on the same page, she asked, "Do you have your overnight bag in the truck?"

"I do. You know, just in case." He smirked while looking adorable.

"You might want to go and get it now so you don't have to later."

He grinned. "Yes, ma'am."

Chapter Twenty-Eight

Rene sighed and stared ahead. "God, I love horses."

Janie followed Rene's line of sight and shook her head. There were horses, all right, but in front of the animals was a line of ropers waiting to move to the other end of the arena, where they'd start their runs.

The cowboys, all dressed in jeans and facing away from the stands as they watched the action of the event before theirs, gave the audience at this end of the arena a perfect view of their backs—and their backsides.

She shot Rene a sideways glance. "Mmm-hmm. Right. It's the horses you're interested in. I'm sure."

"It is." Rene glanced down at Khriste. "It's important to teach my daughter all aspects of equine sports. She can be an Olympic jumper, or a professional barrel racer, or even a team roper, if she wants to be. Right, baby girl?"

"When's Tyler up?" Khriste wasn't interested in the man buffet her mother still ogled. Only Tyler. Much like Janie. She'd been keeping a close eye on the ropers, just as Rene had, but she was concerned with one in particular.

"I don't know, baby. Ask your Aunt Janie. I bet she knows all about what Tyler's doing."

Janie frowned at Rene, then glanced down at Khriste. "Soon. The tie-down roping is up next." She decided to get Rene in trouble, since her friend had no qualms about throwing her under the bus. "I think Tyler already rode in the first event. The bronc riding. You know, the one that we missed because we were late."

Khriste's mouth dropped open and she turned to glare at her mother.

"Mom." The girl made the single short word stretch out extra long, clearly showing how annoyed she was. "I told you we were gonna be late and miss things. *Important* things."

"Yeah, Rene. Important things." Janie smiled as she jumped on board with Khriste's indignation.

"Sorry." Rene wrinkled her nose at Janie, but the damage had already been done, judging by Khriste's scowl.

They'd arrived after the events had already started because Rene had picked Janie up late. Rene had tried to convince Janie that Khriste hadn't been ready on time, but after all the years they'd been best friends, Janie knew the truth. Rene ran on her own schedule, and rarely did it match everyone else's.

Arriving late and not having time to talk to Tyler probably wasn't such a bad thing. What would they have done in public, and in front of her best friend and godchild? Stood awkwardly, like polite friends who hadn't been in the same bed just twelve hours ago?

Things were already complicated enough with their relationship limited to the privacy of her house. She should have known being anywhere with Tyler in public would make it even more so. She should have said no to his invitation. Made up some excuse—

That thought halted dead in its tracks as Tyler turned to face her and scanned the stands. She saw the moment his eyes found her. He smiled wide, and even at that distance, she could swear she saw a twinkle in his blue, blue eyes. Her heart pounded harder. She had to bite back a cuss at the realization that she couldn't even see the man without being affected by him.

It was time for Tyler and the other ropers to move and he had to turn away, but still she couldn't tear her gaze away from him as he leapt easily into the saddle. If she'd thought he was handsome before, she'd been mistaken. There was no sight more beautiful—though that word didn't seem appropriate—than Tyler in the saddle.

He was soon lost to her sight in the group of riders moving toward the ropers' box. Janie glanced at Rene and found she was under scrutiny. Rene's brows rose but before she could utter even a word, Janie said, "No comments, please."

Rene pressed her lips together. "I wasn't gonna say a thing."

Somehow, Janie had trouble believing that. There was nothing Rene could say anyway that Janie hadn't already thought herself as she debated the future of this thing she had with Tyler, including how maybe it wouldn't be so bad if she just gave in and let herself fall for the man.

The wide swing of the pendulum when it came to thoughts of him only proved to her she was crazy. Being with him made her so. Yet here she was, breathless from a smile and craving another.

"I see Tyler!" Khriste's excited exclamation dragged Janie back to the event. "He's getting into that little cage."

Janie raised a brow. Born and raised in Oklahoma and the girl knew nothing about roping. "Rene, you really should have taken her to a rodeo before now."

"Sorry. I had other things to do. You could have done it."

"I had a few things to do of my own." Erasing her scowl, Janie put an arm around Khriste. It was partially her fault. She should have taken it upon herself to bring her godchild to an event. She'd just have to correct that oversight now. "It's not a cage, sweetie. It's more like a starting gate where the ropers have to wait until the calf is let loose and they can rope it."

When Janie had been in college and riding barrels, she always had liked the tie-down event the best, but she'd never given in to the lure of dating a roper.

The fact that Tyler was a roper and she'd always had a weakness for them wasn't helping her confusion one bit. All the old triggers from the past came back with a vengeance, resulting in a visceral reaction based on a long-standing attraction to the men in the sport, right along with her caution regarding getting involved with one.

But she was already involved, wasn't she?

Ironic how she'd managed to get through her teen years and her college years, right up until her meeting and marrying Tom, all without falling for a roper. Not until she was thirty-six had she fallen victim to a rodeo cowboy's charms.

Her, and who knew how many other females. She hadn't missed the number of women—girls, really—who were watching Tyler just as closely as she was. God, how she hated that.

The calf was released into the arena, and it took off in a crooked path across the dirt. Seconds later, Tyler and his horse were in hot pursuit. With the piggin' string held between his teeth, and his legs controlling the well-trained cutting horse, Tyler swung the rope above his head and let it fly.

Even aimed from the back of a horse at full gallop, the loop of the rope landed true, sliding over the calf's head to settle around his neck. Tyler leapt from the saddle. As the horse came to a dead stop, the man ran at full speed to where the calf was held by the rope tied to the saddle horn.

She'd always wondered whether the horse could reason out what he was doing and why, or if he just knew the steps so well he repeated them without thought. Either way, it was a beautiful thing. Man and horse worked in a well-practiced synchronicity that had always fascinated Janie.

The gelding took a step back to keep tension on the rope, holding it secure and taut around the calf's neck until Tyler could get to him. Tyler lifted the two-hundred-plus pound calf and flipped him onto his back on the ground. He took the string from between his teeth, wrapping it around three of the calf's legs, securing it in a half hitch before he thrust his hands into the air to stop the clock.

The entire thing, from Tyler leaving the box to the time he threw up his hands to tell the judges he was done, took only seconds. Eight point nine seconds to be exact, according to the announcer. It was a good time that would possibly put Tyler in the lead. He must have realized it, too. He grinned as he released the calf. It rolled to its feet and took off running as Tyler gathered up his rope and headed back to his horse.

"Aunt Janie, did Tyler do good?"

Janie realized she should have been explaining things to Khriste, but Tyler had been too much of a distraction. Not a surprise. "He did very good, sweetie." The next rider took his position in the box. "Want me to explain the rules to you so you understand?"

"I understand. The cowboy catches the cow and then lets him go."

"You're right. That's exactly it."

Rene smiled. "Can't argue with her there."

"I guess not." Janie laughed.

Leave it to a child to break things down to their simplest form. She could learn something from the girl. Maybe things didn't have to be so complicated all the time.

The rest of the ropers took their turns, but Janie didn't see a whole lot of them since she kept watching for Tyler, who was still at the other end of the arena.

"Mom, I have to go to the bathroom."

Rene glanced at Janie. "I guess we're heading to the Porta-Johns. Lucky me. You want to come?"

Janie laughed. "As tempting as it sounds, no, thanks. I'm good."

"Yeah, I figured. We'll be right back."

"Okay."

As Rene and Khriste headed off to the facilities, the condition of which would no doubt be pretty horrendous, considering the event grounds were packed and it was a hot day, Janie decided she'd be waiting until she got home.

"Did you see Tyler's run?"

The question had her turning, her mouth opening to answer automatically until she realized the stranger was asking the question of her friend. Both girls stood close to the rail, but Janie hadn't noticed them until just now when she'd heard his name.

She hadn't heard the announcers speak about another cowboy named Tyler, which meant they had to be talking about her Tyler. Except, judging by the familiarity with which the girl spoke about him, he wasn't Janie's Tyler at all.

"I did. Isn't he the guy you fooled around with last year?"

"Yup. The very same. Damn, he looks good today. I wonder if he's entered in the team roping, too, or just in the bulls."

"OMG, I hope he is in the team roping. I love ropers. They're so freaking hot."

"Yeah. Me too. But there's nothing hotter than a hot guy on the back of a bucking bull."

"Heck, yeah."

The inane conversation between the two girls,

both so young they probably were college-aged, had Janie's insides twisting.

"Oooh, look. He's coming back this way."

That got Janie's attention and had her glancing up. She could feel the excitement coming off the girl as he approached. The blood drained from her face from the impending collision of worlds— the girl from his past and Janie from his present. She felt cold in spite of the hot day.

Rational thought seemed impossible—she was one big emotional ball of nerves—but the one thing Janie could be sure of as she stood shaking next to these girls was that she didn't want to be there to see them and Tyler together, even if all they did was talk to him. She shouldn't have come here.

He was on his way to this end of the arena now. She knew as soon as he walked his horse to the grassy area by the parked stock trailers, he'd be back to say hello to her. He'd already seen her and knew she'd seen him. He had to come over, even if his former fling was standing right next to her.

What a mess. Like her nightmares come to life. She dared to glance at the girl he'd chosen to be with. Young, and barely clad in the heat. Bleached blond hair that hung down to her ass. Big, bouncing breasts that seemed to defy gravity even without the support of a bra. Legs that reached a mile long out of her cut-off short shorts.

How in the world had Janie ever thought she could hold Tyler's interest for more than a night or two? She couldn't. Not if this was an example of the girls he usually went for. Of the temptations he was surrounded by constantly. In bars. At rodeos. Hell, probably even at that store where he worked.

"Tyler! Hey." The girl's sickeningly sweet greeting was suggestive enough that Janie didn't even have to look at her to know what her expression would look like. She'd be smiling at Tyler, hopeful for a repeat. Thrusting her breasts at him to ensure he took notice.

To his credit, all he did was nod to the two girls before he turned to face Janie. There was no reaction or sign he recognized the blast from his not-so-distant past. Either he had the best poker face she'd ever seen, or he didn't remember the girl. Janie didn't know which option was worse.

That this girl standing right next to them had probably been a one-night stand was hard enough for Janie to swallow. The thought that Tyler could have had so many girls he couldn't remember them all was horrifying.

Would he not remember her in a year, either?

"Hey, darlin'." He smiled wide and looked at Janie as if she were the only female there. Another time, another place, she might have let herself believe that was true. "I'm glad you made it. When you weren't here before the opening ceremony, I got worried."

She forced herself to respond, even though what she wanted to do was sneak behind the stands and hide. "Uh, yeah. Sorry. Rene was late picking me up."

He nodded. "I saw that Khriste is here, too. Where'd they get off to?"

"Bathroom."

"That's good. That means I can do this." Grinning,

Tyler wrapped one hand around her arm. She felt the warmth of his touch against her bare skin as he leaned in for a kiss. She leaned away, which halted his forward progress and brought a frown to his formerly smooth brow. "What's wrong?"

"Nothing." She scrambled for a reason why she'd avoided his kiss. There were many to choose from, but only one she thought they should discuss where they currently were. "I just don't think we should do that here."

"Why not? I don't care who sees me kissing you."

Her brow rose and she fought with all her might not to look toward the girl and her friend. "Are you sure about that?"

Frowning, he nodded. "Yeah. Very sure." His answer was firm, sounding almost defensive.

His second hand came up to grip her other arm. He pulled her close and planted a big kiss on her lips. The kiss wasn't romantic, or even sexy. It felt more like him proving a point, that point being when he wanted to kiss her, he was going to, no matter where they were or what she said about it.

When he pulled back, Janie dared to glance past him. She got a look at the girl's surprised and angry expression as she stood behind him.

He released his hold on her arms and took a step back. Paranoid, Janie wondered why. Then she realized Rene and Khriste were working their way back toward her, and Tyler had stepped back to turn and smile at them.

"Hey, girlie. You see me ride?"

"Tyler! You were the best!" Khriste, of course, had her usual enthusiastic welcome for him.

While he was occupied with the warm reception the little girl had provided, Janie pulled Rene to the side. "Can we go?"

"Now?" Rene's forehead crinkled. "Why? What's wrong?"

"I'll explain later." If she could manage to get the words out without vomiting, that was. When Rene still frowned at her and didn't look as if she was going to let it go with just that, Janie added, "Please?"

"All right." Rene nodded. "Khriste, baby. Say good-bye to Tyler. We have to go."

Tyler and Khriste both looked confused by Rene's statement.

"But why?" Khriste whined.

Tyler's frown deepened as he glanced between the adults. "Everything okay?"

"I'm not feeling real well. I think I'd be better off at home." Janie pressed a hand to her stomach. She wasn't even lying. She did feel sick.

His concern was evident in his expression. "A'ight. I'll check in with you later."

She waved away his offer. "I'll be fine. Really. I'll probably lie down and try to sleep through it."

He nodded. "Okay."

Khriste didn't accept their leaving as easily as Tyler did. She complained and pouted, but Janie didn't hear half of it. She just walked away from Tyler, leaving him wide open to be scooped into the clutches of, if not the girl he'd been with before, then someone new. That thought only made her even sicker.

In the car, Rene glanced at her. "You going to tell me why we left?"

Janie pressed her lips together and considered that for a moment. She opted to try answering with a question of her own. "Do I have to?"

After a pause, Rene said, "Maybe. Then again, maybe not. I'm pretty sure I can guess *who* you're upset about, but what I can't quite figure out is why."

Why was the question Janie had asked herself over and over again since meeting Tyler. Why had she been so stupid as to open herself up to a man guaranteed to hurt her in the long run, even if she had believed she could be physical with him and not get attached emotionally?

Those few nights in his arms, it had seemed worth the risk.

Not anymore. Without the warmth of his embrace, when she felt so keenly the cold emptiness in her life, she knew a few stolen moments of pleasure had not been worth the pain that would surely linger.

She managed to make it the whole drive home without having to answer any more of Rene's questions. That was probably because Khriste was having a meltdown that they'd had to leave the rodeo early. It ended with their dropping Janie off and Rene promising to drive directly back to the arena so Khriste could see Tyler in the final event, the bull riding.

The two drove off in a haze of dust on the gravel and Janie was alone. Again. That did nothing to banish the whirring of doubts and self-recrimination in her head.

She turned toward the barn. She'd check on the horses and then head inside.

It was dinnertime, not that she had an appetite. Maybe she'd heat up some leftovers later, though any food in the fridge would remind her of him. She shook her head.

In a short time he'd pervaded every aspect of her life. The kitchen reminded her of him and all the time they'd spent there. She couldn't look at Bella without picturing him helping Khriste with the mare. The field of cut hay, the tractor parked by the barn, it all reminded her of him.

She couldn't even hear a truck out on the road without her heart leaping. She had to break things off with him. That much was obvious. Far better to do it now, before she got in any deeper, than to wait for later when he left her for the next, most likely much younger fling in his lineup.

Being with Tyler had been like a fireworks display on the Fourth of July. Exciting and colorful, but quick to burn out. Maybe she hadn't appreciated her boring married life with Tom as much as she should have. At least she could count on the steady, uneventful drudgery . . . but not really, because it had all been yanked away when he'd died.

So what, then? Live her life in solitude? That couldn't be the answer any more than trying to grasp at a brief moment of passion with Tyler was. What she needed was a nice, boring man.

Sadly, what she knew she needed and what she *wanted* didn't seem to exactly line up at the moment. After experiencing the brilliance that was Tyler, his exuberance, his energy, his sheer lust for life, anyone else would feel dull in comparison.

She'd left him at the rodeo, with those two girls and many more like them. Janie had to wonder which would have been stupider—staying or leaving.

Chapter Twenty-Nine

Tyler couldn't keep the smile off his face as he steered the truck onto the side road. It had been one freaking great day. He'd placed in the money in three of his events, and he had a pretty little thing riding shotgun in his truck.

He glanced toward the passenger seat and his smile got wider. "Almost there, girlie."

There was no answer, but then again, he didn't expect one. She was a beauty, though, with big eyes a man could easily fall in love with. Hell, all it had taken was one warm, wet kiss and he was pretty sure he loved her already.

There had been no question in his mind she was the one. He'd picked her up and tossed her into the cab, and she'd ridden shotgun like a little lady the whole drive.

He didn't know what the hell was wrong with Janie that she'd left right after the tie-down roping. She'd missed him riding the bronc by getting there late, and she'd left so soon, she'd missed him in the bull riding, too.

Hopefully, it was nothing serious. Whatever was the matter with her, the puppy was definitely going to cheer her up. "Your new mama sure is gonna be surprised by you."

The pup's ears lifted as she wagged her tail and looked excited just at the mere fact he was talking to her. Tyler laughed at the reaction. If only all females listened to him as well as this dog did, Janie in particular, he'd be sitting pretty.

Why did the woman insist on being so contrary? He hadn't missed that she didn't want him to kiss her in public. How uncomfortable she'd looked just talking to him. He'd have to change all that. Hell, coparenting this little girlie could only help. Right?

Who could resist that adorable face? If the puppy didn't melt Janie's heart and convince her she needed to give them a chance as a real couple, nothing would.

His anticipation grew the closer he got to Janie's house, filling him with an energy he couldn't contain and making it hard to sit still. The puppy sensed his excitement. She started to hop around in the seat, running from one side to look out the window before hopping back to the other side to paw at Tyler's leg.

"A'ight. Settle down." Amazingly, she sat her butt down, but continued to stare at him as if waiting for his next command. He snorted out a laugh. "You really do listen to me. Maybe when you meet her, you can convince your mama to do the same."

He didn't need or want a woman who blindly obeyed and did anything he said. Hell, he didn't mind a woman who challenged him. He preferred it, actually. But Janie wouldn't even agree to go on a real date. That she'd come to the rodeo had seemed like a step in the right direction, until he'd seen how strange she acted around him while she was there.

It didn't matter, because he had an adorable little bundle to surprise her with. Tyler pulled into her driveway riding a high, excited about giving her the dog. And if Janie was sick, he could fix her something to eat and the three of them could snuggle in her bed. Maybe watch some television. Have some tea. Whatever she wanted. If she fell asleep, he'd cover her with a blanket and then make her breakfast in the morning. He liked that idea more than he'd ever thought he could.

Throwing the truck into park, he turned to the pup. "You ready?"

More tail wagging said she was. He reached down and lifted her warm little body, tucking her beneath one arm much like a football. He strode to the back door but restrained himself from pounding too hard in case Janie was napping. He knocked softly and then a bit louder when she didn't come right down.

The dog got wiggly beneath his arm but he wasn't sure enough of her obedience to set her on the ground without a leash. Who knew if she'd take off for the horses, or just for the hills? He wasn't in the mood, or in the right footwear, to go chasing a nine-week-old puppy across the fields.

Hindsight being 20/20, he realized he should have stopped by the pet store. It was stupid not to grab some supplies before heading over to Janie's.

She wouldn't have what they needed for a new dog. A leash, some puppy food, maybe a chew toy, and a bed. He'd been so excited, he hadn't thought it through. That was all right. He'd accept Janie's sweet gratitude, see her settled in bed, then run out and get what they needed. Maybe he'd pick up some chicken soup for Janie, too. Though he wasn't sure if she had a cold, it couldn't hurt.

Tyler frowned when he realized she was taking an awfully long time to answer the door. He knocked one more time, louder this time, vowing if she didn't answer, he'd let himself in and check on her. She might be sleeping, but she could also be passed out on the floor for all he knew. He couldn't leave until he saw she was safe.

Finally, she came around the corner of the kitchen door and for the first time since he'd started showing up at this door, she didn't smile.

She unlocked the latch but didn't say anything, so he figured he'd better. "Hey, how are you feeling? Any better?"

Her shorts and T-shirt told him she'd already changed for bed, even though it wasn't long past suppertime. Maybe she'd been lying down and he'd disturbed her. That would explain her lack of warmth, though not really. He'd woken her in the dead of night from a sound sleep to have sex and she'd never seemed as unhappy about it as she did right now.

"Not really." Janie sighed. "What are you doing here?" Her gaze dropped to the pup in his arms.

There was no hiding the puppy, so he should probably explain it. "I thought I'd bring you a surprise to cheer you up a little bit." He thrust the wiggling dog forward. She barely filled his two hands, she was still so little.

Janie shook her head. "What is this?"

"She's for you. Isn't she cute?" For the first time since he'd gotten the idea to give her the puppy, he began to doubt his plan.

"For me? Why? We didn't talk about this."

He pulled the pup back and cuddled her against his chest since it was obvious Janie wasn't going to hold her. Hell, it was looking doubtful she'd take her at all.

"Actually, we did talk about it. Right there." He eyed the kitchen table and chair where he'd brought up the need for a dog as a kind of early warning system in case anyone pulled into the driveway while they were too distracted having sex to notice. She frowned more deeply and he elaborated. "Yesterday morning. Remember?"

"You joking while we were having sex isn't having a discussion about a life change such as getting a dog." The good dose of attitude in her answer made him feel like a schoolboy being taken to task by his teacher.

"A'ight. Just chill, darlin'." He really couldn't argue with her. He hadn't asked. He also had never imagined this would be her reaction. She loved animals. She'd told him all about how as a teenager she'd taken in stray dogs, cats, and even a raccoon.

"Chill? You dump this responsibility in my lap, without asking me first, and that's your advice. That's all you have to say? Chill?" Eyes open wide,

Janie looked about as crazed as she sounded as her voice rose to a higher pitch.

"A'ight. I was wrong. I'll take her back." As if he was gentling a spooked horse, Tyler kept his voice low and calm.

"How can you take her back?" Her outburst got more manic rather than calmer, as he'd intended when he made the offer.

He drew in a deep breath and let it out. "I don't know what you want from me here, Janie."

"Well, I don't want you to take her back. You took her and made a promise that she'd have a home. You'd go back on your word like that? Just because things didn't work out?"

"Then I'll keep her myself. Is that what you want? Tell me what you want me to do."

"I want you to leave." Her flat, emotionless answer surprised him more than her reaction to the puppy.

"This can't be about one tiny dog. Janie. Please. Talk to me. What's wrong?"

"I heard a girl talking about you. She was young. Pretty. Perky in every possible way. I can't—no, I won't and I don't want to compete with her or anyone else."

"It's not a competition. I'm here with you because I want to be. I don't want to be with anyone else but you. That's why I keep asking you out. I want to get more serious with you." All this because some girls in the stands said something about him? How was that his fault? He decided to set Janie straight on how things were. "And really, if you're going to be with me, you're going to have to understand that I can't help it if some girl I don't even know was talking about me at the event. It comes with the territory. That's rodeo."

"Oh, you knew her."

The venom of her answer made him curious. "Who?"

"The girl who said hello to you today when you came to talk to me. Remember her? She certainly remembers you. Apparently, according to her conversation with her friend, you two *hooked up* last year."

Frowning, he pawed through his memory. He remembered the girl saying hello to him, and as he thought more, he remembered the same event the previous year. He hung his head and blew out a breath. "Yeah, I didn't recognize her today, but . . ." He let out a sigh. "I'm sorry you had to hear that, but it was really nothing."

"Nothing? You have sex with a girl, forget her totally, don't even recognize her until I mention it, and then say it was no big deal? I thought I knew you, but obviously I don't."

"Whoa, wait one minute. I didn't have sex with her. We kissed a couple of times during the event and then I drove home with Justin. Ask him if you don't believe me. And the reason I didn't recognize her was because her hair wasn't blond last year. She looks totally different and honestly, Janie, the only person I was looking at today was you."

She looked as if she was considering his explanation. Possibly even believing him, which was good since it was the God's honest truth.

He took a chance and dared to go a step closer.

"You do know me, Janie. I'm exactly the guy you thought I was. Nothing's changed. I'm the same."

"Maybe you are, but I'm not."

Shaking his head, he didn't know what to say. He didn't understand her. Hell, he didn't understand most women. Probably why he'd never had a long-term relationship. It could be his own damn fault. He didn't speak their language or understand the inner workings of the female mind.

The pup whined and he felt her start to shake. She must have picked up on his mood. He could only imagine how his own displeasure with the situation was radiating off him and the puppy sensed it. He held her tighter. At least the dog was one creature of the opposite sex he understood. Horses, too. If only he was as proficient at reading human females.

He looked back at Janie. "What's changed for you? Why is anything different?"

"Seeing that girl—"

"Dammit, Janie. You can't hold against me something I did a year before I met you. I kissed her. I didn't fuck her." He hated that he'd cussed in front of her the moment the word was out of his mouth.

She rolled her lips in, shaking her head. "It doesn't matter. There will always be someone like her between us."

"Why? I didn't know you then. I don't want to be with her now."

"Fine, I understand that she's from your past. But I'll always wonder if the next girl I see will be your future."

Frustration rolled off him and the pup whined

again. "I don't know what to do to convince you that you're who I want. No one else."

"There's nothing you can do. I told you. It's not you. It's me. It's how I feel and I can't change that."

He snorted. "You never tried."

"I take full blame for all this. I slept with you when I knew I shouldn't. You were always too young and I can't blame you for that. I should have known better. Should have known I wouldn't be able to handle it."

"I'm almost twenty-five. I'm not some kid." Even as he said it, he reviewed the evidence against him. He still lived with his parents. He worked for someone else in a dead-end job with no prospects of anything better. She'd met him while he was hiding in her truck like a fool after running from a stupid situation he'd gotten himself into.

"I know you see me as some screwup, but I'm not. Not really. Yeah, I joke around sometimes, and I have gotten myself into some trouble, but that's not who I am. At least, not all the time. I can be serious."

"That's not the problem at all. I know you're not a screwup. You're a hardworking, generous man, but I'm too old for you."

"No, you're not."

She shook her head. "We've been over this before. Over and over again. It won't end any differently this time."

"Why did you let me into your life at all? Why let me be with you, make love to you, sleep in your bed and wake up next to you, only to kick me to the curb after?"

"I told you, I didn't mean to. You got under my

skin. A little at a time. Slowly. So slowly I didn't realize it was happening until I couldn't help myself."

Her losing control because of him was a good thing. Maybe things had started to look up. "Then what's the problem?"

"You're—"

"Younger than you," he finished her sentence.

"Yes."

"So what?"

"We're in different places in our lives. We have different futures."

He didn't miss that her argument was all over the place. First, his bringing the dog had thrown her. Then the girl from the rodeo. Now she was back to their ages with the added complication of their different lives and futures. What crap excuse would she come up with next?

The woman was fighting hard, but doing it badly. He could only hope it was because she really didn't want to get rid of him. Either way, he wasn't going to make it easy.

"How are we in different places?" he countered. "I love animals. I work on a ranch. You have animals. You own a ranch. I want to make a future training horses and raising stock. You have a small herd of cattle and a horse operation. How is that different? Seems to me that you and I are on the same page."

"The same book maybe, but not the same page. You're in chapter one, just starting out. I'm way farther along in my story."

This argument had backfired. "Okay. Enough of this book stuff—"

"No, it's a good analogy. You're starting your life and you need a girl your age to share it with."

Back to this again. He rubbed his temple with the hand that wasn't holding the puppy. "I don't want a girl my age, Janie. Believe me, I know. If I wanted one, I could have one. I've had plenty of them."

"Exactly." Her smile was small and sad.

He knew his mistake the moment he'd made it. Telling her how many girls he'd had was not the best choice for his defense. "That's all in the past."

"It's not. Your past is part of you. You can have— you have had—any girl you want. You're still that same man. It's who you are."

He bit back a curse. She'd said it sweetly, but it might be the worst insult he'd ever been dealt. Just because he'd played the game didn't mean he was and always would be a player. "No. You're wrong."

She shook her head, a slow move that only pissed him off more.

It was likely she was past listening, but he wasn't done talking.

"Listen to me, Janie. Yeah, I have women in my past. Going out was what I did when I was killing time and waiting for the right one to come along. So I've been around the block. That's a good thing. It means I'm sure of what I want. I want you."

He could see in her face she wasn't giving in. He felt like tearing his hair out. Or maybe kissing her until she saw the truth in what he said, what he felt. Instead, he settled on asking, "Why don't you believe me?"

Janie shrugged. He began to see that he could talk until he was blue in the face and she wouldn't believe him, and he was at a loss as to how to change that.

"I'm gonna go." It was either leave or shake some sense into her. Since he'd never laid a hand on a woman and never would, he chose to go.

She took a step forward, mouth open, and then stopped herself. Just the effort, that one move, told him she wasn't completely happy about his leaving. At least not this way, with things so bad between them.

He hiked the puppy up a little higher against his chest and was rewarded with a big sloppy tongue kiss. "Good girl."

Brushing a hand over the dog's head, he shot one more glance at Janie before he turned for the door. He didn't say good-bye, because this wasn't. He'd be back, but only after she'd had some time to calm down, and to think.

He wasn't cocky enough to think he was irresistible, but hell, they'd shared a lot together. She'd think about him after he left. He had to believe that or everything was lost, and he refused to accept that.

Chapter Thirty

The tears didn't come until Tyler was out the door, but once he'd gotten into the truck, they started to flow.

Wiping her hand across her eyes, Janie thanked God that he had driven away and hadn't seen her weep. He'd never know how hard letting him go, how hard watching him drive away, had been. She couldn't have handled him seeing her cry or worse, comforting her. She would have folded. All resolve would have fled if he'd wrapped his arms around her or pressed his lips to her forehead the way she'd seen him drop a kiss to the puppy's furry little head.

Why did he have to be so damn good? Good with dogs. Good with horses. Good with kids. . . . Good in the bedroom. And in the kitchen. And in the bed of his truck.

Tyler was also very good with women. Janie reminded herself of that before she jumped in her car and drove after him. She drew in and let out a shaky breath, uncertain what to do.

Taking an over-the-counter sleeping pill and

knocking herself into oblivion where she could forget this whole horrible day was very tempting. She hadn't done that since right after Tom had died. She hadn't even been really tempted to do so until this very moment.

That realization seemed pretty momentous. How in the world could losing her husband drive her to the same actions as pushing Tyler out of her life?

She suspected she knew the answer. She'd started to fall in love with him.

Had she let herself, she would have turned her heart over to him, and no matter how good a man he was, she still believed he would have broken it eventually.

How would he have felt about her, about them, when she turned fifty and he was still in his thirties? Still handsome. Still the hot rodeo cowboy who attracted the ladies like flies to honey.

Even if Tyler truly believed he was fine with the age difference, and even if she chose to believe him, she wasn't all right with it.

The fear of losing one more thing in her life that she cared about was nearly paralyzing. It had hit her hard today when he'd thrust that little dog at her, and she'd been overwhelmed by memories of watching her and of Tom's old dog slowly fall into a sleep he'd never awaken from on the vet's table.

Having to watch that, just weeks after watching her husband take his last breath, had numbed her to loving anything. A defense mechanism to keep her from crumbling completely. Tyler had reawakened that part of her she thought she'd put to bed forever.

Now she felt, and she hurt, and it sucked.

Maybe she had been living only half a life, inhabiting a world of dull gray until he'd brought back the vivid color to it. But with the vibrancy of really living, all the feelings, both good and bad, also returned.

The house phone rang. Janie glanced at the receiver in the cradle on the counter nearest the stove, half thinking it might be Tyler. Rene's name and number came across the readout. She felt horrible doing it, but she didn't answer. Instead she watched it ring, paranoid the whole time that Rene could somehow know she was there and not picking up. Almost afraid to breathe until, five rings in, the phone finally went silent.

The reprieve only lasted a few seconds before she heard her cell phone sound from where she'd tossed it on the counter when she'd gotten home. She didn't have to look at the display to know it would be Rene. When the beep sounded for a voice mail, she walked over and hit the button to retrieve it, guilt riding her the whole time.

"I finally got home from that rodeo and got Khriste settled, so now it's time for you to explain what the hell happened today. Call me!"

Janie hit the END button and put the phone down gently, to make sure she didn't accidentally hit REDIAL and call back. Rene was a good friend, but the wound was too fresh and the tears too near the surface for Janie to repeat the events of today, even to her. She'd call back eventually. Until then, hiding and avoiding contact seemed like the best course of action.

and avoiding contact seemed like the best course of action.

The house was too quiet. She felt Tyler's absence in the kitchen. Upstairs in the bedroom would be just as bad.

Janie found herself wandering to one of the few rooms that didn't contain memories of Tyler—the bedroom she'd shared with Tom. The room where he'd taken his last breath.

She rarely went in there since moving to the bedroom upstairs. The room would make a good office, but she couldn't bear to spend that much time in it, so she'd left it set up as a guest room. Not that she had any guests.

Funny that she gravitated there now. Even stranger that as she perched on the edge of the bed and ran her hand over the comforter, a sense of calm came over her.

She felt peace, as if the drama the rest of the house buzzed with couldn't penetrate the walls of this room. She felt closer to Tom, or at least his memory here, than she did at his grave site. That cold piece of marble marking his resting place held no warmth, none of his spirit. This room though, did. Even without any personal items remaining in it.

Janie flopped onto her back and stared at the ceiling, her head cradled in the new pillow she'd bought when she'd redecorated this as a guest room. There were cracks and chips marring the white above her. The whole room needed to be repainted. It hadn't been done since shortly after she and Tom had gotten married. She didn't have the energy to do it now, alone.

Rene had told her more than once that Tom wouldn't have begrudged her moving on. That there was no reason for her not to. Still, it had seemed wrong to Janie, but here in this room where she felt Tom so strongly, she somehow knew. He wouldn't want her to go it alone. She felt the weight of guilt lift from her shoulders, but that didn't change things with Tyler.

She couldn't think about him anymore, but she couldn't *not* think about him. Sighing, she covered her eyes with her forearm and willed the thoughts to leave her in peace for just one night.

Amazingly, it seemed to work. Janie felt herself drifting, falling asleep in the one room in this house she'd ever had a good night's rest in. She'd have to go upstairs eventually, but for now, she let herself relax, just for a little while.

The ringing of the house phone extension on the table next to her head startled her out of what felt like a deep sleep. Confused and in complete darkness, she slapped the bedside table until her hand knocked the receiver over. Cursing and still half asleep, she sat up and searched with two hands, scrambling to grab it before the call went to voice mail.

Hitting the button in the process, she finally got the phone to her ear. "Hello?"

"Aw, Janie. Jeez, you were asleep. I'm so sorry I woke you. It's Rohn, by the way."

His voice only confused her more. She'd been expecting Rene. A small part of her had been hoping for Tyler, though if she was going to stick to her guns and make a clean break with him, they shouldn't be talking on the phone. But her widowed neighbor Rohn was probably the last person she'd thought would call.

She glanced at the clock across the room on the dresser. It was just past eight. Still a respectable time to call. "No, really. It's fine. I dozed off without meaning to." Logic began to take over. Maybe her stock had gotten into his fields. "Is everything all right?"

"Yeah, everything's fine, actually. Um, this might sound crazy, but do you want to have dinner with me tomorrow?"

"Um, sure." Still disoriented, she didn't know what else to say.

"Great. I thought we could go to the Italian place in town. I could cook here, but I can only make one thing decent and that's steak on the grill, so I figured you'd rather go out."

"Whatever you want is fine."

"A'ight. We'll go out, then. It'll be nice for both of us to get out of the house. So around six okay?"

"Uh, yeah. Fine."

"Great. I'll pick you up at your house."

"Okay."

"Wonderful. I'll see you then."

"All right. 'Night."

"Good night, Janie." There was a smile in his voice, which only confused her more.

After she had hung up, she could finally take the time to think, which had seemed impossible during the call. She considered the strange twist of events.

What was that about? Janie struggled for an explanation. Surely it wasn't a date. She hadn't exactly been a friend, but she'd been at least friendly, neighborly, with his wife, just as Rohn had been with her husband. He probably just wanted to take her out as a thank-you for the pie. Or maybe he wanted to discuss buying her hay. . . .

The hay. She remembered she'd have to figure out the machines on her own to rake it and bale it herself. Or, a safer bet, give Rohn a discounted price to buy it if he sent Colton over to bale it for him.

She didn't think she could take Tyler working at her place again, even for pay this time. To be as close as they had been and then have him be nothing but a hired hand would be torture.

Janie knew she should call Rene back. It might help to bounce the strange dinner invitation off her friend, but exhaustion won out. She crawled up the stairs and into bed. It could all wait until tomorrow.

Chapter Thirty-One

Morning came much too early after Tyler's sleepless night. He probably shouldn't blame it all on the puppy. After what had happened with Janie, it was doubtful he would have been able to sleep anyway. But the whining when he'd put her on a blanket on the floor next to the bed had lasted so long, he'd given in, picked her up, and let her sleep with him in bed.

Once she could curl up against his side, the puppy had slept, even snored, while he'd lain there with his mind spinning over what had happened and what he could do about it.

He'd woken early and slipped out of the house before he had to explain the dog to his parents, who'd luckily been out when he'd returned home. Immature, avoiding the conversation, maybe, but it was the best he could come up with right now until he figured some things out.

Maybe he could leave the dog at Rohn's house at night if his parents really pitched a fit. He looked at her in the seat, happily watching the scenery pass.

She wouldn't be happy about that. Neither would he, truth be told.

He glanced over as he pulled into Rohn's driveway and she wagged her tail, just because he'd looked her way. As miserable as he was about the situation with Janie, this little dog could still bring a smile to his face.

"You excited for your first day of work, girlie?"

She stood up in the seat, ears forward. This one would make a good cattle dog. She was so eager to please, she'd take commands well.

And dammit, he needed to name his little girl before she only responded to the nicknames he'd been calling her. Tyler slowed the truck to a stop. Colton's and Justin's vehicles were already there. He sighed and braced himself to deal with the guys and Rohn while bearing an unexpected, not to mention uninvited, puppy.

How did he get himself into such messed-up situations? Tyler wished he knew. Hell, he was basically a good guy. Why couldn't he catch a break?

With a sigh he grabbed the pup and tucked her under his arm, mentally preparing to face Rohn. Tyler would grovel if he had to, to get the man to allow the dog on the ranch during working hours, and maybe longer, depending on his parents' reaction later.

He glanced down at the little girl in his arms, feeling her heart thunder beneath the hand that held her. "Good thing you're so damn cute. Let's hope that's enough to make Rohn fall in love with you."

It hadn't been enough for Janie, though. Pushing

that depressing thought aside, Tyler strode to the kitchen door. "Morning, all."

"Morning." Only Colton answered as three sets of eyes focused on the little bundle of tail-wagging joy in Tyler's arms.

He figured he needed a name and he needed one quick. The pup would seem more like an already established part of his life—one he couldn't part with—if she had a name other than *girlie*. The image of Janie's dresser and the old stoneware pitcher filled with white wildflowers hit him. "This is Daisy. She's going to be working with us from now on. If it's all right with boss man here, that is."

Tyler tipped his head toward Rohn, laying the adorable little dog's fate squarely on his shoulders. The older man's brows rose. He no doubt knew Tyler's plan. That he'd look like the bad guy to everyone if he refused to let the dog on the property.

"Where'd you get her?" Colton asked.

"The shelter. She's a mutt, but they think she's got some cattle dog in her."

Rohn leveled a look at Tyler. "She fixed?"

"Yes, sir." Tyler nodded, happy he had an answer that would satisfy Rohn. "The place I got her from won't adopt out pups until they're fixed and have all their shots. You can still see where her little belly was shaved from the operation."

"A'ight." Rohn sighed. "If she and Cooter can get along, she can hang around here."

No problem there. Cooter was so old they'd long since lost track of his age. A bloodhound, he had no interest in herding cattle. His main goal was to wolf down his bowl of food as fast as possible so he could go back to sleep.

"Great." Tyler grinned. "Thanks, boss."

"You're welcome. Now grab yourself some coffee so we can all get to work."

"Yes, sir." Tyler moved toward the coffee machine, but turned back to Rohn. "Here. Hold her for a sec while I grab a mug." It couldn't hurt to get his boss good and attached to the dog, just in case she ended up having to live here until Tyler could come up with a better plan.

Rohn frowned, but took the pup thrust at him. She stretched forward to lick his face and Tyler knew Rohn was a goner. The man shook his head even as his expression softened. "All righty. Enough of that." He pulled her close to his chest and rubbed her ear with one hand.

Justin laughed. "She is pretty damn cute."

"Yeah, she is," Rohn agreed, even if his tone sounded as if he was reluctant to do so.

Mission accomplished. He knew the floppy-eared Daisy with her one blue eye and one brown eye and splattering of brown spots on her short white coat would charm even the hardest heart. Tyler turned toward the cabinet to hide his satisfied grin.

"So, Rohn, you think any more about asking out Janie Smithwick?" At Colton's question, Tyler's good mood fled.

He poured the steaming coffee and managed to get it all into the mug and not on the counter, but most of his attention was trained on Rohn's answer.

"As a matter of fact. I have. We're going out to dinner tonight."

Tyler spun to stare at Rohn. "Tonight?"

"Yup. I'm taking her to the Italian place."

"When did you call her?" Tyler realized he sounded a bit too interested. "I mean, it's just kind of sudden, is all."

"Last night."

Last night, right after she had kicked him to the curb. What the hell? She hadn't wasted any time. Janie had agreed to go out in public on a real date to a restaurant with Rohn. The one thing she'd refused again and again to do with Tyler even though he had asked, and he'd asked long before Rohn had.

Crap. What did this mean? He couldn't think past the noise of his pulse pounding in his head.

Tyler glanced up and saw Justin watching him. Justin was the only one in the room who was aware of what had been going on with Janie. The only one who could even come close to suspecting how hard Rohn's announcement would hit him.

"Good for you." Colton was grinning ear to ear over the news. Seeing his glee increased the sudden bout of nausea roiling through Tyler's gut. Colton shot Tyler a look. "See? I told you she'd say yes. And you, Justin, owe me twenty bucks."

"You two bet on it?" Tyler turned to frown at them.

"Yup." Justin glanced at him. "I never thought she'd say yes if he did ask."

"Pfft. I knew she would. I should have put money on it with Tyler, too."

That would have been a bet Tyler would have lost. Never in a million years would he have believed

Janie would say yes. Not after he'd been in her bed, buried inside her. No more than he'd thought Rohn would ever get up the nerve to call.

He'd called, and she'd said yes. Jesus, he felt even sicker picturing her answering that phone and her agreeing to dinner out. He put his coffee mug on the counter, untouched, as the conversation went on around him.

"So glad I could provide such good fodder for your entertainment." Rohn shook his head, but still smiled. Of course he was happy. He was taking Janie out tonight.

Tyler tried to slow his breaths, which were coming fast and short. He couldn't stay here. He grabbed his mug and dumped the contents down the sink. "I'm gonna head out and get started."

He nearly forgot the pup, still in Rohn's lap, until she whined when he walked toward the door. He turned back and reached for her, feeling justified that she at least still preferred him to Rohn. Small consolation, that, but it was better than nothing. Right now, that was what it felt like he had after losing Janie. Nothing.

Though if he could lose her so easily, maybe he'd never really had her at all.

Tyler pushed through the door of his parents' house to find his brother in the kitchen.

Tuck glanced up from snooping under the lid of a pot on the stove. "Wow, you're home, and early for once . . . and you have a puppy with you."

"Yup." He was in no mood for the third degree or

any attitude after the day he'd had. "And you're here. Still. When are you leaving, again?"

Putting the lid back with a clatter, Tuck raised a brow.

"Tomorrow. And what the fuck crawled up your ass today? I've seen you barely a handful of times since Becca and I have been here, so don't act like we're putting a cramp in your social life." Tuck strode to the table and yanked out two chairs. "Sit your ass down and tell me what's wrong with you."

Now he was in for a lecture. He should have kept his mouth shut.

"I have to feed the dog first." He'd forgotten the bag of food in the truck. Tyler thrust the puppy at his brother. "Be right back."

The expression on Tuck's face would have been funny if Tyler wasn't so miserable. He held the pup in two hands at arm's length. The two were in pretty much the same position when Tyler returned with the bag of food. Tuck and Daisy, eyeing each other as if neither was sure what to make of the other.

"Jesus. Give her to me." Tyler took back possession of the puppy, even though it did make getting a bowl out of the cupboard and pouring the dry food into it twice as hard than if he'd had two hands to use. "You're supposed to hold a puppy like a baby, not like a bomb."

"What do you know about babies?"

"Not a hell of a lot, but I know about animals, and puppies need to feel safe and feel your heartbeat. It reminds them of their mother."

"Oh, really. And how exactly did you become this

particular puppy's mother—or father, as the case may be?"

"I adopted her from the shelter, and her name is Daisy. I'd appreciate it if you'd use it so she gets used to it." Tyler sure as hell wasn't going to explain any more about the events that had led to him being in possession of Daisy rather than the intended recipient, who could at that very moment be getting ready for her date.

The scowl he hadn't been able to fight all day returned. He set the dog and her bowl on the floor and then turned back to the cabinet for a second dish for water.

After she had something to drink, the next stop was going to be the fridge, because he needed a beer. If Tuck had drunk the last of what Tyler had picked up for the family dinner the other night and hadn't replaced it, he might have to knock his brother out on sheer principle.

He yanked the door of the fridge open hard and the dozen or so bottles in the door clattered together. At least that was a welcome sound. First one he'd heard all day. Well, except for Daisy whining every time he left her sight. Sad but true, at least that made him feel loved.

Tyler grabbed a bottle and popped open the cap. "Thanks for picking up more beer."

"No problem. Now sit down and talk."

He sat, but he didn't want to talk. "Nothing to talk about."

"Okay, well, let me suggest a topic. Did you talk to Mom and Dad about a dog? Because they didn't mention it to me if you did."

"No, I didn't."

His brother blew out a sound that said it all, but followed it up by saying, "Tyler, you can't do shit like—"

"Tuck, shut up for a second before you lecture me. She wasn't for me. She was supposed to be a gift. The person I got her for didn't want her." He took a long swallow of beer as he remembered how she didn't want him either, apparently. "And no, I didn't ask her first. I wanted it to be a surprise."

"Her." Tuck nodded. "I figured this had to do with some girl."

"She's not just some girl. She's not a *girl* at all." His stupid brother always thought he knew everything.

"So you were serious about this one."

This one. As if he had a revolving door of females waltzing in and out of his life. It seemed Janie and Tuck shared the same opinion of him.

"I really wish I had half as many women in my past as people think I do. I swear." Tyler shook his head. That was a moot point now since Janie was with Rohn. The puppy, however, chowing down noisily on the food, was not. "If Mom and Dad freak about the dog, I'll just move out."

Probably long past time he got his own place, anyway. Maybe if he'd had one, Janie would have taken him seriously, like she obviously did Rohn, rather than treating him like some kid only good enough to have sex with a couple of times.

He glanced across the table to see Tuck watching him. "What now? Got something else to lay into me about?"

"Nope." Tuck smiled.

"You better tell me what's got you amused before I knock that smile right off your face."

Tuck snorted. "Try it and you'll be looking a lot less pretty in the morning. And I'm amused because I think my little brother has finally gotten his heart broke."

His brows rose. "And that's enjoyable for you."

"That you finally are serious enough about something or someone to care about losing it, yeah, I am happy about that. I was starting to worry you'd never settle down."

Tyler lifted the bottle in a toast. "Glad to oblige."

The clock on the wall high above the sink caught his eye. Five o'clock. What time was Janie's date? And how many more beers would it take before he didn't care anymore?

Chapter Thirty-Two

Janie stared at herself in the bathroom mirror, debating whether it was too late to call Rohn and cancel this . . . whatever tonight was.

Maybe if she knew what this was, it would be easier to decide whether to go or not. Was it a date? A business meeting? A widow/widower support group? Two neighbors just sharing a meal?

She patted more flesh-colored cover-up into the dark circles beneath each eye with the tip of one finger. If she'd actually get a decent night's sleep, she could probably forgo half of her makeup and she'd still look years younger.

With a sigh, she turned away from the mirror and headed for the bedroom. What to wear was the next issue. She couldn't look like she was dressed up since they were only going to the place in town, but she couldn't dress in her usual jeans and boots either. And her outfit couldn't be too sexy. She didn't want to give Rohn the wrong impression.

It had been years since Janie'd had to worry about what clothes she put on. Not during her marriage and not since. As long as she looked presentable for church, the rest of the time she dressed for comfort and utility. Even when Tyler was coming around, she didn't worry whether she was in the soft old T-shirt she slept in or the jeans she'd worn to muck the stalls.

That thought gave her pause. While she'd been in the middle of her fling—for lack of a better word—with Tyler, she'd come up with every opportunity to make things hard. Only hindsight cleared her vision of the situation and made reality undeniable. When it was just them at her house alone, things had been easy with Tyler. She hadn't realized how easy.

It was only her fear of the outside world creeping into what they had that made it seem hard. The problem was, there was no keeping the rest of the world out of her private little space forever. And that was why Tyler wasn't here tonight, and she was dressing for what she hoped was not a date with Rohn, but could very well be one.

A glance at the clock told her she'd better get a move on. He should be over in less than half an hour to pick her up, and she wasn't dressed for the night yet.

Staring at the clothes hanging in the closet didn't help. Nothing jumped out at her and said *wear me*, so she started at one end of the rack and flipped through the contents, one hanger at a time.

Some of the stuff in there hadn't been worn in years. She really needed to go through her clothes. Since she wore the same things—her favorites—over and over again, she could probably donate half of her things to charity and never miss them. The choices began to overwhelm her, until she thought she'd lose her mind if she didn't pick something soon.

The clock was ticking. Janie reached out and grabbed the casual cotton dress she'd worn to Sunday service the other week. It would have to do. If it was good enough for church, it was good enough for the Italian restaurant in town, and it required no thought on her part. No coordinating a shirt with a skirt. It fit. It looked decent, and it was quick and easy to throw on.

Sad that her life and her wardrobe had been reduced to what was the easiest. She should probably work on that, but not tonight. Tonight she had too much else to deal with thanks to this strange dinner invitation.

Another trip to the bathroom to check her reflection, where she fluffed her hair even though it just fell right back to where it had been, and she was done. Janie grabbed the purse she'd filled with the essentials she'd need for her dinner out—she refused to call it a date—and headed downstairs.

Rohn, as she'd expected him to be, was right on time, pulling into her driveway at two minutes to six. His effort to be punctual was endearing, even if his arrival ramped up her nerves.

She was halfway out the kitchen door as he jumped out of the truck and headed to meet her. "Hey, Janie."

"Rohn. Nice to see you again." She pulled the door shut behind her.

"I was gonna come to the door to get you." He looked a little disappointed as he said it.

"No need. I saw you pull in, so . . ." Janie shrugged.

"No use waiting." Rohn dipped his head and smiled. "You always were the kind of woman who liked to do things on her own."

Janie wondered what woman Rohn was talking about, because it sure wasn't her. She'd always felt like she'd relied on Tom and their hired men too much. That she felt the loss of their help so keenly proved that.

She forced a smile. "I'm not so sure about that."

He tipped his head to the side. "Eh, women rarely see their own virtues."

Her brows rose at what seemed like a compliment, though she wasn't sure. "I guess."

"Should we go?"

"Sure."

With a nod of his cowboy hat, he laid a hand on the small of her back to steer her to the truck. The physical contact, even as small as it was, seemed so strange, she was glad when they reached the passenger door and he moved to open it for her.

They lived in a small town, and nothing was very far from anything else. That proved to be a good thing as the small talk in the truck cab lagged.

"So the place looks good," he said, keeping his eyes on the road as he navigated the way to the restaurant.

"Well, all that rain earlier this spring really helped. Last year was so dry." The weather was the best Janie could come up with. How pitiful.

"Oh, I know." He nodded. "Terrible drought last year."

"Mmm-hmm. It was." Janie rolled her eyes at herself as she glanced at the passing scenery out the side window.

With this less-than-auspicious start to the evening, it was going to be interesting seeing what other mundane things they could cover before they ran out of conversation. At least there'd be food shortly. Eating was always good to fill awkward lulls.

"So I hope you like Italian food."

"Love it. I don't cook it as frequently as I'd like to, though. I really shouldn't eat all those carbs too often."

"Oh, did you want to go somewhere else?"

"No, no. This is fine. Really."

"Okay. If you're sure."

"Very sure. Thank you." She let out a breath. A man hadn't worked this hard to accommodate her wishes in—forever.

When she was dating Tom, he'd just make the decisions and she'd follow along. And Tyler—well, there weren't all that many decisions to be made there. Sex in the bedroom again or in the kitchen?

She tore her mind from Tyler. That was over. One day maybe there'd be a time she'd be able to enjoy reliving those memories without feeling the knife stab through her heart, but not yet.

Luckily, the restaurant came into view, putting an end to the painful silence. There was a bit of jostling as Rohn made sure she never got to open any door for herself, not in the truck, nor while entering the restaurant, and they entered the dim interior.

It smelled amazing inside, which was a good topic of conversation actually. Janie jumped on it. "It smells great in here. Good choice."

"Thanks, and it does."

The hostess greeted them. "Two for dinner?"

"Yes, please. I made reservations. Lerner."

"Sure. Right this way." The hostess grabbed two menus, and Rohn waited for Janie to follow her before he brought up the rear, just as he waited for her to be seated before he sat himself.

She buried her attention in the menu, happy for the excuse not to have to make conversation for a little bit. God, she'd turned into a hermit. Maybe Rene had been right. She needed to get out among the living more.

"Anything look good?" he asked.

"Everything looks good." She hadn't eaten much today. Nerves and misery combined had squelched any hunger pangs until she'd walked in and smelled the food cooking. "Maybe the eggplant parmigiana. That's something I never make for myself at home."

He laughed. "That describes pretty much everything on the menu for me."

Had she been interested in Rohn romantically, this would have been the perfect time to suggest he come over for dinner at her house, or that she could cook something and bring it to him. But she didn't make that suggestion. Instead, she just smiled. "Then you have plenty to choose from."

"That I do." After a few seconds, he closed the menu and leaned his elbows on the table. "I have to admit something to you."

"Um, okay." She lowered her own menu, starting to worry a little bit about what this confession would be.

"Colton talked me into calling and asking you out. I thought the idea was crazy at first, but now I'm glad I did it."

So this was a date. Janie forced another smile and looked down at the menu open in front of her.

A server arrived just in time to fill the silence. "Can I get you something to drink?"

Janie jumped at the offer. "Yes, please. Red wine."

"A beer for me. Thanks." Rohn paused for the waitress to leave before he reached out and laid his hand on the table between them. "Janie?"

"Yeah?"

"It's okay. It's just dinner."

She lifted a brow. "Hmm?"

"I can see you're not ready for this yet. It's only been, what? Barely a year for you since Tom passed."

"Yes. About a year."

"I should have realized. I'm a lot of years further along than you are."

It hit her, hard and fast. She was a horrible person because she *had* started to move on, and in doing so she'd done far more than just have dinner with a man.

To her horror, the tears welled so fast, they spilled over her cheeks in quick drops that hit the pages of the menu before she could catch them.

"Shit." He hissed out a curse and handed her a napkin. "I'm so sorry."

She grabbed the soft paper and pressed it to her eyes. "No. Don't be. Believe me, it's not your fault."

Tears not quite under control, she still managed to thank the server who'd appeared to set the wine in front of her.

"Ready to order?" The waitress hovered, just when Janie really wanted her to go away.

"Can you give us a few more minutes?" Thank God for Rohn. He saved the day and saved Janie further embarrassment.

"Of course." The server left and Janie wiped at her eyes again.

"Janie, we can go, if you want."

"No. I'm fine. Thank you. And I'm so sorry."

"No need to apologize."

"Yeah, I really need to." She couldn't have him thinking it was his fault. "The truth is, I have—or I thought I had—accepted that it was time to move on finally. I met a guy."

To his credit, Rohn kept his expression neutral. "A'ight. So what happened?"

"Well, among other things, there's the guilt. It has only been a year." She'd thought she'd made peace with Tom and could move on, but the tears told a different story.

"Janie, I'm sorry I said that. I just wanted you to feel better and to let you know that I understood if you weren't ready. Speaking plainly here, the truth is, Tom was diagnosed more than two years ago with what amounted to a death sentence. He and I talked about it once, back before the disease really took hold. He prepared himself then that he had six months, maybe a year if he was lucky. He thought you'd prepared yourself, too, to move on after. He wanted you to live your life."

The tears misted her eyes again. "Did he say that?"

"He did. So if your guilt over Tom is what's keeping you from happiness with this other man, don't let it. It's not what he wanted for you."

She smiled. "Well, there's more."

"A'ight. I'm listening if you want to talk."

He was a pretty amazing man to take her out on a date and then offer to listen to her talk, and cry, about another man. She hated to take advantage of him like this, but Rohn might be the one person she knew who truly understood what she was feeling.

Rene was a friend, but her spouse was alive and well. Rohn had been through this. Janie forced her eyes to meet his. "He's younger than me, by a lot."

He grinned. "That's okay. Seems like every starlet in Hollywood has a younger man nowadays."

She let out a laugh. "You might not have noticed since I wore the shoes without the manure on them, but I'm no star."

"I know who you are, and I don't think it matters. Did the age difference bother him?"

"Not at all. Just me, apparently. But he's so good-looking, and he's a bronc rider and a tie-down roper and bull rider—he's like one big magnet for the buckle bunnies. I can't compete with them. I'm eleven years older than he is and nearly twenty years older than some of the girls who are after him."

Rohn pursed his lips as he nodded slowly. "Seems like quite a guy."

"He is." She sighed. "And he's so generous with his time and good with animals and kids, but none of it matters because he's young and wild and I'm sure even though he says he's ready to settle down with one woman, it won't last. How long before he's bored?"

"Well, I can tell you this. I have some experience with this situation. Believe it or not, I was young and kind of wild myself back in the day, but the minute I met Lila, I was ready to trade in all my buckle-bunny privileges for a wedding ring."

"That seems like such a different time, when you and I were young. Now they text rather than talk in person or on the phone. I read an article that young girls today, middle school and high school aged, consider"—she lowered her voice to a whisper—"oral sex equivalent to kissing. Can you imagine?"

Rohn let out a burst of laughter. "If that's true, I can't say I'm not a little envious I was born thirty years too early. But seriously, let me tell you this. I've got three young guys working for me. Yeah, they like to go out and get wild, but every one of them is deeper than they appear. Take Tyler, for example." Rohn's gaze pinned Janie. "You know him."

She swallowed hard and tried to breathe. "Yeah."

"He's got a heart the size of Oklahoma, and he'd give you the shirt off his back if you needed it. When he puts his mind to it, he works twice as hard as anyone I know, but he hides it all behind this cocky, devil-may-care attitude, which I'm convinced is a defense mechanism."

Intrigued by his insight into Tyler, Janie couldn't help but ask, "Defense against what?"

"I think he's got big dreams for himself, but I think he's afraid of failing. So he pretends he doesn't care. Like it doesn't matter. He grew up in the shadow of an older brother who could do no wrong. State rodeo champion. War hero. It's hard for a young guy to live up to that kind of standard, so he adopted the persona of the family screwup. That way no one expected anything from him, and he couldn't disappoint them."

Janie's eyes widened at Rohn's analysis. He was a lot more intuitive than she'd ever expected him, or any man, to be. "Wow."

He laughed at her reaction. "Don't be too impressed. I'm not looking to get my own talk show or anything. I happened to grow up with a brother just like Tyler's, so I know more than most how he feels."

Janie nodded, feeling a warmth, a camaraderie with Rohn she didn't feel with many others. "Thanks for this. I know it didn't work out exactly as you'd planned."

He dismissed that concern with the wave of one hand. "Eh, you know what, I'm glad it worked out this way. A good friend is far more valuable to me at this point in my life than a girlfriend. God, how I hate that word *girlfriend*. Almost as much as I hate the term *dating*."

She smiled at his cringe. "I know. Me too."

"So, you hungry? Because I'm ready to gnaw on this here table."

"Yeah, I am." Far more important than dinner, Rohn had given her some pretty heavy food for thought regarding Tyler. What she was going to do about it, she still wasn't sure, but that was something to think about later. Janie tried her best to push him to the back of her mind and give Rohn her attention. "So what did you decide on?"

Chapter Thirty-Three

"You're looking mighty cheerful this morning." Colton tipped his head toward Rohn where he stood pouring coffee. "How'd the date go last night?"

Rohn turned toward the table where Justin, Colton, and Tyler sat. "Dinner was very nice."

"And?" Colton prompted.

Tyler prepared himself to hear the worst and hoped the coffee he'd drunk didn't come back up as his gut twisted.

"And that's all I'm gonna say about it."

Colton frowned deep, looking as unhappy as Tyler felt when Rohn sat, his satisfied smile not quite hidden behind the coffee mug as he took a sip. Justin shot a sideways glance at Tyler, who regretted ever letting him in on his secret. Bad enough to lose Janie, but to have Justin know and watch the whole thing happen made it feel all the worse.

To lose her just because he didn't fit into whatever age bracket she thought acceptable was a bitter pill to swallow. Rohn fit her criteria. Tyler didn't, and his age was the one thing he couldn't change.

At least Rohn was a good guy. Time to man up and stop wallowing. If Janie preferred Rohn, there was nothing Tyler could do about it. That didn't mean he could sit by and watch, though. If Rohn and Janie really were together, Tyler would give his notice and find another job. His heart could only stand so much, and standing by watching Janie with another man was more than he could take.

The puppy whined from the floor, standing up on her back legs to scratch at his jeans with her front paws. "Daisy, be good before boss man kicks you out."

"Aw, she just wants some attention." Rohn reached a hand down toward the floor. "Here, girl."

She skittered across the floor beneath the table to Rohn's side. Tyler pretended to ignore the dog's abandonment, but he feared his mug couldn't quite hide his scowl.

Justin watched the dog's move, shot Tyler a glance, and then asked, "What're we doing today, boss?"

Before Rohn could answer, Tyler said, "If we're not too busy, I wouldn't mind cutting out early. I still need to bale that hay over at the Smithwick place."

If he remembered correctly, Janie had lessons scheduled for this afternoon. He could jump on the machine, get the job done, and leave, hopefully without ever having to talk to her.

Rohn's eyes met his. "Sure. Head over whenever you want. I don't have too much planned for today."

Tyler nodded. "Thanks."

Talk of plans for the day went on around him,

but he didn't participate. With Colton and Justin chattering away, he didn't think anyone would notice.

When the coffee was finished and it was time to start the day, they all stood to head out to work.

Justin and Colton were headed out the door when Rohn laid a hand on Tyler's shoulder. "Can I talk to you for a second?"

"Uh, sure."

Rohn waited for the screen door to slam shut behind the other two before he said, "So, you and Janie?"

Tyler felt the blood drain from his face. "Rohn, you hadn't asked her out yet."

"Relax. It's okay."

He frowned, surprised when it began to sink in that Rohn knew. "She told you about us?"

"No. I figured it out on my own. You don't exactly have a poker face, kid. At first, I couldn't figure out why you looked so strange whenever her name came up. Then last night when she told me there was a young, wild rodeo cowboy she was interested in, it all made sense."

"She said she was interested in me?"

"Yup."

"She dumped me because she thinks I'm too young."

"Yeah, so I gathered, but it was more than that."

Tyler nodded, trying to be a man and accept her decision. "Yeah. It was because she was interested in you."

Rohn surprised him by laughing. "No, she's definitely not interested in me. At least not like that."

"She's not?" He forced himself to meet Rohn's gaze head-on.

"No, she's not. Son, it took me about five minutes to figure out her heart is already promised somewhere else."

Tyler's brows shot up. "To me?"

"Yes, to you. Jesus, I took you for smarter than this when it came to women."

He wasn't stupid, just confused. "But she broke it off with me. I got Daisy for her, and she wouldn't even hold the pup."

"Ah, so that's where the dog came from." Rohn nodded. "Listen, not everything is about you. Maybe you need to consider where she's coming from. She lost the man she thought she'd grow old with, and not all that long ago. Death changes a person. Makes them wary to open themselves up to that kind of hurt again."

The knowledge hit Tyler like a lightning bolt. He couldn't believe he hadn't seen it before, because it was so damn clear now. "You're right. She's lost everyone she's ever really loved. Her mother, her grandfather, her husband."

"Yup." Rohn nodded. "And you couldn't know this, but she even had to put their old dog down, right about the time her Tom died. It was a lot for her to handle all at once."

Tyler felt so stupid. Of course she'd be afraid of loving again. She'd rather be alone than bear another loss. She didn't even want to risk loving the puppy because one day it would be gone. "So what do I do?"

The older man shook his head. "That is up to you. All I can tell you is don't give up too easily on her. Give her time. I think she'll come around. Oh, and take the day off, with pay, and get that hay baled at her place before the rain they're predicting comes. She and I discussed my buying her harvest last night, and I expect a quality product for what I'm going to be paying her for it."

Rohn was like a guardian angel, for both of them. Sending Tyler to her place to work for the day where he'd no doubt run into her and hopefully be able to make things right. Making sure she had the cash she needed by probably overpaying for the hay. Stepping back to let Tyler have a shot at Janie when he'd obviously had an interest in her himself.

Tyler had always liked Rohn, but now he had even more respect for the man.

He dipped his head. "A'ight. Thanks."

"Don't forget to take the dog." Rohn glanced down at the pup on the floor. "If that face doesn't win her over, nothing will."

Tyler had a few ideas up his sleeve that might do the trick, but Rohn was right, the dog couldn't hurt. Daisy following closely behind, Tyler left Rohn's kitchen and headed toward his truck with a lot lighter step than when he'd walked in barely an hour before.

He and Daisy had a big job to accomplish today, and the least of it was baling that hay.

* * *

"Do you feel better now that you finally talked to me about things, instead of dodging my calls?" Rene asked through the cell phone.

"I guess." Janie had known she wouldn't be able to hide from the conversation with Rene forever. Since Rene had cornered Janie after church, there was really no getting out of talking to her.

"Why do you still sound so down? You've got not one but two incredibly handsome and eligible bachelors interested in you at the same time, and you're acting like it's the end of the world."

"First of all, I told you Rohn and I agreed we're friends and nothing more. Second, I was a total bitch to Tyler when he came over last time, so there's no guarantee I'll ever see him again." Phone in hand, Janie walked down the stairs from her bedroom.

She heard the rumble of the tractor and her heart leapt. Tyler. "Oh, my God."

"What?" Rene sounded as panicked as Janie felt. "What's happening?"

"I think he's here." She ran down the remainder of the stairs and to the window. She spotted him bouncing along in the tractor seat, heading toward the hayfield. "He's finishing up the haying. Rene, what do I do?"

"Put on your prettiest dress and some lipstick, and go out there."

Her heart thundered. A sleepless night spent reviewing her conversation with Rohn about Tyler, all while missing Tyler horribly, had her emotions even closer to the surface than usual. "Lipstick isn't going to make up for my acting like a lunatic."

"Not alone, no, but a good amount of cleavage and a sincere apology might."

Hell, maybe Rene was right. It couldn't hurt.

"Okay. That's what I'll do. I have to go." Janie turned back toward the stairs, running up them. She didn't know how much time she had. He'd work for at least a little while, she was sure, even if he had to go back to Rohn's. Long enough for her to get herself together and intercept him before he got back to his truck and left.

"Call me and tell me what happens."

"I will. Bye." Her head spinning from all she needed to do in a short time to make herself presentable, Janie tossed the phone on the dresser and started to strip off her farm clothes.

She ran to the bathroom. One glance in the mirror told her she looked like crap as yet another sleepless night showed clearly on her face. Reaching for her makeup bag, she dug for the cover-up that she hoped would camouflage the dark circles beneath her eyes. But the lipstick she slicked on her lips next wouldn't help if he was past listening to her.

What she was going to say still remained a mystery. What could she say after she'd flipped out on him? She'd have to figure something out, and soon.

Janie reached for her mascara and thought better of it. The way her emotions were all over the place, there was a very real chance she'd cry off any eye makeup the way she had last night during dinner. Poor Rohn. She owed him one for being so sweet during that episode.

The need to catch Tyler before he left pushed

her forward, toward the closet. She stared at the selections for the second time in two days, only this time she glanced past the dresses she usually wore to church and landed on a little red cotton sundress. It was much too bare so she'd never worn it for service, but it would do when she needed to catch a certain cowboy's eye.

She pulled it off the hanger and held it in front of her, glancing in the mirror. The red floral print brightened her features, and the low cut showed a good amount of cleavage. Decision made, she slipped it over her head.

Thinking she might as well go all out since she was pretty over-the-top already, Janie reached into the back of the closet and grabbed her good cowboy boots.

As she sat on the bed to pull the boots on, her wedding ring caught her eye. She swallowed hard and stared at it. Rohn didn't wear his wedding ring anymore. When she'd asked him at the restaurant how long it had been before he'd taken it off, he'd smiled and said about a year, but that he still kept it in the bedroom and looked at it every day.

Reaching down, Janie slid the diamond and gold band set off her finger and saw the white indentation left where it had been for so long. Drawing in a bracing breath, she stood and put the rings on top of the jewelry box on the dresser. It felt like a big step, and she was about to take another one—if Tyler still wanted her.

One more glance in the mirror and she turned for the door, hoping it wasn't too late to win back the man she'd been foolish enough to push away.

Chapter Thirty-Four

Tyler raked the hay in the smaller of the two fields with Janie's nine-inch tractor and had just headed back to the barn for the larger machine to start baling when he saw her. He'd been a little worried when she didn't come out right away. A small doubt in the back of his mind had kept him from going to her first, thinking Rohn might have been wrong about her feelings. That maybe she was avoiding him.

But she was there now, standing next to his truck and looking like a vision. Her dress blew in the breeze that ruffled her hair. She'd left it down and her hat off, and the closer he got, the more he wanted to bury his hands in her long waves and kiss her senseless. He held that impulse in check as he slowed the tractor to a stop and cut the engine.

Daisy wagged her tail, hopping around between his legs. Whether the dog was excited by the prospect of someone new to meet, or she could sense Tyler's anticipation, he couldn't be sure, but the puppy practically vibrated with energy. If he could face the truth, he'd admit he might be shaking a bit himself.

He climbed down and, once his boots were on the ground, reached back up for the dog, who was dancing in the seat. He supposed in her little puppy brain, she thought Tyler had taken much too long to climb down.

"Hey." Puppy under one arm, Tyler forced the greeting to sound casual. No need for Janie to know that he was shaking like a leaf.

"Tyler, I'm so sorry." Her voice broke on the apology. Janie took a step forward, her eyes bright with unshed tears. "I'm sorry for how I acted, and that I was so stupid, and how I wouldn't go out with you. Just for everything."

He smiled. That was all he needed to hear. "I'm sorry, too."

"For what?"

"For springing Daisy here on you. For pushing you into something you weren't ready for." He took a step forward, put the pup on the ground, and laid his hands on Janie's arms. "I want you to know, I'm not giving up on you and me, but I'll wait until you're ready."

"I'm ready now." Her answer didn't quite convince him.

He moved his hands down her arms and grasped her hands in his, wondering if she was really ready. Rubbing his thumb over her fingers, he felt something different. He glanced down and saw her wedding rings were missing. His gaze shot to her face.

She must have seen his reaction. "I figured it was time I took them off."

Emotions ricocheting through him, Tyler pulled her closer. She was in his embrace in an instant, her arms wrapped around his neck, her lips pressed to his.

The kiss could have easily led to his lifting her pretty little sundress up and claiming her right there against the tractor, but he wasn't going to let that happen. They'd already begun this relationship backward. Time to get things back on track.

He pulled away from her mouth. "I want to go on a date. A real one. Out in public at a restaurant, like you did with Rohn."

"Okay."

His brows rose. "Really? You're not just saying that?"

"No, I'm not. Though can I request we go to a different restaurant from the one he took me to? I don't want to look like the kind of woman who has a date with a different guy every night."

"Fine. Wherever you want to go." He kissed her again, only allowing himself a quick peck before he continued. "And I want you to meet my family. Come with me to Logan and Emma's baby's christening next month."

"Okay."

"And no sex."

"What?" Her eyes widened and her voice rose.

He smiled at her surprise. "I know, it sounds funny, but I need to prove to you I'm serious. I want a real relationship with you, not just sex."

Her brow wrinkled. "No sex for how long?"

"I don't know. A month." He shrugged. The furrow deepened in her brow and he laughed. "Okay, how about two weeks?" When she still didn't look happy, he added, "How about we discuss the details later?"

She cocked one brow. "Good idea."

The puppy wasn't happy, either, but for a different reason. She didn't like being ignored and jumped up to lean her front paws on Tyler's leg.

He grinned. "Someone wants to meet you officially. And don't worry. I'm keeping her. I talked to my parents and to Rohn and they don't mind if I keep her at my house at night and bring her to work with me during the day. So I'm not trying to unload her on you."

Janie glanced down at the dog. "I'm sorry I overreacted the other day."

"No. I'm sorry I sprang her on you."

"You named her Daisy?"

"I did." Tyler reached down and picked up the pup. It seemed the only time she was content was when he was holding her. "After the daisies growing along the fence in your hayfield. And the ones on the dresser in your bedroom."

It was as if he could see the walls Janie had erected around her heart crumble. Then Daisy leaned over and licked her face, and he knew she was a goner.

"She is sweet." Janie raised her gaze to his. "So are you."

"I try," Tyler joked, but he also needed to be serious for a moment. "Janie, I want you to know something. None of us knows how long we have on this earth, but as long as there is breath in my lungs, I will never willingly hurt you."

She was quiet for so long, he knew she had

something to say. He put the puppy down again and pulled her to him. "What? Tell me."

Her eyes filled with tears again. "I'm so afraid of losing you."

"I know. But you won't."

"I'm trying so hard to have faith, but you could meet and fall for someone else, and want to be with her instead—"

"Nope. Won't happen." He shook his head, firm in his answer.

"How can you know that?"

"Because I've already fallen so hard for you, there's no room left in my heart for anyone else." The puppy whined at his feet. He laughed and tipped his head toward the dog. "Maybe room for her, but no other woman, Janie. Only you. It's you I love. Nobody but you."

Now the tears did fall, sending long streaks down her face. She opened her mouth and he pressed a finger to her lips. "Don't say it back just because I did. Don't say it until you mean it, Janie. I can wait."

He was doing his best to give her the space and time to move slowly. Like Rohn said, she'd had a lot to deal with in her life, but he needed her to know that he was there for the long haul. If that meant he had to reveal his feelings and risk her not sharing them, then he'd do it.

Janie reached up and, after kissing his fingertips, moved them from her mouth. "It's okay. I made my peace with this, and with Tom. I think I can love the memory of him and still be okay with loving somebody else, too."

"Any chance that somebody could be me one day?"

She smiled through the tears. "It already is you."

His heart full to bursting, he leaned down and gathered her as close to him as he could while standing.

Giving in to the urge he could no longer fight, he ran his hand up her back and into her hair. He tugged her head back and took her mouth with the kind of kiss he'd been holding in for fear of scaring her. He claimed her mouth, but it felt like more than that. It was a promise of love, of their future.

By the time he pulled away, they were both a little breathless.

"Wow." She let out a short laugh, her cheeks adorably pink. "You sure about waiting two long weeks before we have sex?"

"Less sure with every second." One more kiss like that and he'd lose all control. They might not even make it to the house if that happened. He squeezed her harder and groaned. He could feel her, warm and soft, beneath the thin cotton of the dress. "Maybe we could just wait until after our first date."

She laughed. "All right."

He drew in a breath through his nose. "What are you doing tonight?"

"I think I might be going out to dinner with somebody."

Her sly look had him smiling as he asked, "Oh, really. Anyone I know?"

"Some cocky cowboy I can't seem to get off my mind." Daisy yipped and Janie glanced down. "He's got a real cute dog, though."

"Sounds like a hell of a guy."

"He is. I'm hoping he'll be around for a long time."

Tyler leaned in low. "Just try getting rid of me."

"Never." Rising up on tiptoe, she wrapped her arms around his neck and paused with her lips just shy of his mouth. Her eyes on his, she asked, "How early do you think restaurants open?"

"Hungry?"

"Not for food." Her smile looked devilish.

He grinned, lifting her up against him. "God, how I love you."

"I love you, too, Tyler."

After possibly the five most wonderful words he'd ever heard, he figured the day couldn't get any better . . . and then Janie wrapped her legs around his waist and kissed him like she meant it, and he realized they were just getting started.

Read on for an excerpt from Cat Johnson's
next hot cowboy romance,

Midnight Wrangler,

available this December.

Rohn had just stepped out of the truck when a woman who looked too familiar to be a stranger caught his attention. He squinted through the midday glare, frowning, until recognition hit him like a sledgehammer to the chest.

A smile bowed Rohn's lips. It had been a long time, but it was her. Yeah, she had changed a bit. She was older, a bit curvier, but he'd recognize her anywhere. From the blond curls that had tickled his cheek when they'd embraced, to the curve of the hips he'd held on to tight in the bed of his truck where they'd first made love, he knew her. Even twenty-five years later.

In deference to the heat, she wore a tank top that showed enough of her creamy white skin that he could see she was still as fair-skinned as ever. Her shoulders were pink on top, proving that just like when he'd known her, she'd still freckle and burn rather than tan.

Back in the day she would have been wearing cut-off shorts, Daisy Dukes that showed off her legs to such advantage that Rohn had been able to think of nothing else but having her thighs wrapped around him. Today she wore knee-length khaki shorts, but that didn't stop him from picturing what lush curves were hidden underneath.

Gone were the cowboy boots she used to love to wear every day on the farm, even in the summer. In their place were sandals that let her toes peek out.

She stood with her back to him as she held the door open for an older couple walking out. When they stopped to say thank you, she turned her head enough that he could see her face.

If he hadn't been 100 percent certain before, he was now. He took a few long strides in her direction. "Can it be? Bonnie?"

She turned at the sound of his voice. When her eyes widened, he knew she recognized him, too. "Uh, yeah. It's me. I didn't know you were still in town."

"Yup. Never left. I own a place not far from here. Cattle ranch."

"Oh. Nice. Good for you."

"Bonnie Blue Martin. Back in town. Wow." It was still a shock. He'd been thinking about her just last week.

She let out a short laugh but it somehow lacked humor. "I haven't heard anyone call me that since high school."

"That's good to hear." Rohn cocked one brow. "I don't know how I'd feel about some other guy using the name I used to call my girl."